TWINS

ALSO BY
ROXANNE PULITZER

The Prize Pulitzer

TWINS

Roxanne Pulitzer

VILLARD BOOKS

NEW YORK

To Mac and Zac for teaching me how to give
To Lorraine Odasso for teaching me how to forgive

ACKNOWLEDGMENTS

I would like to express my gratitude to my family and to Robert Warren for being so wholeheartedly supportive during the writing of this book.

A special thank-you to my editor, Peter Gethers, for helping and enduring.

TWINS

THE PRESENT

Gracie awoke with a start. She felt the damp twisted sheets beneath her and ran clammy fingers through her tangled long blond hair. Lying still for a brief moment, she stared at the familiar bars across the double window. As she turned her eyes away, she saw with relief her mother's old chipped nursery chair and the blue-lacquered Indian box that contained all her treasures. Like melodies from the past, they lent a note of nostalgia to the room. Carrie must have already been here, Gracie thought tiredly. She reached over for a pen. . . .

Dear Mother,

It seems that I always feel the need to write to you when I am in this place. Dr. Cain approves, but I don't like the way his eyes observe me whenever I mention you. They go blank, like cardboard. I want to take a paintbrush and fill them in with orange or purple.

The last time I was here for a long period, I colored all the sides of the bathroom with the pastels that Carrie had sent me for my birthday. I was tired of staring at those bare walls, my mind etched too many fearful shapes upon them; goblins and hooligans, dragons and cyclopes leered and cavorted around me until I felt that all the bleak Frankensteins of my childhood were inhabiting my bathroom. Once, I was so frightened that I flew off the toilet with my underwear hugging my calves and stumbled down the corridor into the night nurse's arms. Unfortunately, she had little solace to offer; she looked and felt like an oyster, shapeless, slippery, alien-like, and she smelled of iodine.

At present, I feel nearly secure in my plain little room. The bars seem to protect me from the games of the outside world and my own throbbing loneliness within Father's house. I can almost touch your presence now, soothing and strengthening me. Perhaps this is due to the sense of peace and contentment that comes over me after the turmoil.

The last three or four days are one big blur in my memory with flashes of screaming and tears and Carrie's devastated face leaning over me. I think they had to tie me down this time. I kept asking them to bring you a chair. Why is there never a chair for you? Father always sits in it—just like he did on our first-grade Mother's Day celebration at the Palm Beach Day School. Do you recall how excited Carrie and I were that day? We couldn't wait to recite our poem and give you the flowerpot we had made out of papier-mâché with a note glued precariously to the stem of four white tulips:

"To the best Mother in all the world,
with all our love XOXOX,
Carrie and Gracie"

That was our first Mother's Day without you, our first since the divorce. The school had invited all the mothers to join their children.

I recall your dismay when you came into our classroom and saw fifteen smiling mothers already settled behind each little desk with Father unperturbed in their midst, loudly discussing the merits of his children and firmly ensconced in your seat.

I searched frantically for a chair but Miss Williams told me there were no spare ones available. You stood in the doorway during the entire pro-

4

gram looking so proud of us and pretending to be oblivious to the smug hostility that had pervaded the room as soon as you walked in.

The signals were clear: You were an outcast and the pack was baring its fangs. I felt my face flush and was so choked up I thought I would never get through the poem. That day I experienced, for the first time, a strange combination of fear, guilt and pain—a feeling that I was then too young to define. Years later, I understood that this was a form of shame: I had been ashamed of my own father!

As soon as our performance was over, I cheered up slightly at the thought of your smile when Carrie and I would bring you our gift. But as usual, Father made a big fuss over us, clapping loudly and monopolizing the situation. Then Carrie and I were caught up in the confusion of good-byes and when we were free at last to give you the flowerpot, we saw, to our horror, Father ostentatiously carrying it off and out the door.

I cannot erase that moment from my memory. You tried to comfort us as best you could with hugs and love. You told us that in your mind our flowerpot would always be on your bedside table and that this way the flowers would never die. But I never got over that afternoon. I have been committed to this hospital on Mother's Day on and off for many years now. Will I forever be searching for your chair? . . .

How I hated school after the divorce! I remember we were still in kindergarten then. The change in the way you were treated was so sudden and confusing. You used to beg to be included in our activities. I once heard a teacher refuse to let you come to one of our plays and another time you had to bring in a copy of the custody settlement before you were admitted to the parent-teacher meetings. Carrie and I could see the humiliation they were putting you through, but we never dared show our feelings for fear of displeasing Father. We knew instinctively that he needed unconditional admiration and blind followers to maintain his good humor—so we remained quiet and thus played right into his game.

I have never forgotten your words after the Mother's Day scene: "Whenever people draw a circle that shuts you out, you should have the love and the wit to win. Draw a larger circle that takes them in." I keep trying, but I still have a hard time including cruelty in my circle of love.

I am so tired, Mother. I should go soon. But I cannot leave you quite yet. So many thoughts are bursting in me still. They must have filled my dreams these last few days.

I remember how you and Father used to have dreadful fights. Carrie and I would often hear them all the way in our room at night. I remember my heart pounding. I remember praying the yelling would stop. I wished a magic wand would appear and make you like each other again. However, I would take all the yelling and screaming again rather than the silence that followed the divorce. The house was so empty without you, the sadness was overwhelming.

Father had the house stripped of all memories of you; within a week, all the furniture was changed and the walls repainted. I know how sad you were not to be allowed past the front door after the trial was over, but truly you would have hated to see what had happened to your beautiful home. The feeling of loneliness there was unbearable for Carrie and for me. We took to rocking ourselves to sleep, locked like spoons in the fetal position and taking turns sucking each other's thumbs for comfort. Sometimes through our tears, I thought I could hear your voice calling us from the night, aching to come in. How hard it must have been to handle your pain and anger. Yet you always seemed to withstand all your trials with dignity and forbearance. Even when you were first sent to jail that ghastly day, you kept your head high and your voice gentle.

I shudder to think of someone like you in prison. Butterflies and angels should be free to give of their beauty to the world.

It's strange, because since that very first night you were locked in, I began feeling your presence next to me. As a little girl, I could feel your arms around me, and your voice whispering in my ear. Now sometimes when you come to me I can actually see your astral body for a brief wonderful instant and your voice is as clear as music.

I miss you so, Mother.

Lots and lots of hugs and kisses.

I love you.

Gracie

Gracie felt as though a burden had been lifted from her mind. Her letter to her mother had been an instinctive way to cope with the situation. Now, she was simply thankful to be alive after her blackout. She'd forgotten, momentarily, that she was in a hospital, to all intents and purposes a prisoner behind bars.

Gracie was startled by a knock on the door. Dr. Cain, the North Palm Beach Institution's chief psychiatrist, walked in with his habitual, professional "Well, well, how are you this morning?"

Gracie looked up slowly. Dr. Cain's entrance created an all-too-familiar atmosphere in which she found herself swimming like a goldfish in a bowl, wondering how she got in and how she would get out.

"Your sister is waiting outside to see you," said Dr. Cain. "She's hardly left the hospital since she arrived from Los Angeles two nights ago."

"How long have I been in here?" Gracie inquired.

"Your father brought you in three days ago. He told me to call him in Kentucky at his horse farm the minute you woke up. He had a winner yesterday in a big stakes race and . . ."

"Could you please call my sister in now," interrupted Gracie hurriedly.

She had no interest in her father's racehorses, now or ever for that matter. Dr. Cain took the hint and left the room. A moment later, Gracie's spirits rose at the sight of her twin.

Carrie came into the room and immediately slipped into Gracie's bed. They hugged silently for a long, long time. As Carrie held her sister, she felt infinite compassion for her. She wished she could take the pain and horror from Gracie's soul.

When they finally let go of each other, their eyes met in silent understanding, as they had throughout their entire lives. Each loved the other more than herself.

These girls defied the belief, contrary to most theories about twins, that the older one would always be the strongest, the emotional leader. Throughout their twenty-three years, this position of leadership had vacillated back and forth. One was always strong for the other, when needed. However, over the last few years, Carrie had moved into a full, productive married life. She had become a mother at nineteen, yet had remained as social as ever, always seen in L.A.'s newest, trendiest night clubs. Gracie, on the other hand, had withdrawn into herself since her sister's wedding five years before. She showed less and less interest in her friends and their social escapades, preferring to lead a secluded life in her father's house in Palm Beach.

She kept out of Dexter's way as much as possible, dividing most of her time between her passion for photography and her dedication to various causes, usually involving child abuse centers. Her photographs exuded a strange, haunting quality, a uniquely poignant interpretation of reality. Her favorite themes were children and animals. Although she spent many hours on her work and in her mother's old darkroom, Gracie had no desire to embark on any career whatsoever. At night she enjoyed reading books on mythology and metaphysics and the lives of great mystics until late into the next morning.

She had chosen a lonely path for one so young and beautiful. It seemed to Carrie that her sister couldn't sever the cord attaching her to her childhood and that all her creativity, her receptiveness to human suffering, her uncanny understanding of the mysteries of life, only plunged her deeper into her own private abyss. Carrie was clearly now in the stronger position and she knew how crucial her strength was to Gracie's sanity. Her house in Beverly Hills was always open to her twin; it represented, for Gracie, a refuge from pain. There she could laugh and party and play again. She visited frequently, always for just a short time, always when Michael, Carrie's handsome husband, was away on film locations. During each visit, Gracie would bloom forth into the rare and exquisite woman that she was before she returned, as though compelled, to Palm Beach and the chains that were binding her.

"I brought you something," Carrie said as she reached into her Ralph Lauren alligator bag. She handed Gracie an adorable painting done by Kenny and Keith, Carrie's twin boys, portraying people dancing and holding hands, with colorful rainbow halos above their heads.

"Here's a photograph of them. It was taken last month at their fourth birthday party," she continued.

Gracie held up the picture. The children had laughter and blue icing all over their faces.

Carrie was always good with children. They understood her immediately, because there was no facade. If she thought something, she said it. If there was a question, she asked it, often without thought for the consequences, but always without malice or guilt. Carrie had the magical quality of spontaneity, and beyond the frankness that some people found upsetting, there was a great generosity of spirit.

"You and I are the only ones that can tell them apart," Carrie said with an attempt at an energetic smile. It was an infectious one and Gracie smiled back.

As she put the picture on the night table, she thought how the twins looked just like she and Carrie had at that age: innocent and free. She reached over and gently patted Carrie's hand in admiration.

Carrie stood up and adjusted the skirt of her new Armani suit. Her silky blond hair had grown very long and her tiger-green eyes sparkled on her suntanned face as she glanced down at her children.

"At least it happened at home. Last time, when you disappeared, we were worried to death," Carrie said quietly.

"What *did* happen this time?" Gracie sighed.

Carrie hesitated, then decided to tell the truth. It was *always* best to tell the truth to Gracie. "It was the night before you were brought here," she began. "Daddy was giving a black-tie dinner party." Carrie did her best to get the next part out as casually as she could. "I gather you were found huddled, completely naked, in the china closet. You must have been there for hours because it was only at dessert that one of the guests heard you scratching in there." Carrie took a deep breath.

"Father was very upset, needless to say," Carrie said. "He almost choked on his tart, and I don't mean Zoe."

Carrie batted her eyelashes when she referred to their father's latest girlfriend, then continued. "You crawled out in your birthday suit with your drawing pad and purple crayon. Apparently, the Harringtons pretended not to notice." She was going to continue but was interrupted—to her astonishment—by Gracie's laughter. She stood in stunned silence and then, suddenly, she too started to giggle. The thought of Gracie, naked, appearing like Lady Macbeth in the midst of the formal Palm Beach dinner party . . . Gracie was roaring with laughter now. Tears were streaming down her cheeks and Carrie was laughing just as hard.

"The best part," she gasped, "is when Mrs. Felton complimented you on your interesting artwork! She wanted to know why you'd scribbled 'William the Conqueror' under the portrait!"

Gracie was holding on to her sides, out of control.

"Then you explained, at great length," Carrie went on, "how your hand is guided by spirits and you never know what the picture will be until you come out in the light."

"Oh my God! It's not true!" Gracie gasped.

"It is! And all the other guests' noses were glued to their plates since you engaged in this entire discussion while standing there naked as a jaybird."

They both burst into one more round of uncontrollable laughter, tears streaming down their faces.

The nurse came in with Gracie's medicine tray and eyed the girls suspiciously. "You'll have to be leaving now," she said to Carrie, who was trying unsuccessfully to stop the laughter. "Miss Portino must have her sleep."

"I'll be back tomorrow, my Gracie," said Carrie, drying her eyes. She gave her sister a long good-bye hug.

"Thank you for bringing Mother's chair," Gracie replied gently.

The laughter stopped the moment Carrie left. A sadness swept over Gracie as she watched the door close and she became engulfed by the quiet. No sounds filtered in from any other rooms; it was as if she were alone in the world, the last survivor on earth. As she got out of bed and slipped into her satin robe, her fingers touched the back of the tiny wooden chair and her sadness deepened.

She walked to the window. The sky was ominously dark. She could hear her thumping heart and forced herself to focus on how she and Carrie used to dream together. Their mother, Anne, had inspired them with the freedom to dream. They would take turns at night telling each other stories of how happy the family—the four of them—would always be, forever together. Gracie tried to cling to these thoughts, but the reality of what she would go through the next day loomed unbearably before her.

"Father will be here tomorrow," she whispered suddenly into the empty room.

THE PAST

Anne leaned over to view the small, fourteen-mile-long, one-mile-wide island of Palm Beach. Peering down from her first-row window seat, she smiled as the plane made its final approach over Mar-a-Lago into Palm Beach International Airport.

A tiny stretch of land with a gigantic legend, she thought. The island, which meets the Atlantic Ocean on the east and the Intracoastal Waterway of Lake Worth on the west, was emerald-green this evening, with its perfectly manicured hedges and lawns, graceful coconut palms and lush foliage, dotted with pools and tennis courts. Host to European titles, to presidents, kings, tycoons and celebrities, it was an enigma to almost anyone who knew it. To an outsider, Palm Beach was like a movie star—glamorous, larger than life, beautiful and mysterious.

Anne had been coming here to see her best friend, Jane Whitburn, for eight years now, on and off, and she couldn't even begin to figure out the separate tribes, all with their own self-inflicted, inflexible rules and regulations.

Was it a monolithic culture, she wondered, with one level of wealth, one aging citizenry, with conspicuous consumption, an emotionally impoverished, decadent environment? Did its inhabitants, with their abundance of social topspin, thrive on intrigue and manipulation? Was it a land run over by nouveau riche status seekers and pyramid climbers? Was it a Paradise Lost?

Or was it a worldly capital of affluence, a benevolent bastion of money and power? Were its genteel people dedicated to philanthropy and to making the world a better place? With its labyrinthine social machinery and its history unparalleled anywhere, with its freshness of spirit—was it the proverbial Garden of Eden?

Or a mixture of the two? It didn't really matter.

To her, right now, it was simply another resort among the many she had frequented.

Since college, Anne had led a much more sophisticated life than most of her contemporaries. She had fallen in love with a French count while attending postgraduate classes at the Sorbonne in Paris. Later, she couldn't tell if she had fallen in love with the city or with the man, but he had introduced her to European high society and she had fit in as though she had always belonged. During those days, Anne juggled her classes—Comparative Religion, Eastern Thought and other philosophy-oriented subjects—with dinners at Maxim's, balls in private châteaux, racing at Longchamps, polo at Bagatelle, and late nights at Regine's and Castel's. It had been a whirlwind romance which had taken her for enchanting weekends at the Danielli in Venice, the Ritz in Madrid, Claridge's in London, the Excelsior in Rome, and on and on, from palace to palace until the magic faded.

Later, she had fallen for an art collector in Paris who had been buying up all of the great art deco pieces before anyone else had thought of doing so, and she had lived with him among Ruhlmann desks and Gallé lamps. He had given her a Degas sculpture representing a thoroughbred horse and an exquisite Millet drawing, which she still treasured. With him she had roamed through museums, art shows, sales and auctions and he had introduced her to the intelligentsia of Art. By a very young age, she was already well acquainted with European aristocrats, café society, and jet setters, as well as artists, poets, painters and writers, where generally her preference had remained.

Anne was courted by a number of men, but she had always been the

12

one to move on, leaving her partners feeling empty and lost with the sense they would never love again, not quite as they had with Anne. But she knew that when the mental attraction faded, her intense sexuality also waned, and so she had refused to marry any of them.

She was highly sensitive to beauty in all its forms, whether she was living in the fast lane with her rich friends or in Greenwich Village with a wild impoverished Russian emigré, or simply observing drunks, gays and gigolos in late-night bars. She had the ability to recognize the truth in things—what was genuine she made hers, the rest she discarded. She was a sophisticate who accepted bizarre behavior without judging it. Europe may have robbed her of naiveté, but she had preserved an innocence of soul which was apparent in her photography.

As Anne walked out into the tropical humidity, Palm Beach society was the least of her concerns. Her mind was far more intrigued by Jane's urgent telegram, received yesterday, begging her to come for the weekend.

Anne climbed into the midnight-blue stretch Park limousine, as the chauffeur began loading the old Louis Vuitton luggage she had purchased at an estate sale.

"The Southern Bridge is closed tonight. We'll have to take the Middle Bridge," her driver commented.

"I'll keep that bag up here then. I'm going to be late," said Anne, pushing the button to raise the partition.

Anne, as a photojournalist, had perfected the art of applying makeup, on herself and others, in a moving car, racing from one job to another. She highlighted her enormous green eyes and moistened her full, pouty lips with nude-pink lipstick as the limo made its way across the bridge on Royal Palm Way, where the Town-owned docks jutted out into the lake, home to the huge yachts for the season. She passed by the Society of the Four Arts building on the left, dedicated to culture; in front of her, the Royal Palm trees that lined the road seemed like armed guards.

Anne pulled on her nylons over her long slim legs as the car made a right on South Ocean Boulevard. The smooth water was now on her left, the fabulous estates immaculately landscaped with breathtaking flora on the other side. As always, she was overtaken by the sparkling cleanliness of Palm Beach.

Anne slithered into her black silk strapless evening gown as they rounded the corner at Marjorie Merriweather Post's mansion, then swerved left, past the prestigious private Bath and Tennis Club, heading toward the Whitburns' estate, Casa Palma.

13

A sweep of Anne's long blond hair fell back, touching her shoulder blades, as she put in her simple one-carat diamond studs.

"Miss Anne Graham," announced the chauffeur to the guard, as the massive black filigreed wrought-iron gates, with their highly polished brass knobs, opened.

The driveway was lined with banyan trees, floodlit, alive with people and cars.

The Whitburn home, built in the twenties, sat on the eight acres of ocean-to-lake property. The magnificent palatial estate was one of Addison Mizner's pride and joys, the architect who most influenced early Palm Beach, with his artistic Mediterranean flair, accentuated by red barrel tile roofs, arches and stately columns.

A valet parker in a red waistcoat, open-necked shirt and black trousers opened the door for Anne. As she stepped out, the fragrance of the gardenias, which flanked the steps to the front door, momentarily made her dizzy. She suddenly realized she was famished.

A white-uniformed maid opened the huge wood carved double doors.

"Good evening, madam," said a butler in pin-striped trousers and black jacket.

"Please follow me," he added, escorting Anne through the impressive large entrance hall with its grand staircase. They passed along a Spanish-tiled cloister, whose walls were lined with hunting prints. The corridors and stairs were all open-air, and led through archways to the terrace. There were arches on three sides of the pool, all thick with climbing purple bougainvillea, which supported the second floor of the mansion, leaving the coral pool half in the garden, half in the house. Tonight, beneath the stars and gently waving palm fronds, milled a throng of elegantly dressed guests, glittering with jewels.

"Would you care for a drink, ma'am?" asked a young waiter.

"Champagne, please," Anne replied, anxiously looking for Jane.

All she could see were many identical heavily lacquered platinum tresses, styled after First Lady Jacqueline Kennedy, shimmering in the soft light.

Yellow allamanda climbed over the walls that formed the patio, and on a higher back wall, also made of coral, were sculptured heads from whose mouths water gushed to fill the freshwater pool. The house boasted two pools—one regular, one saltwater, with a beach cabana next to the ocean.

"Thank you," Anne said, sipping her drink as she stopped next to an antique urn filled to overflowing with orange and yellow nasturtiums. I'm leaning more toward the Garden of Eden, she thought.

14

Jane's family was rich old guard—old money, old name—blue-blood members of the elite conservative society, which was supposedly so hard to reach out to. But, as Anne heard Jane's loud peal of laughter and then saw her flying toward her in a Burmese silk sarong, with Persian turquoise necklaces hanging to her waist and a gardenia behind her ear, she laughed with delight. There was nothing conservative about this mad friend.

Jane was a graceful, five-foot ten-inch, slender woman with a mane of lustrous, thick, red hair, one blue eye and one green eye, and an exquisite profile with pure, proud lines. She had breeding and had led a sheltered, privileged childhood, beginning with a private tutor the first few years, then attending the exclusive Foxcroft School, which she had loathed. She had gone on to Stanford, as her mother had wished, where she studied Russian and Chinese philosophy and where she had met Anne.

"Anne," exclaimed Jane in a low husky voice, bear-hugging her. "My God, it's been too, too long, my friend," she said, shaking Anne by the shoulders excitedly, looking into her eyes. "Thank you for showing up."

Jane liked few individuals, preferring babies or old people—her pet abomination being stupidity—but oh, how she loved Anne. She was so natural and charming and light-hearted. Anne had in her the receptiveness of a child who looks intensely at the world for the first time—clean and fresh. She had an inner light that seemed to shine from her, and a gift for seeing things more profoundly. In spite of all her worldliness, her mental and emotional life had remained pure, untouched and razor sharp. There was nothing jaded about Anne. Jane always felt spiritually uplifted around her. But, even more than Anne's understanding and kindness, her outstanding quality was her gaiety for life. The two girls' common ground was intelligence; they both gobbled up knowledge with a voracious energy—and humor.

"I've missed you, and your message sounded urgent," began Anne, holding her hand. "Where have you been? Is anything wrong?"

"No, I've been in Africa on a photographic safari for a month," Jane answered, as a white-jacketed waiter handed her a vodka martini, "and then in New York studying theater."

"I think you would be a great stage actress. You have wonderful talent," replied Anne, knowing all too well her eccentric friend with the 150 IQ could somehow never stick to one thing or place for very long. Anne was the opposite—she had great tenacity, dedication and determination when it came to her career.

"How's the doctor and the little missus?" Jane asked.

"They're fine," Anne told her. Her father was a famous heart surgeon, a short, plump, pugnacious man with a prickly outside and a custard-cream center. Her mother was a distant, imposing figure, secure behind the barricades of fancy clothes and exotic hats. "They're still sending me money every month—which I send back. Do you think they'll ever understand I want to make it totally on my own?"

"No, I think they'll try to pamper their little girl forever," Jane giggled.

"What do you think of all this?" Anne waved her hand at the party.

Jane moved her right hand rhythmically to and from her mouth, as she puffed on a cigarette in a big ivory holder.

"You mean, what am I doing in a town where everyone's first name is Muffie or Bunny?"

"I can't believe you're here," Anne told her.

"Mummy insisted. I haven't been home in six months," answered Jane, winking. Being an only child, Jane was extremely close, in her own way, to her mother, even though they were complete opposites. Jane had a loathing for formality and the hollow forms of society. Growing up, she had observed these conventions on the inside and she had never truly conformed to them. She prized her privacy, and her privileged upbringing had given her the tools with which to hide her Bohemian life-style.

"I've got something to tell you," began Jane, her eyes twinkling, "and I wanted to tell you in person. I met this fabulous-looking musician a few days ago, up in the Village," she went on. "He's the *best* fuck." She giggled, then hesitated, aware that the translucent white-skinned, blue-eyed, bleach-blond woman behind her was eavesdropping. "Be careful how you quote me," laughed Jane to the lady. "No naughty language!"

Anne blushed as the woman's long thin face looked as if it had shrunk inward, with the exception of her mouth and eyeballs.

Jane had an aversion to the press, and knew the woman was one of the local sycophants who sold information to the columnists. She couldn't fathom how she had wormed her way into her mother's very private party, where no members of the newspapers were ever allowed.

"Come on," said Jane, picking up a canape off a passing tray and depositing it whole into her mouth, leading Anne toward one of the twenty tables that were set for dinner with sparkling Baccarat and gleaming Wedgwood.

Ice sculptures were scattered strategically among the buffet tables containing silver serving salvers laden with food. There was a sumptuous cold buffet of Scottish salmon, Maine lobsters, Florida bay prawns and

16

cracked crab claws. Another table had hot entrées, including swordfish steaks and boned quail stuffed with foie gras. And one could have anything from the massive mahogany bar—Krug, Louis Roederer, Bollinger.

Anne's stomach growled, but Jane's news was more important.

"Anyway," whispered Jane, "I married him last week!"

"What?" Anne cried incredulously. "You *married* him?!"

"Sh-sh," said Jane, nudging her forearm.

"Mummy doesn't know yet. I've waited for you to get here," she went on. "I thought I could use your support." She grinned maliciously. "Mummy loves you—you're levelheaded," mocked Jane lovingly while Anne stood motionless.

"You'll like him better than my last boyfriend."

Anne remembered Frazier Howell III quite well—and she hoped she would agree with her friend.

"What a stuck-up bore he was," Jane continued, gulping her vodka. "A lazy, pompous ass whose single achievement in life was the accident of his birth. Oh, there's Mummy now—let's go say hello." She grabbed Anne's hand. "Oh, one more tiny thing—he's only eighteen."

"My God! You're twenty-six," Anne said, astonished.

"That's not so ancient," replied Jane, poking Anne in the ribs.

"Is he here?"

"Are you kidding? I wouldn't subject him to this."

The champagne passed, sparkling in the thin-stemmed glasses, the silver trays glowing white and gold as Marguerite Whitburn moved among her guests. Directing here, correcting there, wondering if the food was being replenished properly and counting to make sure there was enough clean silver out, the servants stiffening at her approach. Always prepared, always in control—the mark of good breeding.

Marguerite Whitburn reeked of old money. Her figure was lithe and willowy, her magnolia-white skin accentuated by dark hair, dark eyes and vermilion lips. The patrician line of a salmon-pink empire-style evening gown stressed her well-kept body. A simple cameo, an heirloom from her mother, hung at her neck. She stood like a person proudly in control of her proper background, presenting strength, confidence, authority and status, based on ancestry and heritage. She belonged to that exclusive clan who ganged up with exquisite politeness to keep others out of their domain. People were always trying to cultivate a sense of belonging to Marguerite's Palm Beach but most ended up in no man's land, looking in but unable to join the exclusive Bath and Tennis and the Everglades Club. Marguerite was a patron of the arts, heading up committees at the Society of the Four Arts and the Garden Club, loved by everyone for her extraordinary contributions to the Red Cross, heart and cancer charities. As Anne watched her, she wondered if she was aware how well her daughter Jane understood the purity of giving, anonymously donating one million dollars of her own money each year to her own pet charities.

"Hello, my dear," said Marguerite, holding Anne's hand a second longer than the greeting required. "This is an unexpected pleasure."

"It's so nice to see you, Mrs. Whitburn," replied Anne. "It's a lovely party."

"I hope you'll be staying with us for the weekend, my dear. It's been nearly six months since you honored me with your company."

"She promised, Mummy," Jane interrupted.

"Yes, yes, that would be lovely," stammered Anne, Jane's news pounding in her brain.

"We're playing bridge tomorrow, if you care to join in," Marguerite went on, one eye on Anne, one eye on the party. "You'll have to excuse me—I'm needed. But we'll have a nice long talk tomorrow." She patted Anne's hand, then swept toward the butler's pantry.

"She's going to be furious," Anne whispered, sipping her drink.

"That's why I'm leaving the day after tomorrow," said Jane, as the cream of the town's society began to dance to the music of Neil Smith. "We're going to spend some of my money and sail around the world, so Paul can write his music."

"She'll be livid," Anne reiterated, shaking her head.

"I know, I know. She'll say: 'Rich days will be followed by empty ones. Don't squander.' Then she'll . . ."

She was suddenly interrupted.

"Jane Whitburn, darling. I haven't seen you in so long," cooed a woman, the muscles of her face performing a smile.

"Gertrude," said Jane, rolling her eyes to Anne.

"Excuse me," said Anne politely, suddenly deciding she needed to use the powder room. She wandered toward the gracefully arched opening to the formal living room, where Renoirs and Monets decorated the off-white plaster walls that soared twenty feet to a beamed ceiling. There were long, dark oak sideboards, intricately carved, containing alternating bowls of pink azaleas and white gardenias. Waiters circulated unobtrusively with trays of champagne.

The alternating bronze and alabaster faces peered at Anne with the interest of a stranger in their midst.

"It's Anne Graham, isn't it?" said Mrs. Rhineland, a wrenlike woman in a green Galanos chiffon gown, her face powdered flour-white, her eyebrows plucked away and replaced by two exaggerated half-moons. "Yes."

"Why, dar-r-ling, I attended your one-woman exhibition at the Museum of Modern Art last year. It was exquisite. You must be very proud of your success."

"Divine, your book was simply divine," chimed another woman, waving her hand with long blood-red nails in the air.

"What a talented photographer you are, Miss Graham," said a tall gaunt man with a courteous manner.

"Thank you."

"What made you choose photography?" asked a soft, gentle voice with a hint of a French accent.

"It makes me happy," answered Anne. The expression on her face held the soft hint of a smile.

It had all begun with no clear-cut sense of direction or obsession. Anne's father had given her a box Brownie camera for her twelfth birthday, and she had dabbled with black-and-white photography throughout high school and college. She had graduated with honors from Stanford, majoring in English Literature, all the while experimenting with pictures, influenced by the work of Bill Brandt and Ansel Adams. After a year at the Sorbonne, Anne began work as a photojournalist for *Life* and the Sunday *Times*, traveling the world, interviewing and writing to complement her photographs, her eye developing unconsciously and coming as something of a surprise. Her work started appearing in *Stern, Paris Match, Vogue*. Her love of adventure led to the photographic travel books. It was the sixties, and the era of the hippies had arrived, confirming her tendencies toward the unconventional, and they had been the first to appreciate her as an artist, when her first book of photographs of Buddhists in Ceylon came out. It became sort of an underground password between them, for Anne spoke in a language of peace and compassion, which rang a bell with these flower children. Anne then became obsessed with the beauty of India, and tried to capture its spell on film. She accompanied her pictures with her written impressions of the country, and a few poems. This second book was an overnight success in the traditional publishing world, and no one was more astonished than Anne herself. She was critically acclaimed and, though her royalties were hardly making her rich, she was definitely self-sufficient.

While the reviews of her work had been very positive, when all was said and done, Anne did not really know how she took her pictures. Her response to India had been such a matter of instinct, she didn't know how to describe it to anyone. She knew that she loved her work and put a great deal of psychic energy into it. She had her own personal philosophy of photography—simplicity. Anne believed in a rigorous lack of affectation, wanting to capture as nearly as possible the emotional, as well as the objective, reality. She had been able to visualize the scenic effect of India in her mind's eye well before taking the photos. Somehow, she could squeeze the subject into her mind—but from there, it was magic. She didn't feel at all in command of the technique.

Now, suddenly she was interviewed, recognized in restaurants. Although her public was a small one, her name had become synonymous with purity.

"I would be thrilled to have a small dinner party for you," commented Mrs. Rhineland.

"Thank you for offering," began Anne, "but I'm only here for two days. I have an exhibition opening at the Victoria and Albert Museum in London, next week."

"May I be introduced to this charming young lady?" asked another.

"Excuse us," said Jane, with a wondrous blend of delicate dignity and unapproachableness, sweeping her friend away.

"My God, Anne! Is this the story of your new life? How ghastly for you. I can see that if I ever become a success on the stage, I'll have to give it up immediately. I couldn't stand the notoriety," she added, her eyes wide with genuine horror. "Let's get away from this rat trap," she added, wiping her brow with a theatrical gesture of humor.

"Who *was* that woman?" Anne asked.

"She's the one who has the servants iron her money—so it's crisp!" The two girls stared after the woman. As was her fashion, Jane jumped right into a new subject. "Remember that one party we had in my apartment off campus? When we sat in the bubble bath drinking champagne, while our guests cavorted around us?" Jane beamed. "I wish we were back there."

"I remember your pet monkey was perched on your shoulder," chuckled Anne.

"It's nice to see you back in town, Jane," said a tall dark-haired figure, in a low sexy voice. "Who is your beautiful friend?" he added, turning to Anne, holding a cigar tranquilly in one hand.

"Goodness, Dexter, you must be the only one here who doesn't know her," grumbled Jane indifferently, introducing them hurriedly.

"Oh, but of course." His eyes rested thoughtfully upon Anne. They lingered so long she felt uncomfortable. No, not uncomfortable, she thought. Almost the opposite, almost hypnotically calm, as if his gaze were stripping her bare, right to her soul, and it was as if he were saying, "It doesn't matter what I find there—it's all right."

"I'm a fervent admirer of your work, in particular the series of photographs you did on Iranian women," he murmured softly. "May I get you a drink?"

"No, thank you," she replied. "Please excuse me." Taking a glass of pink champagne off a moving silver tray, she followed Jane off into the crowd, shivering.

"That man you just introduced to me is vaguely familiar," Anne said. "Who *is* Dexter?"

"Oh, he travels around the polo crowd. He likes to be where the action is, always seen with the right people. He's completely surrounded by an aura of glamour that totally conceals the man." She hesitated, grabbing a hollowed-out grape that was filled with a tiny dollop of cream cheese. "But he's supposed to be an extraordinarily gifted lover. The women can't get enough of him!"

"Ugh, that's all I need, a new lover," laughed Anne.

"Let's go upstairs, take a plate of food, and chat in peace. These people all sound like broken records. It's flattering, but it does get boring. Originality, my dear, as you and I well know, is sadly lacking in this dreary world we live in," pronounced Jane, in a loud stage whisper, as they fled upstairs like guilty teenagers to their room.

Dexter Portino leaned against the mantelpiece, underneath the oil portrait of the Whitburn family, taking up his favorite position, that of observer. The sparks of light on the crystal and the shifting colors of the evening gowns gave the room an air of brilliant gaiety. Or was it the woman he had just met? A slight smile flickered over his handsome, softly cruel features.

The morning sun broke clear at dawn with all the pure tints of a fine opal radiating in the cloudless sky.

In his elaborate flower chintz–covered four-poster bed, Dexter was breakfasting on Earl Grey tea, a large glass of freshly squeezed grapefruit juice, thinly sliced toast and a bowl of fresh cut melon, all served on a large white wicker tray. A single red hibiscus flower floated in a small crystal bowl. One side of the tray was filled with the morning papers—

The New York Times, The Wall Street Journal, industry journals, and *The Palm Beach Daily News,* "the Shiny Sheet," which was only good for news of the social events in town. The other side of the tray held financial reports from his businesses, and the information he had had a detective gather on Anne Graham.

Dexter couldn't forget the first time he had been brought face to face with Anne. It was a vague and fleeting impression suddenly drawn into amazingly clear focus. She looked at him from an imperial height of untouched purity and pride. He was struck by an undefinable expression of mingled receptiveness and indifference, as she lifted her green eyes slowly from the shadow of their dark lashes and rested them upon him.

Dexter studied a picture of Anne attending the J. H. Lartigue show at the Museum of Modern Art in New York last month, and pictures of her from her exhibition at the Norton Art Gallery in West Palm Beach last year. All of the social register in town had shown up. Dexter was amazed as he sipped his tea. Everyone who came to Palm Beach was guilty until proven innocent—why was Anne different, he mused. The WASP natives were usually suspicious of everybody, but all of them seemed to embrace her.

Also included was detailed background information on her as well as her parents, a schedule of her shows for the next year, taped interviews, social events she had attended lately with a list of her escorts, reports of conversations from her friends, even the fact that she collected china dolls. Dexter's report also told him Anne was now in Paris.

Dexter gazed at the photos. He had seen many beautiful women in his life, but the face of this woman he had run into a few weeks ago haunted him. The clean, proud strength she faced the world with stared back at him. So, too, did the white-blond hair and intense green eyes.

Suddenly, at this stray and solitary moment, the past turned back upon him like a revolving picture in a mirror, with a flash of unwelcome recollection—and he saw himself, a teenager with the wrong color skin, eyes, and dressed improperly.

Dexter had been born in Frankfurt, the son of Willem Schmidt, a German general, and Rosa Portino, a wealthy Argentinian. He had had a privileged childhood, until age thirteen, when the war had broken out, and he was yanked out of his English boarding school, his father fearing mother and son—because of their dark looks—might be mistaken for Jews. They had fled to Buenos Aires, taken his mother's maiden name, and he was forbidden to speak of Germany ever again. All he had ever overheard was that his father had been tried and convicted after the Holocaust and killed for his participation in committing war crimes.

Dexter then divided his time between his mother's huge *estanzia* near Buenos Aires, where there were thousands of acres of gardens, fields and mountains slashed by pits of red ore, and an apartment in Washington, where he had resided during his prep-school days. Over the years, Dexter and his mother had visited most of the fashionable resorts and towns in the United States. On their first trip to Palm Beach, his mother had anxiously anticipated shopping on the world-renowned Worth Avenue, where several fountains graced hidden enclaves and the best-known names in fashion, antiques and art were housed. "It has the glamour of Faubourg-St.-Honoré, the quality of Bond Street and the style of Via Veneto," Dexter's mother had whispered to him with awe.

As she spoke, Dexter burst into laughter. He was looking down at something he'd never seen before—a dog bar. It was a semicircular trough, decorated with colorful mosaic tiles and topped with a silver spigot that provided fresh running water. A pug, with a mink collar inlaid with diamonds, was taking a leak in it. Still giggling, Dexter had meandered along behind his mother on the tree-shaded avenue, where the Mediterranean-style vias were framed in vivid red and purple bougainvillea and oleander, until they had stopped for lunch at Petite Marmite. He and his mother had stood in the entranceway for what seemed forever, as the maitre d' gave them a derisive expression. Dexter was learning early that Palm Beach didn't like foreigners—unless they had a European title. A title was a prestigious symbol more valued than a Rolls-Royce. He fidgeted as he watched a Russian prince being escorted to the front table, before he and his mother had been led to a table practically as far away as Siberia. On the way to the table, two women had snickered at his overweight mother.

"Ignore them," his mother said ruefully.

"Look at that ghastly dress," said one in a voice that could have cut glass.

"You look ridiculous in that floral circus yourself," Dexter retorted flippantly. Later he had learned they were wearing the brightly colored floral patterns of the prized "Lillys."

Over the years, Dexter grew to hate having to wait to be invited to the private clubs. He loathed the way many waiters and salespeople in Palm Beach held peculiar airs of contempt for him. It was an attitude that was commonly displayed by insolent menials here, as they whispered "probably Jewish" behind his back. This had infuriated him. Dexter hated Jews more than any of them would ever know. Why hadn't I been born a blue-eyed blond, he asked himself. Why don't I have a title? It was then he swore to himself that one day he wouldn't need one. He would watch, learn, listen and prepare. "I will be king of all this," he had vowed. A white-hot desire for social acceptance had burned within him. It still did.

Back home, Dexter worked hard to build up the already vast family copper and meat-packing fortune, expanding into silver, sugarcane, wheat, livestock and ranching. He practiced doing *everything* well—his mother helping him, polishing his already courteous manners into ones which suggested centuries of breeding and drawing rooms. He danced well and could speak five languages. He spoke a precise, cultured English, without the trace of an accent. He knew just what wines to order, what flowers to present, which places to frequent. He was an outstanding athlete determined to master everything, and he became a fantastic tennis player, a scratch golfer, a nine-goal polo player, a yachtsman and a crack shot. After he had returned from Harvard, he became an obsessive businessman, a tyrant who squeezed his workers dry, and lured competitors into copper mines he knew were worthless.

Dexter slid into his slippers, his brow clouded. The bitter lines around his mouth deepened and hardened. He stepped out onto the expansive bedroom terrace with its dozens of stone-potted geraniums that overlooked the grapefruit, banana and lemon trees in the gardens, and the one-hundred-foot-long turquoise swimming pool, with its yellow and blue mosaic tiles that lined its edges. Dexter lit a cigar with a preoccupied air as he descended the sweeping outdoor staircase through the islets of palms and age-old banyan trees, heading to his gymnasium.

Dexter did ten more repetitions on the quadricep machine, thinking back to the money he had spent to be accepted, and how he'd learned to fit in.

He had played the game of lending his name and photos discreetly to the press over the years, securing invitations to the right parties, setting up introductions for himself and taking up hobbies such as ballooning, fencing, auto racing and hunting, all of which made colorful newspaper copy. There had been years of bowing, scraping and ass-kissing. Dexter had been around Palm Beach so long, and had been invited to the clubs so often because of his expert skills in tennis and golf, that by the time his own application came up, it was somewhat automatic. After the acceptance by the Bath and Tennis membership last year, the Everglades Club followed, then the Sailfish Club, and the Seminole Golf Club in North Palm Beach. He had done it all, and brilliantly. Now he was a member of the Coconuts—the exclusive club of bachelors who held the most coveted party invitation of New Year's Eve; they gave one party only to pay off their social obligations for the year.

Dexter's body glistened with sweat from his morning workout as he walked back into his dressing room to look at the calendar his secretary, Millie, had prepared.

In Palm Beach, most people did not talk business; that was regarded as an ugly necessity which had to be performed but never mentioned. He laughed to himself. Those people were becoming an endangered species. Inherited wealth could be certain death to ambition. Their trust funds paid low interest rates if they had poor personal executors; there was also inflation to whittle away the fortunes. Some of these aristocrats were no longer able to entertain in a grand manner. Dexter would never become one of them—he kept his eye on his money. Even though he used Morgan Guaranty's Trust Department to invest quite a bit of his money, he never presumed anyone foolproof—and he loved outmaneuvering his peers while looking for more investments.

Dexter Portino had a very diversified investment portfolio. He had money in oil, gold, rolling stocks, long-term treasury bills, real estate. He also banked much of his profits in Switzerland, at Julius Baer.

His first phone call every day was to his broker in New York; it lasted a minimum of an hour. On this day he then began ringing up his managers in South America, and spent the next hour and a half talking to them, uninterrupted.

He knew his phone would not ring until he gave Millie the okay to forward his calls to his master suite of rooms. She was absolutely loyal, and guarded Dexter's privacy with the ferocity of a Cerberus.

"Millie, get me Carlos. He's at the Tucumen plant," Dexter said from his intercom system at the head of the bathtub.

"He called fifteen minutes ago, Mr. Portino. There's a shipping problem—he'll call back at eleven-thirty," replied Millie efficiently. "And Franco is on his way to Bolivia. The government is tightening their hold on the tin industry. And another file on Miss Graham arrived for you," added the dependably discreet woman.

"Invite Wally Barker for dinner," began Dexter. "Cancel my tiger shoot in Africa on the fourteenth—I'm going to Paris. Book me a suite at the Ritz for eight days. As a matter of fact, cancel all my engagements for two weeks." He then pushed the servant call button.

"Have Irma bring me the file on Anne Graham. I'm in the tub. Also tell her to get me the manager of the Burning Tree Golf Club in Maryland. Arthur's having trouble getting his new son-in-law in."

"You are having lunch with Congressman Kingston at one, re: the oil cartel, a golf game at the Everglades at three with your lawyer, massage at six-thirty, and dinner on the yacht at eight-thirty. Also, you haven't rsvp'd on the square dance this week at Marjorie Post's."

"I'll get back to you," answered Dexter, picking up the folder his personal maid, Irma, had just brought in.

> "Anne Graham has the sense of wonder of a traveller who enters a strange country."

> "Anne Graham's brilliantly witty work is a refreshing reminder that life is fun."

He flipped through other reviews.

> "Anne Graham knows how to draw the elusive secret to create great pictures. Her work stands on its own—essentially inexplicable."

> "She sees in a different and illuminating way."

> "An original way of visualizing."

Throwing on a towel, Dexter read on and on. He was impressed with her knowledge of politics and her wit, but it was her boldness in interviews that captured his attention. She advanced her views with spirit and vigor. There was a note from Frank attached—she planned to sail the Aegean this summer. Oh, she knows how to work hard *and* play hard, he mused. Dexter greatly respected that.

Stepping into his dressing area, he pulled the draperies, leaned back on the quilted chintz sofa and reran a tape of Anne. She was beautiful, talented, intelligent—and she had her own money. Sitting before him on the screen, in a simple pure white dress, she was full of grace and charm. Her face was startlingly alive, her smile was radiant. Anne was outgoing, full of life and verve. The shape of her mouth was clear-cut, a sensual mouth held closed with precision.

Dexter's eyes shone like those of a cat in the darkness. He had always sought new, exhilarating company. And as far as he'd been able to discern, she had no lovers in Palm Beach. Yes, he decided. He would have her. She would be a clean slate upon which Dexter could write his own tale.

Dexter raced over to the Norton Gallery on Olive Avenue after his golf game. Acclaimed as one of the nation's leading small museums, it was well known for enriching the cultural life in the Palm Beaches. The gallery houses a prestigious permanent collection signed by such masters as Matisse, Degas and Gauguin, and has an impressive display of Chinese art. Dexter had spent time at many notable exhibitions here for business reasons, but even though he had his own impressive gems, in actuality he knew nothing about art.

"Mr. Portino, this is all we have left of Miss Graham's work," said a gray-eyed man with a head of curly white hair, as he handed Dexter three photographs taken of children in the Far East. "Also, here are the books and periodicals on Ansel Adams and Brandt from our library, as you requested."

Back home, Dexter laid his keys down on a table inside the marble-floored curvilinear foyer, where a magnificently handsome hand-painted oak railing swept upstairs with the utmost grace. He slipped his feet out of his shoes, leaving them for his housekeeper to pick up. He gathered his messages off the desk in his booklined study as he went over the evening's menu with the chef—"a cheese soufflé, swordfish steaks, fresh asparagus, salad vinaigrette, chocolate mousse for dessert, Montrachet," he said on the intercom.

"I want white orchids on the boat," he added before taking the elevator.

The masseuse had strong, gentle fingers that kneaded Dexter's muscles and worked out the knots of tension.

"Get my accountant, Millie," said Dexter. "Tell him to go ahead with the municipal bonds we discussed this morning. And fire that new assistant to the chef—the one in charge of shopping. There were no Kellogg's Corn Flakes in the entire household for me yesterday after my polo game," he added furiously.

"But . . . I'm sure . . ." began Millie. Dexter didn't let her finish, punching off the power button on the intercom.

27

Dexter stood at the teak railing, in a navy-blue double-breasted blazer, yellow silk tie, dark gray razor-creased worsted pants and Gucci loafers with no socks, his severely handsome face cooled by the gentle, salt ocean breeze. His one-hundred-twenty-foot yacht edged out from the dock into the smooth waters of Lake Worth. He leaned back, looking at his fifty-five-foot Rybovich fishing boat, bobbing gently against the bejeweled skyline of Palm Beach.

"Why don't you be my guest and take some of your friends out fishing tomorrow on my boat?" said Dexter to one of his guests who was on the board of a company he was trying to take over.

"Thanks, Dexter. I just might take you up on that."

A white-coated steward passed among the guests with Taittinger champagne, the color of crushed rose petals, in elegant Baccarat glasses.

"I have five hundred thousand dollars to play with tomorrow morning," began Dexter. "Are there any new issues?"

"I have three or four coming out this week that our company is underwriting," replied Hank, Dexter's broker, a small rotund man, slightly stooped and completely bald, in spectacles. "The one I recommend is the fast-food chain. All my indications are this will be the hottest stock this year," he added confidently.

"How many can I get?"

"I only have sixty thousand shares that I can give to my clients, Dex, and I already have commitments for forty-five. Do you want fifteen?"

"I want all sixty. Fuck your other clients," replied Dexter in a low voice, as cold as a skeleton, naked of emotion.

Hank downed his bourbon, then peered at Dexter from behind his steel-rimmed glasses.

"You want your job, don't you?" Dexter said.

Dexter noticed they were being watched and he suddenly laughed easily, attractively, bringing the scene back to its normal mood.

"I'm sure you'll work it out, Hank. Also, put me into Manhattan Cable TV networks and those brownstones we discussed." Dexter patted his shoulder, as the beleaguered broker walked away.

"Senator Braxton," Dexter said to a tall heavyset man with snow-white hair and a carefully trimmed mustache and beard. Dexter took the senator's arm and guided him to a corner of the deck.

"You know that favor you owe me? Well, Sam, I need to borrow your yacht for a month this summer. You still keep it in Piraeus, right?"

"After your campaign contribution, you can have it all summer." The senator arched his eyebrows in surprise. "I thought you were going on safari. What's happening in Greece?"

Dexter said nothing, slipped into that inscrutable expression of his in which no feeling whatsoever could be discerned.

His date for the evening sat across from him at the table for sixteen. Andrea Warfield had a delicate, haughty face, a milk-white throat, beautiful arms and bosom, and rich, long brown hair, the shade of a ripe chestnut, which was pulled back in a diamond and ruby clip. Her eyes were vaguely pale, neither gray nor brown; they were lifelessly empty of expression—detached and aloof. In Palm Beach, this was supposed to indicate high breeding—but to Dexter it was repulsive.

About all she'll be good for tonight is fellatio, he thought to himself. He looked forward to relieving her of the boredom of her privileged life.

The sumptuous feast went on in the fashion of most dinners—commencing with arctic stiffness and formality, thawing slightly toward the middle course, attaining just a pleasant warmth of understanding as the guests fawned adulation at each other over the main course.

"Wally, I recently purchased some of Anne Graham's work. Have you thought about having her to your Worth Avenue Gallery?" asked Dexter nonchalantly, motioning to have his plate removed.

"I tried, my dear man. She's soooo in demand, I couldn't get her."

Dexter remembered Anne's naked shoulders, and the figure underneath her revealing black dress. She was a mystery to him—belonging to everybody and yet to nobody.

Dessert was offered; Dexter passed. He believed only contracts should be served with liqueurs.

"You know, I met Anne Graham at the White House," commented the old senator. "She was dating the vice-president's son—and boy, was he pushing for her to be his daughter-in-law." He pulled at his white whiskers while he spoke. "She must be some catch. He usually doesn't think *anyone* is good enough for his old political family."

Dexter managed a thin, tight smile.

The guests chatted in the usual frivolous way of after-dinner guests and started their good-byes. When the yacht pulled back into the mooring, they descended the gangplank.

Dexter bid them good-bye, then silently led Andrea to the library, pushing the button behind the draperies. The secret panel opened to the private room. There, glowing in the light of a Lalique lamp, were mahogany shelves containing hundreds of albums of erotic photographs—of sadomasochism, homosexuality, bestiality, ménages à trois, incestuous situations. Dozens of catalogs advertising artificial genitalia and aphrodisiacs were in drawers. Glass cases contained spurs and the most beautiful whips made of the finest leather from Hermès.

Andrea stood with the usual scornful uplift of her eyebrow; however, her nipples were erect under her pale satin shirt.

Dexter twisted them roughly.

"Get me hard," he ordered, pushing her to her knees, shoving his penis into her mouth.

THE PRESENT

G racie pulled out, stem by stem, daffodils, tulips and irises from the dozens of spring flowers in the large Lalique vase Dexter had had delivered by Old Towne Florists earlier that day. She scattered them in small vases all over the room. The words "All flowers are stalks of sunshine" were ringing in her mind when she heard her father's voice in the corridor.

"Nothing is too good for my daughter," she heard. "She *must* have the best care and service. You may call me at any time, day or night." His deep voice was growing nearer. She could see the doctors' heads all leaning in his direction, nodding eagerly. "I want her to stay here a little longer this time, Ms. Hatch," he added to the head nurse. This last was spoken with such authority that something of an electric thrill passed up and down Gracie's spine. "I'll take it up with Dr. Cain."

The door to her room opened and Dexter strode in. Gracie was struck by the apparent sincerity and kindness that he wore on his smiling face. She was tempted to drop her guard and longed to be swept into his charm, along with everybody else. But she shivered instead. His charm could never touch her. Not after what he had done to her mother.

"Hello, my dear," Dexter said placidly.

"Hello, Father," Gracie replied in a monotone.

"How are you?"

He didn't kiss her. In fact, he hadn't even touched her so far. And he didn't wait for her reply.

"It's wonderful having Carrie and the boys living at home," Dexter said eagerly. He was already pacing the floor incessantly. "I'm looking forward to giving lots of parties with her."

"She's a lovely hostess, isn't she?" Gracie said.

She watched closely as, discussing Carrie, he slowly dropped his mask.

"Being here will take her mind off that Michael. An awful man, she married an awful man," he sneered, with cold distaste. The lines on his face appeared more pronounced; they seemed to deepen by the minute. Then he added with distinct pleasure, "Thank goodness the twins don't take after him. They could nearly be my own sons."

Gracie stared, astounded by his ego, and fascinated at the decay settling onto his face at an alarming speed. She wondered if he would turn into Dorian Gray's portrait before the end of his visit.

"I've arranged for tennis lessons for them at the Bath and Tennis Club with Mitch," he continued. "I hope to God nobody traces their father's ancestry back too far. You know how difficult these clubs are about Jewish blood."

Gracie tried a yellow mustache on her father, and inserted agate stones in his eye sockets.

"Nothing I can't handle, however," Dexter went on arrogantly. But to Gracie he had begun to shrivel up and was turning into a weasel. The agate stones suddenly popped out and Gracie was startled back into reality.

As usual, Dexter did not have a real conversation with her; he did *all* of the talking. He never sat down, he never asked her another question after asking her how she felt. Gracie's detachment was wearing thin. She was weary and irritated.

Dexter turned away. "Well, I'm on my way. There's so much to do." He left the room without pausing for a good-bye.

Gracie felt drained with anger and resentment. I ought to know better, she thought. Remain still for a while, then perhaps peace will return.

Gracie suddenly felt her mother's presence next to her. She smiled. Turning to the center of her room, she was aware of a vast calm that encircled her, sheltering and soothing all cares away.

Dr. Rob Cain got up stiffly from his desk and opened the window with a small sigh of discouragement. He breathed deeply, trying to shake off the atmosphere of gloom and depression that had settled on his shoulders. As he leaned out, a few drops of rain ran down his prematurely aged face. He wished they could wash away the frustration and self-loathing he always felt after one of Dexter Portino's visits. Oh, how he longed for the rain to erase his weaknesses and let him return to being a whole human being before Gracie's scheduled session. Closing his eyes, he wiped his brow with a white cotton handkerchief. Why did Dexter always leave him feeling totally emasculated, with his professional integrity shattered and his self-esteem way below ground level? God, if he's capable of doing this to me, he thought, an adult and a professional, what can he do to a child?

Dr. Cain lowered the window and went to his file cabinet. How can I be of any help to a patient right now, he wondered, particularly to such a sensitive, intuitive person as Gracie, when my own strength and dedication are impaired? Shaking his head, he pulled out the top drawer.

Rob Cain was a big bear of a man, with exceedingly gentle eyes. He was well loved by his staff and patients because of his sincere devotion to each and every case. His whole life revolved around his work; nothing was more important to him. Even as a young boy, Rob had instinctively known how to talk to people about their problems and troubles, and had dreamed often of having his own clinic one day. He had put himself through medical school, then invested his life savings, and the savings of his parents, in this private institution in North Palm Beach. However, not knowing enough about the business end of it, he had almost lost his hospital to the bankruptcy court a few years ago. Feeling tremendous responsibility to his patients, he begged for and borrowed money so as not to shut down, knowing there was so much more for him to do. During this period, he had accepted a large loan from Dexter Portino. Effectively, Portino now had total financial control over the clinic. *His* clinic.

Dr. Cain smacked his lips despairingly and tossed three manila folders onto his desk. He was well aware he possessed a rare sixth sense that allowed him, more often than not, to understand and feel compassion for a wide range of human behaviors and oddities, but . . . Dexter's behavior was such that he simply rejected it with distaste and repulsion. He was unable to cope with the situation in any cool or detached manner. Dexter had him by the balls, professionally and personally. Damn the man!

Gracie was the sacrifice. Cain had to sell his soul on her treatment if he wanted to remain open and help the hundreds of others in his care. Over the years, the parameters of her therapy had been carefully and deliberately laid out by Dexter. The pure hell of this was that Gracie had always known of her father's monetary claim to the institution, thus, rightfully so, she could never totally trust Cain as her doctor. He completely understood that. So what would he ever be able to do for this lovable girl? He wondered if the poor child knew that she was being kept in the institution longer than necessary as bait to bring her sister, Carrie, home to her father's nest—the selfish bastard . . .

Dr. Cain massaged his temples as he leaned back in his chair, recalling the previous year when he had given Gracie's case to a wonderful female counselor named Rosie, who he felt could help her. However, Dexter couldn't control Rosie, so he ranted and raged and threatened to shut down the whole bloody clinic unless she was dismissed directly.

Dr. Cain had thick eyebrows that nearly grew together, and as he frowned now, the brows became a horizontal straight line.

What Dexter is doing to his daughter is criminal, he thought. If only rich people would construct or at least reconstruct instead of delighting in their power to destroy. He glanced at Gracie's file and pondered the girls as he turned his chair toward the open window. The twins looked identical to the eye, but their personalities were so strangely contrasted.

Carrie was an energetic, spontaneous optimist, with an unconsciously selfish and possessive side to her that stemmed from her highly competitive spirit. Gracie was introverted and moody, yet quietly courageous and compassionate. However, there also had crept into her personality an unforgiving mental block concerning *anything* to do with her father. Gracie thought of her mother as a saint; Carrie felt the same about her father. Where was the truth? He certainly wasn't going to get it from Dexter, he thought, glimpsing his near-empty file, nor Anne. Dexter had always refused to participate in any family counseling with Carrie or Gracie, and absolutely never spoke of Anne. *Never.*

Cain tried to calm the frenzy of his thoughts. Why did Dexter favor Carrie so? Had Anne favored Gracie? Was there anything to the "abnormal" relationship between Carrie and Dexter that Gracie had hinted at in anger a few times? Or was it just that peculiar mixture of passion, jealousy and misunderstood affection that ties many fathers and daughters together? He had witnessed Gracie's crestfallen face in the past when Dexter catered only to Carrie. Yet, there was no apparent jealousy between the girls over this. What had been Anne's role? And why was Gracie so guilt-ridden?

Dr. Cain scratched his balding head and forced himself to focus on the one consoling thread in this pattern. No matter what the girls' differences were over their parents, nothing ever interfered with their feelings for each other; the twin bond was unequivocally the stronger love. *Twin bond*—the words acted as a stimulant to his tired, struggling brain. So he mused, still gravely searching, still struggling to solve what promised to be unsolvable.

Gracie ambled down the long, quiet corridor to Dr. Cain's office. Seeing the door open, she made her way toward the familiar sofa. The room was tastefully decorated in desert tones, with a Navajo rug in the center of the Mexican tile floor, and four cactuses in huge Indian pots.

"Hello, Gracie. How are you?" Dr. Cain looked up compassionately. He got up from his swivel chair to give her a hug.

"Hi," Gracie replied simply, not registering surprise, delight or displeasure. She was fond of Dr. Cain, felt sorry for him, in fact; however, her senses immediately picked up her father's presence lingering in the room. She felt it oozing out from under the desk and behind the curtains. It's a muddy brown today, she thought, as it spread from the pages of the heavy files before her, sneaking up Dr. Cain's chest, then clinging to his solar plexus. Gracie could smell danger—Dexter danger, she thought grimly. Fear has a sound and scent all its own.

"Please sit down," Dr. Cain said, pulling his armchair closer to the sofa.

Dr. Cain perplexed her. How could the purse strings so effectively rule this otherwise kindly and dedicated man? Gracie knew he didn't approve of her father, yet he went to extraordinary pains to conceal his dislike. No one, except Mother, had ever dared stand up openly to Dexter; no one, Gracie realized.

She filled a glass with water as she recalled all the "nice doctors" from her childhood. "He's your friend, Gracie," she could hear her father say. "You *must* talk to him." Menacing figures from her past peered at her from behind Dr. Cain. She looked at them with interest over the rim of her water glass. Each one had attempted to mold and control her thinking, her feelings. Most had been very clever, knowing just what to say—candy men, like those who lure little girls into their cars. Somehow they had all worn her father's face. Why didn't I ever say, "Take them away"? she wondered, tossing down the last drop of water with a gulp. The Queen of Hearts would have said, "Off with their heads," but then queens are blessed with authority, whereas lonely little girls can only retire into muteness.

"Is there anything in particular you'd like to discuss this morning?" asked Dr. Cain, watching her attentively and seeing that she was absorbed by some deep-seated intellectual irritation.

"No, not really," she responded in a half-whisper.

Dr. Cain's eyes questioned the secrets which she appeared to hold in her mind, but the quiet composure of the girl's beautiful face stopped all inquiry.

The clock ticked relentlessly; the phone never rang.

"What happened last Sunday?" the doctor asked.

"Nothing," replied Gracie calmly, even though she felt the anger swelling.

A tension-filled silence went on for several minutes. The two simply stared at each other, as Gracie twisted her hair with her forefinger at the base of her neck.

Dexter may as well be in the room with us, concluded Dr. Cain, as he surveyed her passive face and furious eyes. The poor, sad little thing knows she can never trust me. An agony of shame possessed him.

"How was your visit with your father today?" he asked, leaning in closer to her.

Gracie fixed him in her gaze; her eyes flashed a warning.

"He never changes," Gracie began. "Father follows *The Prince* by Machiavelli. 'The man who would be prince must be unencumbered by morals and ethics; he must be part lion and fox,'" she quoted directly, wishing once again she were the Queen of Hearts.

"Do you still believe he doesn't love you?" Cain asked solemnly.

"The ability to communicate an honest emotion is a rare gift that Father does not possess."

Gracie reflected upon the word *father.* He *was* her father, yet curiously he was a stranger to her, a remote, enigmatic figure. How could he appear so warm and loving to Carrie? Even in the way Gracie addressed him, thought of him—"Father." To Carrie he was always "Daddy."

36

"Father loves Father," she continued, twisting her hair. In a mechanical tone she repeated, "Father loves Father."

Dr. Cain intently studied Gracie's delicate, classic features. Why was the issue of Dexter so painful for her? He watched her slowly shake her head and to his surprise, she inquired wearily, "What do you want from me? Shall I tell you all about Father's affairs after the divorce was finalized? Shall we discuss how Carrie and I were subjected to sleeping in his bed alongside his current girlfriends?"

"What do you mean by 'subjected'?" Cain asked.

Remembered pain swept over the girl's features. "Simply that it was a choice between the nymphettes or our lonely, haunted nursery, so most nights we chose to creep upstairs to the master bedroom, wishing Mother would somehow be there again. We were only five, you know."

Dr. Cain nodded silently. After a short hesitation, Gracie continued. "Or do you want to hear about Father 'getting religion' a few months before he broke up with Mother?" In a slightly stronger voice: "Huge white Bibles suddenly materialized in every room along with pamphlets and hymn books. A succession of mean nannies entered our lives, introducing notions of straight and narrow paths which simply added slippery bottomless ravines to our list of nightmares. Gone were the parks and the birthday parties; in came sermons, punishments, quizzes and sin. How do you like that for sudden contrast?" Gracie looked up at her doctor with tortured eyes. "Small children are meant to have consistency in their lives, but Carrie and I were condemned to emotional seesaws from then on. Mother fought with the nannies and quarreled with Father. She lost on both accounts.

"Soon after Mother got the boot, so did the religion." Gracie's tone was bitter. "But the new friends stayed. At least time enough to make excellent character witnesses for Father during the trial."

Dr. Cain shifted his weight and took a deep breath. "What about forgiveness, Gracie?"

Gracie took in Dr. Cain, a tense cord seeming to snap suddenly in her brain. "I *can't* forgive him," she cried. "It's impossible! What he did to my mother . . . when she went away . . . what he's done to all of us! . . ." Her voice grew louder; Dr. Cain's office seemed cramped and suddenly narrow.

Dr. Cain, riveted to his chair, stared, spellbound.

"And *I* . . . I helped to . . ." whispered Gracie, but broke off suddenly before she could finish the thought.

"Helped what? Who?" urged Dr. Cain, a faint hope beginning to kin-

37

dle in him like a tiny flame. Raising himself a little, he looked at her more closely.

"Help me, Gracie. Help yourself," he pleaded.

Entranced in the past, old thoughts began to hover round Gracie's soul like homing pigeons—sweet and dear remembrances of her once-happy family began to shine through the darkness of her brain.

"Mother," she said softly, her sweet eyes full of tenderness and yearning, and her hands clasped on her breasts.

"Let go of your will, Gracie, forgive yourself," Gracie heard her mother's gentle voice in her ear.

"Gracie . . . Gracie," whispered Dr. Cain tremulously, but she was not hearing him anymore. He was all too aware that his patient feared a particular set of painful childhood memories. He could not get her to accept the fact that life was about movement. For her, life was all too clearly stuck in the past. As long as that was true, she would keep returning to the hospital until she could reason with her nightmares. He sighed and gazed at her wistfully. Oh, how he wished he could help her through her bouts of anger and guilt which over the years had led to her sudden blackouts and her tragic emotional fragility. He considered anger, anxiety and grief as fairly easily dischargeable emotions—guilt, however, was not. It was one of the most serious causes of depression a patient could be afflicted with because of the resulting loss of dignity and self-respect. But where did Gracie's guilt lie? He didn't know. After all these years, he simply didn't know.

Everything was so still he could hear his own heart beating forth in irregular pulsations.

Then Gracie smiled, a sad, peaceless smile.

"I'm tired," she said, and looking altogether unearthly in her beauty, she rose and left the office.

Are there some things even the passing of time can't obliterate? Dr. Cain thought, staring into space. It was as if certain recollections were stamped on Gracie's memory as faithfully as scenes flashed by light on photography plates. Would these vivid pictures ever fade into pale negatives for Dexter's daughter?

With a brief silent prayer for guidance, he pushed his gray hair back from his brow and walked slowly to his group session.

38

THE PRESENT

Dexter arrived home from the hospital and immediately called out for Carrie.

"She's out on the pool terrace talking on the phone, Mr. Portino," Irma told him. "And Kenny and Keith are in the pool with the new temporary nanny you hired." Irma was a tiny Spanish woman as wide as she was tall, who had been with Dexter for twenty-five years. She reported only to him and knew where everyone connected to the household was at all times. Through the years, Irma had never fraternized with any other household help, had consistently viewed all wives and girlfriends as intruders and, not coincidentally, had outlasted everyone. She had never married, had always lived in, knowing Mr. Portino demanded total loyalty, which she gave to him unconditionally.

"Thank you, Irma. I'll take a Perrier on the terrace," Dexter murmured and headed outside.

He saw Carrie, looking exquisite in a stunning black one-piece bathing suit, talking vivaciously on the patio phone. She waved to him, whispered with her hand over the receiver, "It's Michael," then resumed her conversation. Dexter hesitated, then proceeded back into the house. Through the glass, he could see Irma head down the servants' path to the pool, carrying a lead crystal glass of Perrier decorated with slices of lime.

"Gracie was still very depressed when I saw her this morning," Carrie was saying to her husband. "Daddy just walked in. He's back from the hospital."

"How *is* your father these days?" Michael inquired. Carrie could hear the not-so-subtle dislike in his voice.

The hostility between the two men had not lessened over the five years since she had married.

Up until her wedding, the motivating factor in Carrie's life had been trying to please her father. She adored him, had since she'd been a small child. He was the ideal in her eyes. She'd thought he was perfect. But when she was eighteen, Dexter had let her down. He'd surprised her by marrying his second wife, Helena, who was her mother's look-alike. Helena was petty, mean and far more interested in spending Dexter's money than in helping to raise his twin daughters. Her three favorite activities were, as Carrie saw it, snorting cocaine, dancing all night and driving Carrie crazy. Helena was jealous of Carrie and tried to keep her away from Dexter. So she decided to keep far, far away. One month to the day after Dexter's marriage, Carrie eloped with Michael Donovan and moved to Los Angeles. Her father was not pleased.

Michael was thirty-seven at the time and had never been married either. He was one of the most successful movie stars of the decade. He had played a detective on a highly rated TV series in the early seventies, then proceeded onto the big screen with even more success.

Carrie pictured her husband on the other end of the line—his just-mussed sandy hair worn long, his ruggedly handsome face etched with suntan lines and character.

She remembered the night they had met, during a black-tie party at the Polo Club in Wellington, following the Cartier Match. She had never seen such a good-looking man, except possibly her father. He was tanned, lithe and muscular; his posture was erect and assured. His casual easy attitude along with the incredible sexual energy he gave off left her breathless. When their glances met, a light color had danced into his cornflower-blue eyes and she knew that she had to have him. And Carrie Portino was used to getting what she wanted.

"What did you say, Michael?" she murmured into the phone.

"I asked how Dexter was," he repeated.

"Oh, he's fine. You know Daddy. Everything is under control."

Michael felt a twinge when he thought of Dexter. Dexter was the one man Michael knew he couldn't quite measure up to in his wife's eyes.

"Daddy's giving me a party next Friday," exclaimed Carrie. "Can't you come? *Everyone* will be there." But she knew, even as she said the words, that they would not entice Michael. Unlike most of the people she now saw on a regular basis in California, missing a party where everyone would be was of no concern to him. Especially a party given by her father.

"I can't make it, Care," replied Michael tenderly. "Look, I miss you and the boys and would love to see Gracie. But we have to shoot the ending of the movie in Venice next week."

She knew he would not change his mind or his schedule. That he *couldn't* was something Carrie had never understood. Even the biggest stars were at the beck and call of their producers. A party in Palm Beach simply wouldn't fit into Paramount's calendar.

Dexter walked into the den and saw that the red light on the phone was still on. Christ, he thought. It had been forty-five minutes since he arrived home and she was still talking. Irma had informed him she'd already been on for an hour *before* he'd arrived. He cursed the special Toshiba phone system he'd installed, precisely so that no one could pick up any receiver and eavesdrop.

"When can you come home, Care?" Michael asked anxiously.

"It all depends on Gracie. As soon as I can, I promise. Do you want to talk to the boys once more before we hang up?"

"No, it's all right, don't make them get out of the pool again."

"Okay. I love you, Michael."

"Me too. Talk to you soon. And give the boys a hug."

Carrie felt an incredible longing for her husband as soon as she put the phone down. But she was immediately distracted as Dexter came bounding onto the patio.

"I thought we'd have a nice dinner at Café L'Europe tonight," he announced. "Just the two of us." Carrie, lost in her thoughts, didn't reply.

"Are you all right?" he wanted to know. "Did *he* upset you?"

"Oh, Daddy, of course not. I'm sorry. And yes, yes," said Carrie apologetically. "Dinner would be lovely." She gave her father a hug. "How was Gracie this afternoon?"

"She's fine." Dexter walked past Carrie. "I made a reservation for nine o'clock. I'll be down in the poolhouse working out if you need me."

When his daughter glanced at him curiously, Dexter added, "I put in new equipment since you were here last. I even have that Stairmaster machine you told me you were so crazy about."

Carrie beamed. She knew the machine was really all for her. He was always so generous. "I'll walk you down," she said, knowing that would make him happy.

"You haven't met Jock, my new trainer, yet," remarked Dexter. "I've been working out with him for a few months now," he added, vainly patting his taut stomach.

"You look better than anyone to me, Daddy," Carrie replied admiringly. She had never seen her father anything but fit, and she knew how important it was to him to stay that way. When she had lived at home, they had jogged and worked out regularly together.

"Well, Jock'll be here in a few minutes and we work for two hours, if you want to join us. We're also going to do a short run up the Lake Trail to the Breakers and back."

"No thanks, Daddy, not today."

"Oh, you think he's not as good as your 'Body by Jake' man," Dexter grinned as he pinched her rear.

"I'll run with you tomorrow, but I really must make the kids some dinner now," she continued.

"That's what I hired the nanny for, darling," Dexter said as firmly as he could.

"Well, Michael believes nannies inevitably separate you from your children, especially at mealtimes. You know I've never had a live-in," replied Carrie, turning away.

Dexter just shook his head. He took a key from his wristband and unlocked the poolhouse. She had a fierce sense of loyalty both to her children and Michael's wishes. In that way, she reminded him so much of Anne. The thought made him angry. But he immediately wiped the frown off his face. He didn't even like Carrie to see him upset.

"Please be dressed by eight-forty-five," Dexter said to her.

"Yes, Daddy," she said.

As he watched her walk away, back toward the pool, he thought again, *just like Anne,* but he began to work out, harder, then harder still, and by his twenty-fifth push-up he'd forgotten about his ex-wife and was thinking only of the pleasant dinner he'd be having with his daughter later that evening.

C arrie and Dexter walked into Café L'Europe and, of course, all heads turned. Carrie had always enjoyed the way everyone smiled, took long sips on their drinks, practically held their breath whenever her father entered a room. People loved to watch him and she loved being on his arm. He made everyone feel beautiful.

"Good evening, Mr. Portino," said Bruce, the very handsome maitre d'. He shook Dexter's hand and kissed Carrie's. "And how lovely to see you, Miss Portino." Carrie was surprised at how pleased she was to hear "Miss Portino," instead of her married name. It seemed to make her feel more like herself. "You're more beautiful than ever."

"Oh, Bruce, you never change. Thank you," Carrie smiled demurely and winked behind her father's back.

Bruce had been the maitre d' there for years. Carrie used to go out dancing with him in the wee hours. They had been quite friendly. In front of her father, however, Bruce had to remain in his place. Dexter did not believe in consorting with the help.

"Your table is ready, sir, or do you prefer to have a drink first at the bar?"

"We'll stop at the bar a few minutes."

"Mr. Portino, how are you," inquired Peter, the bartender, as he reached across the bar to shake Dexter's hand. "The usual?"

Dexter nodded.

"And you, madam?"

"The same, thank you," Dexter answered.

Dexter held up his flute of champagne with Framboise and gently clinked Carrie's.

"Cheers, my dear. Welcome home."

"Thank you, Daddy. Cheers," Carrie kissed Dexter on the cheek. "You're looking very handsome tonight."

Dexter beamed and sat a little straighter on his stool as Lydia, the owner of the restaurant, came over and kissed him on both cheeks. "You look lovely, my dear," she said turning to Carrie. "Although, to be honest, I've never been able to tell you and Gracie apart. How nice to see you." Lydia extended her hand and Carrie clasped it warmly.

"Thank you, Lydia," said Carrie, accepting her compliments with grace and charm.

She had always made Dexter proud.

43

"Let me show you to your table," said Lydia, pulling back Carrie's chair. "Leave your drinks. The waiter will bring them."

As they crossed the pink flower–filled room, several people nodded their heads, but there was no one Dexter deemed important enough to stop and chat with. Instead, he kept his eyes on Carrie. Seeing her in her black, figure-hugging dress, long-sleeved and bare-shouldered, he was once again overwhelmed by thoughts of her mother. With her long legs and huge green eyes. Her luxuriant thick blond hair framing an exquisite face.

Lydia seated them at the number-one banquette where they had a full view of the mahogany and mirrored dining room.

"We'll stay with champagne, Lydia. A bottle of Taittinger Rosé Comtes de Champagne, please."

"Fine. Enjoy your dinner. And again, it's nice to have you back, Carrie."

"It *is* nice," Dexter said, as Lydia slid over to another table. "You should come more often."

"Daddy, we've been through all that."

"And we'll go through it again. This is your home."

"It *was* my home."

"It still is. It will *always* be your home."

Carrie smiled gently. She glanced around the room at all the familiar faces and said, "Palm Beach is the same as ever. Nothing changes here, does it, Daddy?"

"The restaurants have lately. This is the only decent food in town now since the Epicurean closed. Petite Marmite and Taboo have changed hands since you left. Even the old family business, Testa's, is for sale. Now we have Renato's, Wilson's, Lulu's and I don't know what else," he continued. "I haven't been to any of them—they all come and go so fast now."

"You're never here anyway, Daddy," commented Carrie, as she patted his hand.

"I would be," he said, "if *you* were here."

Carrie looked down, avoiding her father's stare. "How does it feel to be single again?" she asked as brightly as possible.

"You think I'd learn, eh? Well, at least I made it five years," Dexter said.

Romantic longevity had never been Dexter's long suit. He was used to the adoration of two or three women at a time. He loved the chase, the seduction and the conquest, as well as the thrill that came with each new partner. He had never answered to anyone for his time or affection, not even his wives, and he liked it just that way. During his marriages, his affairs were brief, one-night stands or long weekends, after which the relationships usually ended.

"Are you getting along with Zoe?" she asked. But she knew he wouldn't answer. He never discussed his women with either of his daughters. She was right—he was as evasive as ever.

"Tell me, how is Michael these days?"

"Busy, Daddy, *very* busy."

"Too busy for my daughter?"

Now it was Carrie's turn to be evasive. She thought of how hard it had become lately for her to be the wife of a huge superstar. After Michael had won the Oscar last year for *One Fool Too Many*, it seemed his fans couldn't get enough of him. She had grown up used to being the center of attention in Palm Beach where everyone had always made such a fuss over "the twins." Now she was just Mrs. Donovan, very much in the background. She didn't realize just *how* much in the background until she'd returned this time to Palm Beach.

Carrie was staring at her champagne and Dexter sensed the subject was dropped. This was very contrary to the way she usually went on, prattling about life in L.A. His eyes narrowed and, with a perverse thrill, he realized he had an opening. There was something wrong—and he determined to find out what it was.

"Should I order for both of us, darling?"

"Yes, please," answered Carrie, still lost in thought. But she smiled as she spotted Mrs. Van Buren across the room.

"Oh my God, has she had another face-lift? Her smile looks like it's made out of porcelain!"

"It's her fifth," Dexter told her. "And it looks more like she's wearing a Halloween mask, if you ask me."

"Why would anyone do that to themselves?" Carrie asked incredulously. "You're so lucky, Daddy. You look younger than ever."

Dexter automatically ran his finger lightly over his right eyelid. He had just had his eyes done two months ago in Miami by one of the top surgeons in the United States. Carrie hadn't noticed, so it obviously was a good job. No one was supposed to be able to tell; one should just look very well rested. Dexter had decided long ago that he'd never accept the aging process—and he felt the eyes were a good place to begin. He'd had the operation in the doctor's office, then stayed two days at the doctor's private inn, under supervision. He had then flown his jet to Lausanne, staying at the Centre de Revitalisation for four weeks so he could get sheep-fetus injections, telling everyone he was in Zurich on business. No one knew about this except Zoe, his latest girlfriend, and she knew better than to say anything.

"Are you ready to order, sir?" a tall, blond, gay waiter asked.

"Yes. Madam and I will have the buffalo mozzarella and tomato salad with basil to begin and then we'll have the baby rack of lamb for two— rare, please."

"Will that be all, sir?"

"Yes, we'll look at the dessert cart later."

"Thank you, sir," he said, pouring Dexter and Carrie some more champagne.

They talked effortlessly for hours—discussing Kenny and Keith, Carrie's social calendar, their homes, politics and travel. Everything except Gracie, whom Dexter refused to discuss. Carrie was the only person Dexter could talk to without strain. The only one he'd *ever* been able to talk to. Even when she was a little girl, six years old, he would take her out to lunch, tell her about his business schemes, gossip about friends, everything but the truth of his romantic affairs. He had never encouraged close, intimate relationships. Carrie was as close as anyone would ever get.

"Would you care for dessert?" asked the waiter, with a feminine lilt, as their table was cleared.

"No, thank you, just espresso please. For two," Dexter answered.

"Are you sure Gracie didn't want me to bring her anything tomorrow?" Carrie asked anxiously.

"Carrie, I've told you fifteen times exactly what she said today. She's going to be fine, just fine. She always is. Please don't worry any more tonight."

"But . . ."

"Please. I want this to be a night just for us. I don't want Gracie with us tonight."

"Gracie is always with me, Daddy. You know that."

"Yes, I do know that." But I don't have to like it, he thought to himself.

Dexter signaled for the check and glanced at his black Hublot watch which matched the one he had given Carrie on Valentine's Day.

"Why don't we go dance for a little while? It feels like I haven't been out since my divorce." At least in town, he thought.

Carrie had become warmed by the champagne and a bit giddy. "Sure, why not."

They said their good-byes and made their way down the stairs to the valet.

"Thank you for a lovely dinner," Carrie said, reaching for Dexter's hand.

"You're welcome, sweetheart," he said affectionately.

Just then there was a huge crash of metal. They both turned and saw Hector Simpson's Rolls-Royce door lying on the pavement, in front of the idling automobile. The car parker was in shock but Hector did not seem fazed in the least.

Dexter roared with laughter. "Hector's had the driver's door stuck on by a metal pin for ten years now," he said, trying to catch his breath. "He always crawls in from the passenger side. Must be a little too drunk and forgot to warn the new boy. Poor fellow. He's only worth about three hundred million," finished Dexter, wiping his eyes.

As Dexter climbed into his Jaguar convertible, he put the top down and headed down Worth Avenue for the bridge.

What a perfect night, he thought, glancing at his beautiful daughter in the passenger seat. *And not over yet.*

THE PRESENT

Sunshine poured into Gracie's room as she lay listening to her favorite Bryan Ferry tape, *Avalon,* that Carrie had brought her that morning. Music, like no other language, has the power to speak from the heart to the hearts of others, she thought, turning up the volume on her earphones. For her, music was able to absorb some of her emotional tensions and clarify feelings that otherwise remained dark and obscure. She wanted to crawl inside its inner symmetry, for she was sure many secrets of life dwelt there.

Suddenly, Gracie was rudely interrupted by a tugging on her arm. She removed her earphones to hear the nurse, finishing her sentence: ". . . group therapy in the library has already begun."

"Okay," replied Gracie, getting out of bed. She headed half-heartedly down the corridor.

Gracie opened the library door quietly and eased toward the small group of people conversing on the floor.

"You live in a totally different world from the rest of us, Nicole," said a very frail, mustached man, dressed all in white. "You believe in things that I can't even understand."

Victor, the man in white, began tugging at the knot of his silk scarf. "You actually think there's a God and that each human being has a soul," he exclaimed in disbelief.

Victor skewered her with hard cynical eyes and suddenly the woman was at a loss for words.

"Well, aren't you taught the same in your church?" Nicole stammered, sitting cross-legged and fidgeting nervously.

"Oh, I suppose so, but then I never think seriously about these things," retorted Victor. "You know that if we did, we could never live as we do."

Gracie sat down next to Nicole.

Nicole Sebastian was a roly-poly, wide-eyed brunette. When Gracie had first met her, Nicole had a bubbly, effervescent personality. But, gradually, she had come to resign herself to being committed to the institution. She'd come in a year and a half ago, put there by her mother, the witch. Mrs. Sebastian was an overpowering, opinionated woman who'd become incensed when her own father died, leaving his entire estate, amounting to ten million dollars, to eighteen-year-old Nicole. The only way she could enjoy and continue her free-spending ways was to have Nicole out of the way. So she told everyone poor Nicole had gone crazy after his death. As Victor spoke, he reminded Nicole of her mother, whom she disliked just as intensely.

The pale, sickly man continued.

"Just think, if a soul has never died, and never *will* die, its burden of memories would be ghastly, horrible. No hell could be worse!"

Victor began to tremble.

"But suppose they're beautiful and happy memories?" interrupted Gracie.

Everyone stared at her. Nicole smiled.

"They *couldn't* be," Victor responded. "We all fail somewhere! Remember we're all born with original sin and must atone, or so they say," he added with a shudder.

Victor had been in the institution for ten years, and thought of himself as the resident psychiatrist and "king" of group. It had been a long time now since that cold November evening he had walked in on his gay lover with another man. He had attempted to cut off both their penises on the spot. Temporary insanity—bullshit, he thought. Victor loved to relive that moment, over and over in his head. Holding the knife, watching their petrified faces. The two of them neutered—that's what keeps me alive, he thought, half-smiling.

"My views obviously don't interest you, Miss Portino," Victor continued. "You appear to be on some plane of thought I shall never rise to."

Gracie and Victor had had their run-ins before. Finding common ground had always escaped them.

"Of course," he hurried on sarcastically, "I don't *want* to rise. I'm perfectly content to live in a moderate state of happiness, then drop into oblivion in my grave."

Gracie looked at him compassionately. "Perhaps if you thought in terms of ignorance versus illumination instead of sin versus payback you might be on a happier track."

Gracie firmly believed that God was all tenderness, love and justice. She could not think God created love only to end in death. *He* doesn't allow anything to be wasted—not even a thought. Nothing goes unrecompensed, either in good or evil, she mused to herself.

Gracie looked around at the people in group and felt there wasn't a space for her there. Just as there had never been a chair for her mother at Father's religious meetings either.

Carrie and she had once overheard their father explain to his new group of friends: "Well, Anne is very unconventional. I fear she has a tendency to fall for the teachings of the devil."

There had been shocked silence after this statement and everybody had stared very strangely at Anne when she came in a little later. She'd greeted Dexter's friends with her usual warmth, Gracie recalled. However, the warmth was met with chilly hostility. The rumors had already started—about her mother's drug abuse, the sexual infidelities, the breakdowns. Who were these people who thought themselves so religious, yet showed themselves so judgmental—who were so ready to believe any and all lies about the baseness of human nature?

After that session, she and Carrie had nightmares for weeks; they needed to sleep with a night-light for months.

When they had finally asked their mother what Dexter had meant, Gracie remembered Anne smiling gently and saying: "If your souls are filled with love, evil cannot touch you." She had then gone on to explain tenderly, "Sometimes there are misunderstandings between people on different paths, but don't be too concerned. With more learning, these will be smoothed away."

In spite of these words, Gracie had always felt uneasy whenever those meetings were held at the house, just as she felt uneasy now.

Victor interrupted her private meditations. He was becoming agitated.

"Well, if your knowledge is so vast," he sneered, "and your faith so pure, why don't you enlighten us with your high-powered mysticism?" He continued petulantly, "Perhaps you should start praying for the redemption of all the rest of us poor lost souls?"

Gracie looked up and decided Victor had such a sour look, he must have need of divine aid to digest his breakfast.

Nicole wished she had a Quaalude, but finally dared jump in.

"Nobody will ever understand us," she said, lumping herself with Gracie.

"I'm going back to my room," said Victor, a tone of finality in his voice.

To Gracie's relief, Dr. Cain brought the meeting to a close.

"We'll meet again on Thursday, same time," he said.

Jane leapt out of the driver's seat of the stretch limo and fairly flew into the North Palm Beach Institution. Her oversized black Ray-Ban sunglasses dangled precariously on her high cheekbones and a mane of glossy red hair floated out behind her.

Her entrance into the subdued hospital lobby created an immediate sensation. Clad all in black, from soft Italian boots to tight leather jeans up to a panther pendant from Cartier hanging above a minuscule silk camisole, Jane swept toward the information desk with long, swift strides, a silvery fake fur jacket flung carelessly over her arm. She radiated a crisp vitality that was as foreign to the laid-back atmosphere and tropical environment as her outfit was. Barely waiting for the receptionist's directions, Jane was already ushering a bewildered-looking chauffeur —who was trundling scores of beaten-up Gucci suitcases along with too many bundles of various sizes—to the elevator. Prattling instructions to him to meet her on the third floor, Jane proceeded to race up two flights of stairs and gallop down a long corridor to Gracie's room.

At the door, she checked herself, stopped and took a deep breath, dropping the role that had long ago taken over her public life. She began tapping softly, a short coded message. Receiving no response from inside, she bent over to pull off her boots, and was turning the doorknob with the utmost stealth, when the chauffeur appeared at the end of the hallway, huffing and puffing loudly under the mountain of bags. She motioned urgently for him to be quiet, and with one finger on her lips, she crept into the room.

The chauffeur stood frozen in his tracks, surrounded by the luggage. A very bizarre woman, he thought—a cross between a wild mare and an overgrown Irish wood sprite. He had picked her up at the Miami airport a couple of hours earlier and instead of resting or drinking in the back of the limo like most of the overseas travelers he was accustomed to, she had told him she preferred to drive and that he might as well enjoy the privacy and luxuries of the backseat for a change.

He'd become very official, and expressed with vehemence his concerns regarding company policy, insurance, and other red-tape considerations. But the lady had merely assured him she was excellent at driving farm trucks and tractors and that she had qualified as a Red Cross ambulance driver some years earlier. She had added that she would get them to their destination "in no time flat." So, in the back he sat, stiff and straight for the whole trip, adamantly refusing the drinks and peanuts she had urged him to sample, and praying his boss would never find out.

Jane sat down carefully on the edge of the bed and watched Gracie dozing with her Walkman on. She looked at Anne's old nursery chair and felt a lump rise in her throat. All these years, Jane had kept her promise to her best friend to stay in close contact with her godchildren.

Anne need never have asked. Jane loved Carrie and Gracie as if they were the children she had never been able to have, due to a botched-up illegal abortion back in the sixties. She'd always been able to give the twins a sense of their own value and had managed to keep some fun and laughter in their lives. Oceans of unspoken tenderness united her to the young girls.

Gracie appeared so peaceful. Jane remembered Anne looking that way. Until she lost custody of her daughters. As Dexter, inch by inch, took away *everything* that Anne deemed important, Anne's life was eventually reduced to a shell. When even the *hope* that she could recover her family and her old life was removed, the shell got emptier, more tortured. It seemed to Jane that her friend's exquisite face had, from then on, been hidden behind a mask of pain.

Gracie awoke, blinked slowly and a delighted smile spread slowly over her face. "Hi, Auntie Jane," she mumbled sleepily.

"Hello, my dear," Jane responded eagerly, swooping down to hug Gracie and knocking most of the air out of her body while doing so.

"Did you bring me anything from Mother?" Gracie inquired as soon as she could catch her breath.

"Of course," Jane beamed. She bounded to the door and summoned the chauffeur to bring in his load. "I don't remember where I packed anything, but I can search through my things while we chat." Whereupon Jane set to opening case after case, pulling out or tossing to the side the most extraordinary assortment of belongings Gracie had ever seen. Books, drawings, medicinal herbs, Burmese silk cushions, a Russian samovar, antique music boxes, Dijon mustard, a hammer and chisel, amber beads, quartz crystals, a Ming Dynasty toad, juniper berries, bongo drums, dog vitamins, pre-Columbian pottery, and on and on and on. Tearing her eyes away from the extravagant mess piling up rapidly around the room, wondering if her mad godmother ever considered packing anything as mundane as clothes, Gracie lay back against her pillow and smiled again. After a short pause, she asked, "I suppose you heard what happened."

"Yes, indeed, I did. Carrie called me in London as soon as she'd arrived in Palm Beach. I'm having lunch with her tomorrow." Jane was now kneeling on the floor and fumbling under a small Aubusson tapestry. "It's been too long. I can't wait to see her. Unfortunately, I can't say the same for your father."

"You know, Auntie Jane," Gracie began wistfully, "whenever Mother would talk to us about Father, there was no anger, no coldness, no hate in her voice. It was as if she were telling a story. She always told me and Carrie to love him. And I was desperately confused because I felt something else inside, a dark feeling toward him."

Gracie turned and stared out the window.

"Mother couldn't have been all wrong about him," she murmured. "I wish I could understand it all."

Jane knew Gracie never truly understood her feelings about Dexter. How could she? My God, the things he'd done to her, to everyone she'd loved. To everyone who'd loved her. She wanted to suddenly hug her best friend's daughter, to assure her that she would, from this point on, be safe. But she knew she couldn't make a promise like that. Not while Dexter still had control of her.

"I found them!"

Jumping up suddenly from the floor, Jane exploded with a triumphant exclamation. "This is from your mother, my dear, with all her love."

She handed Gracie a light-blue felt jewelry bag from Tiffany. Inside the bag were two silver picture frames. A long blond lock of hair was glass-encased in each, with Carrie's and Gracie's names engraved on the bottom.

"What a lovely gift," Gracie said with a small catch in her voice.

"And this is from me, to add to your collection." Jane handed over an exquisitely crafted gold and enamel Fabergé Easter egg. "I could have strangled Dexter for changing his mind and spoiling our spring holiday plans at the last second. I missed you in Aspen." Jane shook her head in exasperation. Her red hair seemed to float through the room.

"Thank you for spoiling me so, Auntie Jane." Gracie leaned over and kissed her gratefully.

"Well, how was your day?" Jane asked brightly, beginning to stuff everything back into her bags.

"I had an awful session with Dr. Cain," Gracie told her.

"Nothing ever changes." Jane grinned.

"Then I went into group and the subject was religion and three of us did all the talking. On the way back to my room, though, one of the girls pulled me aside and told me yesterday's subject had been masturbation and was far more interesting than today's."

"I would have enjoyed *that* discussion," Jane laughed. "Next time it comes up, let me know. I have an interesting list of techniques and procedures that are used in different parts of the world that would boggle your Dr. Cain's mind."

Gracie admired Jane. She was a very successful sculptor now, close to fifty but looking ten years younger. She had been married three times. Her first husband had tried to blackmail Jane during the divorce for hundreds of thousands of dollars. Jane had laughed at him, knowing there was nothing to blackmail her with. When he'd pleaded with her, she'd written him a check for twenty-five thousand dollars and told him never to bother her again. Her second husband had been even wealthier than Jane. The problems were that he was thirty years older and had a strange predilection for vacuuming the house at five A.M. Her third husband, it turned out, didn't like vacuuming—but he did like other men.

So Jane was currently single again. Aware of her charms and which men were attracted to them, she didn't feel remotely threatened by the younger girls in Palm Beach and was always in greater demand than they were.

What a great choice for a godmother, thought Gracie. And I know Carrie loves her as much as I do.

"If you had had any kids, Auntie Jane, would you have chosen Mommy for their godmother?"

"Of course, my dear. Who else?" Jane responded emphatically.

"I wonder why none of her other girlfriends asked her."

54

"To be honest, my dear, your mother thought Andrea would when Chessie was born, but she wasn't even invited to the church service."

"Why not?"

"The scandal. The fear of guilt by association."

Gracie shook her head in disbelief.

"Listen to me, dear. Your mother defied convention, dared to be herself and lived fully and wholly at her own discretion," Jane explained with pride. "She was immeasurably superior to the lot of them."

"Don't talk in the past, Auntie Jane. Please."

"I'm sorry, Gracie, I only meant that it was a long time ago." Jane reached for her hand.

"Last night I felt Mother at the foot of my bed," Gracie began. "I watched her for what seemed two, maybe three minutes, until she faded away. She vanished like a rainbow in a swirl of cloud," Gracie said sleepily.

"I'll let you rest now," Jane said in a husky voice. She kissed Gracie on the forehead and tucked her blanket under her chin.

"Come back soon, Auntie Jane. And thank you."

Gracie closed her eyes and thought of the many nights she had lain in her own bed as a child listening to the ocean, alone in spite of Carrie's little arms encircling her. Tonight that same cold loneliness seemed to lie in wait for her, hovering on the other side of the door. It's ready to engulf me, she thought. Here it comes. Closer . . . closer . . . here . . .

Gracie tossed and turned. At one point, she dreamed of golden doors. She opened one and stepped through.

Looking around, Gracie realized she was standing in the enormous audience hall of a great gold palace where there were crowds of slaves, attendants and armed men. These men were guarding a most impressive throne set high above the rest of the crowd. On the throne sat a woman, crowned, veiled and erect. Her right hand held a scepter blazing with gold and hundreds of colorful gems.

Suddenly, Gracie perceived the object on which the general attention was fixed—the swooning body of a wounded man. Heavily bound in chains, he was on his knees at the foot of the throne. His head was carefully placed in a guillotine.

Beside him stood a tall black slave, dressed in vivid scarlet and purple and masked with a dark hood.

Gracie wanted to rush to defend him, but she was forced to stand helplessly, watching the scene.

At this moment, the veiled woman rose slowly.

Gracie could hear her own voice, straining and ripping at her throat. "No, no, please!" she cried, her eyes blinded by her tears.

Then with a commanding gesture, the queen stretched out her glittering scepter—the sign was given.

Swiftly the blade gleamed through the air and struck its deadly blow. Gracie turned away in horror, but was compelled by some invincible power to raise her eyes again. She saw the slain victim, the tumultuous crowd, the queen.

Gracie stared with loathing as the woman threw back her golden veil. Her own image looked full at her.

As they lifted the body and head of the murdered man, Gracie could see his face for the first time.

It was her father, Dexter.

Then came silence and utter darkness.

Gracie sat straight up in bed, a cold sweat beaded on her chest. There was a storm raging outside. Lightning flashed outside the windows.

Gracie stretched out her arms to the picture of her once-happy family next to her bed, and sobbed.

THE PAST

The outdoor restaurant Le Pirate, a few miles east of Monaco on the shore of Cap Martin, was alive with the sounds of laughter, clapping and flamenco music.

The owner, Pirata, a slim, intense man with dark Mediterranean features, was singing a deep throbbing melody to the accompaniment of his guitar. The wild passion of his young gypsy wife dancing barefoot under the yellow moon had caught Anne's imagination as she sat entranced at the long candlelit table, oddly silent and detached from the merriment and noisy chatter surrounding her. As an artist, Anne was always appreciative of style and movement, and tonight, the familiar scene was enhanced by the gypsy girl's skillful use of castanets. They added a new dimension to the dance, and the dark-haired beauty's supple body moved to the rhythm with a greater fire than usual.

Anne watched the performance, quietly sipping her sangría, oblivious to the conversation of her friends.

"Come on, Anne, dance for us tonight with Pirata, like you did last year. Remember? Up on a table," called out an Italian friend, suddenly interrupting her thoughts.

"Yes, come on, Anne," urged another voice. "You look great in that tight Pucci. Let's see you move."

Anne shook her head. "Another night, Philippe. I'm not in the mood now," she answered with a smile, tossing long blond curls away from her lovely face. She felt estranged from her group tonight, and couldn't quite get a grip on her mood. Something was lacking for her this summer, but she was having trouble understanding her feelings.

Perhaps I'm just tired, she thought, reviewing the past three days in her mind. Lunches at the Monte Carlo Beach Club, boat rides, water skiing, cocktails at the bar of the Hotel de Paris, gambling at the casino, a visit to St. Tropez that had lasted until 4:00 A.M. at L'Esquinade, and dancing again until dawn last night, at the Maona. Or perhaps I'm getting bored with the wildness; perhaps I feel alone amid it for the first time, she mused.

A companion offered her a cigarette. She took it mechanically without lighting it, reading signs of cocaine on a couple of friends' faces. She wondered, vaguely curious, if it had been brought in from Milano yesterday. A slight wave of irritation passed over her. Some people here are going to have another late night again, probably ending in a *partouze* in a villa or pool somewhere, she reflected without humor. It was unusual for Anne to judge or to condemn the actions of others, preferring to make her own decisions as to the way she led her life, and therefore allowing for others to do the same without uncalled-for criticism. However, tonight she felt impatient, as one might with a bunch of difficult children.

Suddenly, she wished she hadn't refused Dexter's casual invitation last week to meet him in Salzburg for the closing day of the Music Festival. She pictured the streets of Salzburg, glistening under the rain, with the great huge posters of the maestro Herbert von Karajan staring down from all directions, at his chosen people, like an arrogant god. Anne visualized him leading the Berlin Philharmonic in his flamboyant style, and could almost hear his magnificent rendition of Brahms's "Requiem." She wanted to kick herself for not going.

The flamenco was over, and Rubirosa had borrowed Pirata's guitar and was playing "La Vie en Rose." David Niven had risen to pull up a couple of chairs for the Kennedy sisters.

Brigitte Bardot was dining at the next table with a group of handsome young cinematographers and reporters from *Paris Match*. Would they all drive back later to La Madrague, her house in St. Tropez, or were they staying in Monte Carlo for the night?

A striking Brazilian boy, whose bare chest gleamed with gold chains above his open, white shirt and who could dance cha-chas and rumbas like no other, suggested the party move on to the Pirate's nightclub across the street from the restaurant. He grabbed Anne's hand and pulled her up a few stairs into the disco.

Wilson Pickett's "In the Midnight Hour" was playing and Anne found herself propelled by enthusiastic partners onto the dance floor, where for the next hour she let loose her pent-up emotions.

Yet, even as she sat back down on the banquette, pleasantly exhausted, and ordered a crème de menthe on crushed ice, she knew she hadn't resolved her problems. Yes, something this year was missing. The Riviera seemed to have lost some of its magic for her. The warm air was as fragrant as ever, the crickets sang just as loudly, the men were still among the most privileged, handsomest escorts in Europe, but somehow Anne was no longer quite as receptive to the romance and glamour surrounding her as she had been in previous years.

I'm getting too old, thought Anne, dejectedly. I'm losing my enthusiasm. I've been a nomad too long. What was wrong with her? She had worked so diligently all year preparing three major exhibitions and a project for a new book. She always enjoyed her work, but usually she appreciated her playtime as well. Why wasn't she having much fun this vacation? Usually, she fit into different speeds with the immediate ease of a chameleon. Anne knew this was one of the reasons she loved to travel so much; every city, every culture offered a new vibration for her to tune in to. So where was her zest for life right now?

As if controlled by a magnet, her thoughts returned to Salzburg. Until this moment, Anne had not allowed herself to face the answer to her questions, but a line from the French romantic poet Lamartine—*Un seul être vous manque et tout est dépeuplé* (One person is missing and the world becomes empty)—burst into her mind with the intensity of lightning. She tried to push away the image of a tall, slender figure, with an air of distinction and the vitality of a healthy animal. The features had fine precision like those of a sculpture, and the broad shoulders suggested security and power. A finely shaped head with black hair swept back, full, brilliant dark eyes, and a remarkably determined mouth with its radiant mockery, seemed to stare back at her with enigmatic insistence.

Anne's heartbeat quickened as she let herself dwell on pleasant, if all too brief, memories of dangerously unpredictable amusement. The picture haunting her regarded her with an elusive, yet strangely attentive look, almost tender at times, gently ironic at others. Bits and pieces of unfinished conversations on subjects as widespread as modern architecture, South American Indians, cinema verité, great navigators, Baroque music, and Madame Blavatsky were ringing in her mind. She was dying to resume them.

A pretty brunette squeezed into the empty space on Anne's right and began an earnest monologue on the various sensual thrills associated with the use of the word *flesh*. Gazing longingly at Anne's décolleté, she slipped a deceptively innocent hand onto Anne's thigh, and left it resting there, high up near the crotch. The girl's speech was delivered with wide-eyed candor; the words were disconnected and slurred, punctuated by inane giggles and suggestive little shivers.

What next? thought Anne, faintly amused. She disengaged herself from the attentions of her female admirer, found her purse and rose to kiss her host, Rubi, good-bye.

Driving back to Antibes along the winding curves of the Moyenne Corniche, she glanced at the clock on the dashboard of her Alfa Romeo —2:00 A.M. If she hurried, she could call Jane in New York and catch her just after breakfast.

Jane had always been an early riser; Anne recalled when they were roommates in college, how Jane would often get up at dawn to run barefoot in the morning dew, an exotic figure gliding about the campus lawn in the early light, vaguely reminiscent of Isadora Duncan. Anne smiled at the memory.

Back at the sumptuous Mediterranean villa in Antibes, where Anne was visiting a delightful elderly Italian couple, old friends of her parents, she raced up the stairs to her bedroom and flung herself on the bed. She dialed Jane's number in the Village. Her friend's low familiar voice answered and at once, Anne was bursting with the need to express the confusing emotions that had been nagging her more and more steadily these last few weeks.

"I think I'm falling in love," she blurted out somewhat gloomily to Jane, drawing a mermaid on a scribbling pad next to the phone.

"I can't believe I'm hearing this," replied Jane with a whoop of delight. "The goddess is returning back to visit planet Earth. At last— who's the lucky man? I hope he can make you stay down here for a while with the rest of us common mortals." Jane was thrilled.

"You know him—Dexter Portino. Remember? You introduced him to me months ago in Palm Beach." Anne pulled the cord as far as it would go and reached for a nail file in her Vuitton cosmetic bag.

A short silence ensued; Anne reiterated in a faintly accusing tone. *"You* were the one who remarked he was every woman's dream lover, or something to that effect. Remember?" insisted Anne. "The night of your mother's party?"

"Yes, I remember," answered Jane, stretching lazily out on her bed and peeling off the clothes she had just put on. "I just have never pictured *you* as 'every woman,' you should know. Anyhow, Dexter is hardly your type; you seldom fall for businessmen. But there's a lot to say for those dark romantic eyes," she added hurriedly, conscious of the unusual urgency in her friend's need to communicate her feelings. "So, well, tell me all the wonderful details. First, the basics. By that, I mean, is he good in bed?"

"Well, I don't know yet. That's the problem," hesitated Anne. "I just don't understand. I think he likes me, at least I can feel electricity, you know, but then nothing happens."

"What do you mean *nothing* happens," giggled Jane. "What kind of nothing? No erection? Impotency? Is he gay?" She had finished stripping and was stretching her long, naked body in every direction like a cat.

"I'm taking an air bath," Jane remarked unexpectedly. "You should too—it's very healthy. Twenty minutes minimum every day. So go on, tell me more about the intriguing Señor Portino. Apart from a passive penis, what else?" she urged, chuckling at her own joke.

Anne laughed. Her friend was so outrageous, it was impossible not to lighten up. She propped up the pillows behind her and continued.

"Well, it's quite bizarre actually, the way he's been popping up everywhere. He came to the show in Chicago at the Art Institute, back in January, with a very beautiful girl that looked a little like Audrey Hepburn. He bought a couple of photographs, which is always flattering, and came over to ask me where and how he should have them framed. Then, a few weeks later, I ran into him again, playing backgammon with some Greek shipowner, in the hall of the Palace Hotel in Gstaad. Anne, reached for a glass of Evian before adding, "By the way, I met the Shah while I was there that week, and he invited me to Teheran to photograph an important religious celebration next month. Maybe I'll get to taste that famous golden caviar that's reserved for the palace only."

"Yumm," answered Jane enviously. "Wait, I'm starving, I only had juice for breakfast, don't go." She rushed off to investigate her refrigerator and came back with a couple of rolls of sashimi on a small plate. "Okay. Go on."

"Well, I introduced Dexter to some of my friends in Gstaad, and we all had lunch together the next day at the Eagle Club on the Wassengradt. He seemed more interested in Geraldine than in me that day, but back then I didn't care."

Anne's voice sounded a little forlorn.

"Have you done the tarot on all this?" inquired Jane. "You're so good at that. The cards always answer for you."

"No, I haven't," replied Anne. "I've only just become really aware of the attraction Dexter has for me."

"Goodness, I always can tell on sight!" exclaimed Jane. "But go on with your story."

"The next time I saw him was at my exhibition in London, two months later. I declined his invitation to dine with him at Annabel's because I was simply too busy that night. The next day, he sent me flowers to congratulate me on my success in the morning press. But it wasn't until he showed up in France this summer, when I was staying on Onassis's yacht, that I started to really like him."

"Aaah!" breathed Jane. "I hope we're getting to the spicy parts."

"I told you," groaned Anne. "There *are* no spicy parts. . . . We had great walks all over Crete together, though. Dexter is mad for archaeology," she finished lamely.

"Walks!" Jane wailed, in mock horror. "What is your life coming to? Is this the girl who has all the men of Europe lining up for a peek at her belly button? . . ." Jane broke off. "Wait. Sorry. Don't hang up. There's the doorbell—can't think who would bother us this early. Paul's still asleep in the den," she added, her previously loud chatter dropping to a barely audible hiss.

"We had a fight last night. Wait," she repeated, bounding off. A moment later, Jane was back. "An electrician," she explained. "I'd forgotten him. I told him I couldn't open the door for another eight minutes precisely. He's gone away in a huff." Jane twirled around as she spoke, looking at herself in the full-length mirror behind her dresser. "He would have interrupted my air bath," she said, examining her magnificent figure with a critical eye.

Anne grinned. She knew her friend rarely bothered with robes or cover-ups or other such minor details.

"What's this about a fight with Paul?" she asked, concern creeping into her voice. "Is there a problem?"

"Psychedelics," answered Jane briefly. "I hate the stuff. I just don't do well on them. Paul insists it's part of being creative. I don't agree. I couldn't handle him last night, but not to worry . . . The mood will pass." Jane stared at the dark circles under her eyes, knowing full well the problem would *not* pass. Paul invariably became violent on alcohol as well as on drugs. "Go on about Dexter."

"Deauville I think was next," resumed Anne. "We went gambling together at the casino in Deauville, about three weeks ago. Dexter did very well at chemin de fer. I just played a little roulette. We had lots of fun. Unfortunately, I was staying with Antoine at his house that weekend, and there was no way I could just go off with Dexter and dump him at the casino. You remember Antoine, don't you? My sweet pansy friend? He was buying horses at the Deauville yearling sales, and I was delighted to accept his invitation because I very much wanted to photograph the Normandy beaches. Instead, I went horseback riding with Dexter on the Trouville Beach the next morning. I was dying to go out with him alone that night, but he didn't ask!"

Anne's voice rose three pitches. "I watched him play in the afternoon polo game, though. He's very good."

"Señor Portino does get around, doesn't he?" murmured Jane, but Anne wasn't listening.

"Then last week, he called me to invite me to join him in Salzburg for a lunch at von Karajan's and a concert in the evening. I was booked up with interviews that day and couldn't cancel them. I came here to Antibes on Thursday. It's absurd, but I just can't keep my mind off him."

Anne sighed, staring at her bare toes and wishing she had painted the nails peach instead of vermilion.

"I'm so baffled by this man . . . that evening in Deauville, it felt like sparks would fly if we as much as brushed against each other. Poor Antoine was seriously in the way. . . ."

Anne stopped for a moment to gather her thoughts. "What's come over me?" she asked pitifully.

"Hormones, my dear," retorted Jane. "There's no doubt, we are going to have to fix this dilemma." She paused to debate within herself the idea that was forming in her mind. A split instant later, Jane plunged into the suggestion that was to change Anne's life forever.

"You need to come spend some time in Palm Beach, that's obvious. It's ridiculous to have both of you globe-trotting hundreds of thousands of miles to merely exchange polite conversation in various hot spots around the world. In your case, Palm Beach is the place to be. It's Dexter's home base and it may be yours, too, at this point in your nonexistent romantic life. Who knows? . . ."

Jane was throwing her clothes back on in a frenzy of sudden energy. "When you've finished tasting caviar with the Shah, come stay at Villa La Palma in October and I'll meet you there. I need to get away myself, anyhow. Let's do this. Say yes, Anne," Jane pleaded. Characteristically, she considered decisions as valid only if they were made on the spur of the moment.

"Mummy won't arrive until the Christmas holidays, so we'll have the house to ourselves for months. I'm sure it's the fastest way to find out how serious you really are about this Dexter, and to tell you the truth, I really must take time out soon from Paul and his crazy trips to find out if our relationship is going to survive. So let's get together in October. We'll take Palm Beach by storm. What could be better?"

"Sounds fun," Anne acquiesced sleepily. "I'm tempted to say yes, but I'll have to check my schedule." The potent magnetism of Dexter's presence flashed before her.

"Oh, to hell with all schedules. Just dream about the elusive Dexter tonight, and call me collect again. Paul couldn't care less. He lives in a world where bills do not exist unless they're rainbow-colored."

Anne muttered thanks and a tired good night. She fell asleep relaxed and happy with Jane's last words ringing in her ears. "My nanny used to say, 'Never say no.' "

Anne's eyes were bright with excitement; there was a warm flush to her cheeks and her white-gold hair cascading loosely past her bare shoulders was softly swept away from her face by the ocean breeze. She stood on the wet sand, inches away from Dexter, one hand extended, palm-up, to display a pair of brightly colored shells that had caught her fancy. The air between them was charged like a magnet. Anne's smile, the look in her eye, held promises that were almost too much for Dexter's self-control. His senses were burning. He wanted more than anything to fuck her right now, here on the beach, on the edge of the water. It took all of his willpower to check the impulse. His blood racing, he turned away to pick up the snorkeling equipment at his feet, and without a word helped Anne into her mask.

Even though the beach appeared deserted, Dexter had waited too long for this day to take the risk of blowing everything for the sake of a quick screw in the sand. An embarrassing interruption could prove fatal to his long-drawn-out plan. Another time, he promised himself. Not now . . . Anne was a prize worth waiting for.

There was nothing that Dexter understood better than women. He could sense Anne's brand-new vulnerability; he was aware she was at last ready for him, and he was going to make sure this was a day in her life she would never forget.

Dexter had read the body language between Jane and Anne during the light lunch they had finished a short while ago at the Whitburns' villa, and he had picked up on most of the unspoken signals between them. Jane had excused herself early, claiming an afternoon appointment in Miami, and had left Dexter and Anne drinking coffee and sunbathing by the pool. Dexter could tell that Jane wanted them to have the house alone to themselves and he had also noticed that Anne was staying in the poolhouse at the other end of the garden. There were many private hours ahead for them to play; there was no need to rush things. Last summer in Greece, Dexter had described to Anne the strange fascination of underwater life, and he had promised to introduce her to the pleasures of the ocean. Today, he had brought her a mask, a snorkel and fins, and he was aware that Anne was thrilled that he had remembered their conversation.

Dexter appraised Anne's breathtaking beauty as she bent over gracefully to slip her flippers on—the long, sleek limbs, the gentle curves of her full breasts above the tiny pink bikini, the flat velvety stomach, the slim naked waist . . . every part of her turned him on; he wanted to possess her body completely and fuck her like a wild man . . . God! She was even more ravishing than he remembered! Struggling to master his senses, he took Anne's hand in his and pulled her into the ocean.

As they headed out toward the reef, Dexter concentrated on his role as teacher, and soon they were swimming slowly, facedown, still holding hands and experiencing together the magic of the scene beneath them. Exhilarated by the colors and the beauty, Anne was grateful to Dexter for caring enough to unveil it to her. A wonderful sense of belonging came over her; she knew at this moment that she trusted this man and loved him more than she had realized. The shields that were still protecting her private world a few hours ago had disappeared, swept away by the ocean.

The hand leading her was strong and purposeful and Anne longed for its caress. Finding foot in the waist-high water, she stood up and lifted her mask. The sun was beating down on her wet hair and shoulders, and her bikini top had twisted to the side, baring one beautiful breast. As Dexter came up beside her, pushing up his mask and staring at the creamy skin and the erect nipple, Anne pulled away the small piece of pink cloth and with a laugh of pure happiness, allowed her full breasts to burst free. Dexter's mouth was already on them, kissing them hungrily with exquisite tenderness, his lips moving lightly up the curve of her throat below her ear, and reaching her own lips with tantalizing slowness; his arm encircled her small, firm waist and he pulled her to him as their kiss deepened. Anne could feel his erection pulsating against her navel; her body undulated against him, a subtle motion of extreme sensuality, teasing, pressing, caressing . . . Her hand reached down into his bathing suit and a small gasp of pleasure escaped her as she touched his hardness. Dexter's tongue was playing with her lips; his eyes held hers as his hand stroked her hips, the small of her back, her thighs . . . she moaned as his palm cupped the throbbing flesh between her legs, and gentle fingers found the softness inside her bikini. Anne's whole body shivered, she wanted him with a frenzy she had not felt since she had been a teenager. Suddenly, Dexter's hoarse whisper was in her ear. "You're so beautiful, Anne. I want to know your taste . . . your smell. . . ." he murmured. "Let's go back to the house."

Anne's legs nearly gave way under her; she wanted to stay here in his strong arms, feeling the heat of his desire; she wanted to move with his passion and with the waves, and drown in his fathomless dark eyes. But the urgency of his tone was a command, and his words vibrated with a magical sexuality that touched her femininity. She pulled away and strode out of the ocean bare and beautiful, and onto the beach. Dexter gravely wrapped a towel around her and they raced, laughing like adolescents, through the tunnel that led under South Ocean Boulevard, from the beach to the villa.

Anne and Dexter stood breathless in the poolhouse gazing at each other's nudity as though transfixed by the intensity of their desire. Anne could feel the pulse beating in her throat; she quivered as Dexter's fingertips touched her feverish skin, gently tracing patterns around her breasts, over her nipples, down her belly, along her inner thighs, "so soft . . . like satin," he whispered. With sudden passionate hunger, he kissed her roughly on the mouth, pushing her head back against the wall and pressing his hard body against hers. His hands were on her firm young buttocks, pulling them up and toward him. A moment later, Anne was pinned against the wall by his weight; her limbs were burning and her flesh wet and yearning for him. Dexter lifted her up and as she wrapped

66

her legs around his waist, he allowed their sexes to touch at last, barely sliding into her moisture, teasing her for a few exquisite instants before plunging into her. She cried out with pleasure, and with long slow strokes, he brought her to the tumultuous climax she had dreamt of for months. Dexter pulled out of her and carried her—still trembling and softly moaning—to the bed. Holding her lips, he thrust his tongue into her most intimate part, tasting her orgasm and kissing her and mouthing her, until she felt she would never stop coming.

Twisting her body sideways, Anne rested her head on Dexter's thigh and took him in her mouth, her lips and tongue wise to his needs, sucking and licking, as her expert fingers stroked him gently. With a soft sigh, Anne came in Dexter's mouth again, ready to receive his own release, and amazed at his control when he didn't come.

Dexter pulled Anne back up to his mouth, their scents and tastes commingling, as they rolled in each other's arms, kissing passionately. Anne sensed Dexter's needs and, her body on fire again, rolled on top of him and guided him into her. Pushing down hard, she straightened up, her hair disheveled and sexy, her eyes wide open, watching his pleasure. She moved with a slow languorous rhythm, twisting her hips and squeezing her muscles until a new urgency took over, and her movements quickened and deepened and she called out for him to come as she climaxed. Watching this beautiful girl make love to him with such passion, her soft white skin an exciting contrast to his tan, her proud breasts shivering under his touch, Dexter could hold back no longer, and he exploded into her with a long intense shudder that brought a faint cry to his lips.

Anne sat still, savoring the warm lingering pleasure between her thighs until she finally slipped off him and into his arms.

Later, as they were playing in the pool, their bodies ached for each other's touch again. Sparked by an insatiable erotic electricity, they made love in the azure-blue water with a magnificent surge of energy. Sliding Anne's bikini bottom to the side, her bare breasts at his mouth, Dexter finished what he had started in the ocean, and took her with a power and a hunger that left her breathless.

The hours flew by and the magic lingered on as Anne was reclining in a lounge chair, next to Dexter, in the late afternoon sun. "I have to go to California in the morning," he announced abruptly. Panic gripped Anne. Was this wonderful man going to disappear from her life again? Would he call her when he got back? Or was today going to be simply an exciting sexual adventure with no future to their pleasures? She was amazed at the control he already seemed to have over her emotions.

Dexter watched her face. Youth and innocence, mingled with that amazing female abandon he had discovered in her today, were written all over her countenance. Women were so easy to manipulate, he reflected, with a cold secret smile. He could read her panic in a second.

Dexter leaned over to kiss her one last time before leaving. She took his hand and put it between her legs. "I can't believe I want you again," she said, as she pressed his fingers onto her warmth. Dexter looked down at her with a triumphant smile and answered, "That's the way it should be."

Yes, she was hooked. He wouldn't have to play any more games with her, he thought to himself. He had Anne in his power. He could control her through sex.

Dexter left the villa with long supple strides. He was planning where and when the wedding would take place.

THE PAST

The morning light played hopscotch on the white eyelet canopy of the crib over which Anne was leaning. Two sleeping infants lay in identical positions with tiny fingers interlocked.

A faint rainbow weaved itself in and out of their golden curls, and Anne recognized the indescribable thrill of wonder and joy that would so often surge through her whole being, ever since that wonderful night three months ago. For an elusive instant the mystery of life and death had become crystal clear to her and she had grasped the mystical lesson of childbirth. At the first whimper of her newborns, unconditional love had burst into her life.

Anne straightened up reluctantly and glanced over at the second crib, which had remained empty since the very first day home—it was as if her twins insisted on sleeping together, refused to ever be parted. She smiled at her useless purchase, and spread over its sides the two lace christening robes that she had ordered at Braun's on Worth Avenue earlier that month. With a start, she remembered that Dexter had asked her to wake him at ten.

On her way through the living room, she paused to look out onto the lake through the large glass sliding doors that opened directly onto the flowered patio and pool area. A three-mast sailboat was gliding by with an air of calm dignity. Anne was reminded of a huge mythical swan on a solitary quest, sailing majestically through the waters of time.

The luxurious abundance of tropical flora, palms, crotons, bougainvillea and wild oversized hibiscus blooms filled her senses with lavish abandon and seemed to add to the moment's unreality.

She turned to survey the magnificent arrangements of lilies and roses that had been artfully dispersed throughout the rooms. They stood out beautifully against the white wicker and rattan furniture. As ever, Dexter had seen to every detail with his usual precision. The sound of music piped through the house told her he was already up.

Dexter was in the midst of combing his tousled dark hair and exchanging a secretive knowing smile with his reflection. He struck a flattering pose, cocking his head to the side and flexing his biceps. Yes, his daily workouts were definitely paying off. He pondered with satisfaction the upcoming day: his wife and the baby twins would look exquisite for the news release.

After the church service, everybody who was anybody would come over to his house for champagne and caviar, and later he would go out to the Polo Club with his Argentinian friends and celebrate some more. Yes, Palm Beach society should be properly impressed by this event! An arrogant look crept over his handsome face as he finished shaving.

Anne walked into the large pink and white marble bathroom and smiled indulgently at Dexter's preening. She loved the way he moved with supreme self-assurance, totally at ease with his power. Sex appeal and charisma oozed from his pores.

Anne let her robe slide off her slim tanned body and pulled her long blond hair up into a barrette. She felt the weight of Dexter's stare on her breasts. She stepped slowly into the steaming bathtub and relaxed contentedly amid the Guerlain scented bath oils. She knew Dexter would climb in with her any moment.

Anne laid her head back against the marble and savored her happiness. Fifteen months ago she would have laughed if anyone had suggested she would so easily and so soon put her career aside—even though she was sure it was only temporary—to become a thoroughly ecstatic wife and mother. But she had been taken by storm and loved every minute of it.

Her thoughts were interrupted by a slight ripple of water. She kept her eyes shut as she anticipated Dexter's hand gently soaping her body. She looked straight up into his enigmatic brown eyes and stretched out languidly with a soft sigh of pleasure.

Anne and Dexter parked their black Aston Martin along County Road and walked across the church's immaculate grounds toward a group of people already standing under the covered archway. They made a striking couple. Two nannies dressed in crisp uniforms followed behind, each carrying one of the babies. A caravan of Rolls-Royces, Bentleys and Mercedes, mostly driven by solemn chauffeurs, pulled up one by one, to let their occupants out. Soon a parade of haute-couture silk dresses, topped with wide-brimmed hats and escorted by an assortment of bright trousers and identical navy blazers, marched two by two up the front steps.

Dexter spotted his secretary and publicist and nodded to them. He was well pleased—*Town and Country* had sent two photographers; the Palm Beach Shiny Sheet reporters were buzzing, and the New York columnists had all shown up as planned. Tomorrow, all the columns would surely be filled with the gossip.

Dexter looked approvingly at Anne, now holding her little girls next to the altar, and thought they made a perfect picture. The yellow St. Laurent dress he had specially ordered from Paris showed off her long graceful figure and flawless complexion.

This past year, Palm Beach's upper class had marveled at his lovely California wife. Society was entertained by her wit and charmed by her honesty. Dexter was also pleasantly, if surprisingly, proud of his latest accomplishment—the twins, Carrie and Gracie.

This christening at Bethesda-by-the-Sea would look well on their future application to the select Day School. All in all, his status in the town was growing by leaps and bounds. Soon, people would forget his South American origins and accept him as a bona fide member of this discriminating community.

Dexter began to fidget slightly as the service lingered and the hymns multiplied. He bowed his head to hide his impatience and dismissed the irritation by visualizing a victorious polo match for himself and his team later that day.

71

Anne was also lost in a private world. However, she was oblivious to everything but this moment with her babies. When the priest sprinkled Gracie's and Carrie's blond heads with baptismal water, a thrill of emotion stirred her heart and tears sprang to her eyes. She felt awed by the rite that had just been accomplished. Indeed, St. John the Baptist had always been one of her favorite saints. She reflected on the ancient symbolism of water, the purification in the Jordan, the miracles at Lourdes, the mystical Celtic springs, the Ganges. Her thoughts dwelled for a moment on Banares, India's holy city, before drifting off toward Katmandu. . . .

Anne spent the rest of the day in a dreamy mood. She seemed to float on top of the champagne bubbles, impervious to the chatter and gossip during the party that followed the ceremony. Later, she politely declined Dexter's invitation to ride out with him and his vast entourage to watch his polo game at the Club.

Jane lingered a little while after the last guests had chattered off. They both laughed at the day's extravaganza.

"The four of you looked like you'd popped out of a fairy-tale book today. Everybody was under the spell," Jane commented.

"Well, *you* were very much a part of it too—the ravishing fairy godmother," answered Anne. She paused, then added, "It's funny. During the ceremony, my mind was filled with images of India and Nepal. Do you think it was a sign that I should take my girls there one day? I wonder if Dexter would come along with us."

A doubtful expression touched Jane's face, but she tossed it away with a giggle. "You and your signs! How do you ever know which ones to follow? I would get lost if I found as many on my path as you do," exclaimed Jane.

"Like Ariadne in the labyrinth," laughed Anne. But she added, suddenly serious, "You know, there never are any coincidences in this life. They simply do not exist. That's *my* thread and it's a pretty strong one."

The two friends walked out onto the Lake Trail to admire Dexter's new hundred-foot yacht.

"I can't wait to decorate the cabins. Dexter's given me carte blanche," Anne began. "I'd love to go really wild and Oriental, but I sense he would rather I stay conservative." As an afterthought, she added, "Italian design is always great-looking; I'll probably go that route."

Anne chattered on happily as they sat on the edge of the dock watching the pelicans swoop down into the lake against the reddening sky.

"I'm surprised you didn't go to polo today," remarked Jane. "You never turned down Dexter before." Before Anne could answer, Jane continued, "By the way, how are your riding lessons coming along? Are you going to become the first American ten-goal lady polo player one day?"

"I'm still sliding all over the saddle, so I don't see how I'm ever going to swing a mallet, let alone hit the ball," Anne muttered. "I'll just have to conquer my fears—mind over matter. . . . I want Dexter to be proud of me."

The two friends smiled at each other; their eyes met in complete understanding. As they kissed good-bye, Anne felt fortunate to have Jane in her life. Their friendship was a monument of strength. It could be picked up at any time wherever they had left off.

When Jane's white Porsche backed out of the winding driveway, Anne closed the front door. She gave the servants a few last-minute instructions before dismissing them for the evening, and retired to her bedroom.

Anne pulled the blue-flowered Porthault comforter back on the antique brass bed and glanced at the picture on the night table. It was a Betty Kuhner black and white photograph taken of the four of them out on the lawn after the twins were born. When she looked at the eyes staring back at her, an eerie thought passed over her. She felt like reaching out and touching these four recently intertwined destinies with the magic of her love, holding them still at this point in her life. Motionless herself, she savored the moment before setting it free.

Her favorite Beatle album, *Rubber Soul,* was gently playing in the background as she moved gracefully around the room lighting candles and a small delicate incense holder she had brought back from Ceylon.

The Dom Pérignon '57 was in the silver bucket on Dexter's side, as well as a bowl of iced Beluga left over from the party.

Anne walked out onto the balcony and was immediately taken by the brilliant full moon set against an exceptionally clear and starlit sky. Her thoughts went to Dexter and the love she had for him. She loved him at neither best nor worst, but simply and entirely with all of herself. The heady fragrance of the night-blooming jasmine, so aptly named Dama de Noche, enveloped her body and led her into a deep romantic reverie. She was startled by the sudden hum of the Aston swerving into the driveway below. Her pulse raced faster as she listened to Dexter's familiar step on the stairs leading up to their room.

A moment later, Dexter sauntered onto the balcony, flashed his dazzling smile and Anne was as mesmerized as ever. Whenever he would enter a room, she became consumed with excitement and the outrageous desire to keep him there with her forever. They had had many glorious nights together—nights of arousal, passion and fulfillment.

"Hello, darling," Dexter said putting his arms around Anne. "I missed you at polo today."

They hugged for what seemed a long time.

"I missed you today, too, but I would have felt guilty leaving the girls," said Anne, hesitating. "And now I feel guilty about you."

"Don't be silly," Dexter murmured, cupping Anne's cheeks with his hands and softly kissing her lips. "Let's have some champagne and caviar in bed. We won the match, by the way, seven to four."

Anne gave Dexter his nightly backrub with her rosewater lotion. He loved to have his sore muscles soothed after polo. When she got to his face, she switched to a night cream and admired his tension-free look. His face glowed with health and strength and she especially loved the sun creases at the corners of his eyes. When they opened, she saw the flecks of gold in his irises.

She continued to massage him as an insatiable heaviness began to spread through her thighs. She brought her lips to his and his mouth began to make gentle intimate love to her. Their bodies slowly became electrified with passion and excitement. And before she knew it, they were panting and sweating in each other's arms. Anne felt a warmth spread through her as if it were radiating out from a center point and she suddenly wanted to move, to ride with him, but Dexter kept her still. All of a sudden she cried out and arched her back in overwhelming pleasure. Dexter merely held his breath—then let it out slowly. He closed his eyes, rolled onto his side and laid his arm across her stomach.

Anne listened to his breathing as they began to drift into sleep, and then, as if in a dream, she heard the faint cry of a baby. Immediately rising, Anne felt Dexter's hand on her thigh. "Stay with me. The nanny will take care of it," his voice cut into the silence. "Stay with *me*."

Anne's heart gave a quick throb, as some strange fear touched her soul, but what it was she could not tell. A moment's stillness followed—a stillness that seemed heavy and dark, like a passing cloud.

THE PRESENT

J ane executed a short intricate tap-dance step on the front veranda of the Portino villa, and rang the doorbell again. After a long pause, she cleared her throat and yodeled with gusto. As the sounds faded into silence, Jane tilted her head to the side, a quizzical expression on her face. She listened once more for signs of welcome. A large macaw, perched on her shoulder, experimented with an inconclusive attempt at yodeling. It cocked its head at the same angle as Jane's; it, too, listened with riveted attention.

"Lorenzo, my friend, I fear that His Grandeur is up to his little schemes again," said Jane at last. "It seems that we are not expected today after all."

Lorenzo fluffed out his turquoise and yellow feathers, hunched himself indignantly into his shoulders and let out a series of ear-shattering screeches.

"My God, what the hell are you doing?" growled a startled Dexter, opening the door a split second later. He scowled, first at the woman, then at the bird. Lorenzo glared back, stretched his neck out and hissed at Dexter.

"Good morning," Jane answered cheerfully. She looked at Dexter full in the face. "May we come in?" She put up a hand to calm the bird, stroking it gently under the throat. "Lorenzo's a surprise for Kenny and Keith."

Dexter was tempted to send Jane packing, with her goddamn imbecilic presents and her exasperating self-confidence. But the Whitburns were one family he did not wish to alienate, so with a huge effort, he controlled his temper and managed a reasonably pleasant smile.

"But, of course, do come in, Jane," he said. "It's so nice to see you." She watched him stride ahead of her in his faded blue jeans, brown crocodile loafers with no socks and aqua short-sleeved polo shirt.

He still has a great body, she thought. He's either working out with Lalanne or "La knife"—or both.

They walked into the spacious living room. Jane didn't recognize the interior decoration; it changed with each new wife or girlfriend. All exterior traces of Helena's five-year marriage to Dexter were already obliterated, even though the divorce had been finalized hardly a month earlier.

Poor Helena. She had turned out to be just another of Dexter's makeovers. He had sent her to modeling school for six weeks before marrying her, then had told her exactly how to wear her hair, precisely how to apply her makeup and insisted on buying all her clothes. He wouldn't even allow her to have a credit card, for fear she might buy something he didn't first approve. When he had finished with her, Helena had looked and walked and dressed and posed just like Anne. Then he dumped her.

Jane wondered if Carrie was helping Dexter with the new decoration. Two walls were lined with bookcases; a fireplace took up a third. The fourth opened onto a terraced back lawn. There were deep comfortable sofas, thick glass-top tables with bowls of gardenias and a Bösendorfer grand piano covered with photographs of Dexter, alone or with his two generations of twins. There were also framed pictures of Dexter shaking hands with celebrities and various magazine articles and cover stories featuring him. Plants splashed color amid the otherwise oatmeal-shaded room.

Dexter moved toward the mantelpiece and leaned against it with studied nonchalance. Jane knew his attitudes were memorized, not inherited. She'd had enough practice with his kind, having watched many would-be

76

Dexter Portinos come and go in Palm Beach. There was no doubt that he was good at what he did, he certainly knew how to hone all his techniques to perfection. He didn't make mistakes; at least, he hadn't so far. She hadn't liked him when she'd first met him and she didn't like him now, though as she got older she was beginning to pity him. She also knew he was somewhat afraid of her. Perhaps because she was untouchable. Perhaps because she knew him so well.

"Carrie will be here in a moment," Dexter was saying smoothly. "She's out on the boat, giving instructions to the staff about some of the improvements we're making." He added steadily, "Irma must have garbled your message this morning. We thought you weren't lunching today." Dexter stared straight at Jane, keeping a perfectly blank face. Oh, how he hated this woman! But God, how he would like to fuck her! She was still so lithe and firm. She was so sure of herself, and that certainly gave her an overwhelming sexuality. Looking at her now, he wanted to throw her down on the floor, to render her helpless, to *keep* her helpless while he fucked her long and slow and hard.

But he shook himself out of his reverie. There was no chance of having sex with this woman. She loathed him.

Long ago, she had opposed him as Anne's *only* character witness from "old" Palm Beach society, and since, she had remained aggressively and assertively in his children's lives, all these years, no matter how cleverly he tried to prevent it, to eliminate her. But one couldn't eliminate "old money," at least not in Palm Beach. One could only try to use it, to control it. But Jane was also uncontrollable.

"Dexter, you know perfectly well I've never canceled a rendezvous with Carrie, nor with Gracie, for that matter. Now why don't you just go get her so we can avoid any unpleasant scenes. And while you're at it, have your butler bring in Lorenzo's perch from my car. My little friend's heavy."

Almost immediately, the butler carried in the perch. The parrot ran from side to side on his bar in a frenzy of energy and squawked several times at the top of his lungs.

"Lorenzo speaks Italian, Dutch and Arabic," Jane informed Dexter. "In English, he has the foulest mouth this side of Hollywood."

"Auntie Jane!" Carrie called out, running into the room from the terrace. "What a perfect surprise. I thought we couldn't have lunch today." She gave Jane a huge hug.

"But indeed we are, my dearest. I have a picnic basket all prepared for you and the boys. I thought we'd eat in a shady spot at the Dreher Park Zoo, then go on to take a flying lesson at Lantana Airport."

"Oh, what a wonderful idea." Carrie sparkled all over like a diamond. "And I suppose this great big fellow is a new friend for Kenny and Keith! What fun!" Carrie approached Lorenzo and scratched his head. "They'll love him. But right now, they're at the Everglades. A tennis lesson. Daddy thought they ought to begin young. . . ."

"Hello, darling," Dexter interrupted hurriedly, rising and outstretching his arms to hold her.

Jane watched them embrace, then kiss, and was as amazed as ever at Dexter. He had always had an aversion to showy displays of emotion, preferring to love and hate undercover—even with his wives—except when it came to Carrie. He was a different person with Carrie. Tender, caring, gentle.

Jane looked at her goddaughter with deep tenderness. She looked so young and fresh standing there. It was hard *not* to be tender and caring around this young woman.

She had on blue jeans with a hole in one knee, black pumps, a white Hane's T-shirt and a man's white tuxedo jacket. Around her neck were six gold-plated bronze chestnuts on a black silk cord that went to her waist.

"Are you ready?" Jane asked. "We ought to be going."

"What time will you be home?" inquired Dexter in a concerned voice.

"I'll be back before five and we'll do the aerobic circuit workout I told you about," Carrie replied, kissing her father again. "You'll love it!"

"Okay, but try to get back a little earlier. Millie needs you to choose those new bathroom tiles, so that she can get the order in by this afternoon."

"Shut up, you fucking moron!" screamed Lorenzo unexpectedly. "Shut up! Shut up!"

Jane couldn't keep a straight face as they bade Dexter good-bye, amid the ruckus. On her way to her open-air jeep, she turned back and announced cheerily, "Lorenzo laid an egg last week. So you might want to rename him . . . her. You might also want to find out what should be done if it happens again. A nest might be appropriate. . . ."

Carrie waved to Dexter as the car leapt out of the drive. Paula Abdul was playing on the radio. Jane reached over to turn the volume down.

"I went to see Gracie yesterday," she said as they pulled out onto North Lake Way.

"What did you think?"

78

"I'm happy you're here for her," Jane said.

"Always," Carrie told her.

"I don't know what would have become of her without you." After a pause, she added, "You're a good sister."

Carrie wore a pensive expression. "But you don't think I'm a good daughter, do you?"

Jane knew that Carrie was referring to Anne. This was dangerous ground. This subject always came up with Carrie; there was so much emotional residue to sidestep, it seemed nearly impossible to get to the core of the question.

Luckily, Carrie didn't wait for an answer. "I know how you and Gracie feel about Mother. You think of her as God's gift to Earth. But I don't. Not by a long shot." Her tone was bitter.

"I know that," Jane said in a soothing tone. "You were hurt long ago. Strong feelings were formed back then and they don't just miraculously fade away."

"Yes, but you and Gracie believe Mother was the *victim* of the divorce. I don't." Carrie's eyes flashed as she continued. "*She* was the one who filed. *She* was one hundred percent responsible. *She* ruined our happy life together. Daddy told me he was in a state of shock when it happened."

Jane sat very still in her seat. She knew that Carrie's thoughts often dwelled on her mother's "defection," and that her moods could swing from joyous appreciation to bitter loneliness at the most unexpected moments.

She said gently, "Your mother had great problems to deal with in those days. You mustn't think she didn't love you with all her soul."

"Mother *promised* she would always be there for us, but she lied. I remember waiting by the phone for weeks, but it never rang." Carrie's lip quivered. "Daddy told me. He explained that she was busy with her 'new life' and she didn't have time for us anymore. At first I was so young and confused I couldn't believe him. I longed for her so. But eventually I had to face the facts—he was right."

For a moment Jane's eyes turned raw. Her own emotional scars were still there and she winced secretly at every mention of her best friend's name. She recalled Anne's sobs when Dexter would leave the upstairs phone off the hook for days on end, usually at the most crucial times, such as the girls' birthdays and holidays.

There was nothing Anne could do to counteract such cruelty. Dexter's selfishness was all-consuming; he believed he could only totally possess someone or something by destroying it.

Why didn't this girl realize it? Why didn't she ever see through her father's lies? Jane realized the answer was simple: because she didn't want to. She didn't have the strength to confront the truth.

"Judge Hawthorne couldn't have been wrong, anyhow. Daddy told me he was the best judge in all of Florida," Carrie continued. "Mother is responsible for a great *many* things. Just look at Gracie." There was deep accusation in her voice.

"Well, my dearest, all I can say is, thank God the two of you had each other then . . . and now." Jane squeezed Carrie's hand. It was all she could do.

"Are you hungry?" Jane asked suddenly. "What if we just munched on our sandwiches now, in the car, since Kenny and Keith aren't with us? Let's skip the zoo and go straight to our flying lesson. We'll have more time to soar."

She gestured to the picnic basket in the back of the jeep as she demanded, "Now, tell me *everything* that's going on in your life. How's Michael?"

"Oh, he's fine. Very busy," replied Carrie evasively. "Daddy's so happy to have us home," she changed the subject immediately. "He adores the boys, you know."

"What do you think of his divorce from Helena?"

"I never liked her. She was too cold. Too British. Daddy loved playing to it, it was a game for him, but I never got it."

"Does he have a new girlfriend?"

"Her name's Zoe. I haven't met her yet—she's off at etiquette school." When Jane shook her head, Carrie just said, "You know Daddy."

Unfortunately I do, thought Jane to herself. Another twenty-year-old bimbo, I'm sure.

"Did you hear that terrible storm last night?" Carrie asked. "I thought it was hurricane season already."

When Jane nodded, Carrie went on. "I had a terrible nightmare. I thought I couldn't hear Gracie breathing, and I sat up in sheer panic thinking she'd died. All I could hear was my own breathing in my ears."

Jane shifted in her seat. "Talk about a *nightmare*," she exclaimed, trying to lighten the subject. "I had been thinking of having a touch of plastic surgery. The breasts just aren't the same, you know, when you reach fifty. So I thought I'd have a little lift. Why *not*? But then I dreamed that I was in the hospital and when I woke up, the doctor had made a horrendous mistake and had sewn one nipple on my right cheekbone, and the other on my chin!" Jane made a circle with her fingers on the two areas. Carrie burst into laughter. "That was the end of that idea."

"For *now*," Carrie said, and giggled.

"Exactly," Jane said. "Just for now."

When she pulled into Lantana Airport a few minutes later, they were both still giggling.

THE PAST

The four-year-old twins came running across the lawn, ringlets bobbing, sparkling with happiness. They were physically indistinguishable except for a tiny mole Carrie had next to her mouth. In the womb, they had only one heartbeat, and even now their pace of breath was the same.

Anne looked at the identical girls, against the backdrop of the jewellike water of the Atlantic Ocean. There is always a need to explain a divergence from the common order of things, she mused. When she first was made aware she was having twins, Anne read everything she could lay her hands on—*My Twin Joe, Twins in History and Science, The Cult of the Heavenly Twins, The Intellectual Resemblance of Twins* and at least thirty more books. She smiled. Twins certainly were fascinating, and it was true, there was a whole network of codes, customs, body language and private signals—verbal and nonverbal systems—laced throughout the world of twins, but most important, Anne had learned that their

82

mystical twinship was the central core of their young lives. Identical twins had the closest possible human relationship, the bond between Carrie and Gracie being greater than that between mother and child. Anne had accepted that.

"Look, Mommy, look . . ." began Gracie, wiggling her toes in the sand.

". . . at the pretty shell we found," added Carrie, finishing her sister's sentence, as usual.

"It's beautiful," replied Anne. "*Very* beautiful."

Anne had always been able to tell the two apart. To her they looked very different, even though to most their nuances of expression were imperceptible.

Gracie wore a look of fragility, that of a princess who awakens bewildered, unsure of things; while Carrie's face was always animated, determined and full of life.

The girls ran on ahead, splashing in the waves, while Anne strolled behind them, catching a handful of salt seaweed, enjoying the sunshine and the flower-laden fragrance of the ocean breezes. She sighed. Life was supposed to be perfect. She had two beautiful children and a handsome husband who loved her, but . . . Anne was disappointed in her marriage. She had been infatuated the first couple of years but she was beginning to realize Dexter was not really the man she thought she had married. He was not as bright; nor was his personality as she had believed. There was an intellectual loneliness here in Palm Beach for her. There seemed to be no one to talk to, least of all her husband. Dexter was totally uninterested in her career, her interests, her *thoughts.*

Some months ago, Anne had accidentally found in his trophy room every interview she had ever given, all her books, varied articles written about her and an in-depth detective report on herself. At first, this had just been another disillusionment, another realization that in Palm Beach there was no such thing as spontaneity. She put it in her head that he must have wanted her so very badly back then that it was nearly touching in a way. However, lately, not even her sexual passion—still strong, still consuming—could blind her. She was having difficulty adjusting to this person who had absolutely none of her interests. She could no longer reach him—perhaps she'd never been able to. He seemed most interested in her as a trophy, not a wife with whom he could share his life and his self. And the twins—how *did* Dexter feel about the twins? He said he loved them but he showed no affection, no interest in their lives when they were babies beyond spending a few minutes with them at bedtime. It was as if she had performed a service, given him what he needed—two beautiful children—and now that they were older he treated them as if they were just two more valuable possessions—cars or boats or pieces of jewelry. She couldn't penetrate the shell he had created for himself when it came to his family. No, Dexter was shrouded in a secrecy purchased by his vast wealth.

Anne beachcombed along the soft sand, watching the scurrying land crabs and the pelicans as they soared overhead. She could not repress a slight nervous shudder as she turned to watch her children chattering volubly with each other in their own private, extraterrestrial language. The family unit was what mattered now.

"Help us, Mommy," squealed Carrie, her bright cheeks soft and pure in their bloom, as a wild rose.

The three of them spent the next few hours building a sandcastle where the princess could live happily ever after.

"**Y**ou're late," said Dexter, as he dismounted and threw the reins to a groom, who had cantered up after him.

"But, I'm here now. Doesn't that excite you?" smiled Anne, kissing him on the lips.

Dexter looked at Anne's profile—the proud purity which he had sought in marrying her. "I'll meet you up in the box after I shower," he replied, patting his mare as the groom led her away, the foam of her hard ride still flecking her glossy chest and forelegs.

"Do I have to go so soon?" asked Anne sensuously, pulling him toward the back of the stables.

"No, you don't," replied Dexter, feeling a slight erection. Anne did have that quality that kept him off balance, and sparked his fantasies.

Anne's mouth was dry. She felt a certain hunger for sex herself—it hadn't been that good for her lately, and it had been much too long.

She trembled as he slid her sheer organza blouse over her shoulders, so that she stood utterly exposed in the sunlight. Dexter's hands, surprisingly gentle, like they used to be, sculpted her body, mastering the shape of her neck, shoulders and breast. His fingers lingered on her nipples, circling them with his forefinger, as they went to the ground together, never breaking their lips apart.

Anne's eyes told him how badly she wanted him. He quickly stripped, then tugged her skirt down, stroking her stomach, her hips—moving slowly downward, tracing the delicate skin hidden between her thighs.

84

His fingers slid deep inside her. He knew what she wanted, even if she herself had forgotten.

Anne's heart was pounding. It had been months since he had done this. He kissed her between the legs, at first softly, then more passionately. She groaned, and then thrust her aching hips forward to capture Dexter's face. He buried his head there for several minutes, his tongue knowing all her hidden, most sensitive places. Dexter didn't stop until she came, crying out his name.

When he finally kissed her, she could taste herself on his lips. His moan pierced the stillness as he thrust into her. She cried out a moment later, another climax triggered by his.

The Pimm's was flowing as Anne sat in her private box with its panoramic view of the cool, green polo fields. Dexter was once again going over the intricacies of the game, play by play, providing biographies of the players, on and off the field.

"Enrique's girlfriend was found in the Dempsey dumpster next to the Publix yesterday morning," he said. "She'd OD'd on heroin."

"Oh my God," muttered Anne, distraught, subconsciously playing with her latest gift, a glorious sapphire necklace, framed in shimmering mother-of-pearl.

"Dear, will I be seeing you at my Planned Parenthood ball next month?" interrupted Thelma Wolcat, dressed in a chartreuse Chanel suit and looking a decade older than her admitted seventy years.

"Well, actually, I'm planning a working trip to Egypt next month," replied Anne, adjusting her skirt so the grass stain didn't show.

"Nonsense, you'll just have to put it off and lend your support," commanded the dowager imperiously.

"Yes, we'll be there," asserted Dexter.

"Good, good," replied the haughty matriarch, patting Anne's arm with her soft liver-spotted blue-veined hand as she walked off.

"You mustn't shirk your social responsibilities," began Dexter, tipping his cigar to a photographer. "This is where your children will be growing up. We must nurture our community, it is our duty," he averred.

"I have to get going on my new book, Dexter. I've been trying to get started for over a year. I'm under contract," pleaded Anne. "Before we married, you encouraged my work."

Even though Anne dutifully attended Dexter's polo matches, horse races in which he had entries, yachting events and hunting parties, he no longer believed in the reciprocal understanding he had espoused earlier for respect in their mutual independence.

He had built her a magnificent studio on his property as a wedding gift, but now he didn't want her to work. Anne's time was so occupied by the children and Dexter's hectic social calendar, that she now had few opportunities to devote to her photography.

She missed her craft desperately. Her pictures were becoming part of the permanent collections in numerous museums and galleries around the world, but she was disconnected from it all. The one thing in life she had never doubted was her talent. It had always seemed an inextricable part of her. But now . . .

She was losing herself. She knew it. She was losing the part of her that made her *her*. For a moment, she wondered how it could have happened. Then, of course, she understood. It was love. She gave up too much when she'd fallen in love with Dexter. But that love was dead. Or if not dead, she realized with a frightening start, dying. Decaying. So why don't I just leave? Pick up and start anew? For one exhilarating moment she decided she'd do just that. And then she felt it—a clutching in her stomach, a pull far greater than she'd ever felt for Dexter. This was also love—love for her children, the twins, Carrie and Gracie. She couldn't leave. Not now, perhaps not ever. Love was keeping her there once again.

Through the rest of the match, Dexter led polite conversations through and around many subjects. A strange, subtle smile Anne had noticed once or twice before lighted his face, but not another word was said about Anne's work.

THE PAST

Anne's peach terry-cloth robe was strewn messily across a white wicker chair in the master suite. She had created a totally white bedroom, with an immense antique four-poster brass bed, canopied in lace and covered in plump, white silk pillows. Her nightstand was littered with dozens of books, which she devoured hungrily in the small hours of the night. Dexter's table was bare, except for a clock and a silver and gold monogrammed cigarette box. Anne was standing in an ivory lace bra and panties in her adjoining dressing room, waiting for Carrie and Gracie to come out of her massive walk-in closet.

The room was filled with dreamy pastel flowered fabrics, antique white lace curtains, family pictures, rare potted palms and orchids. She had worked for months unleashing her creative passions, using all her energy, taste and enthusiasm to create a rich, glowing environment. In the corner, on a rose upholstered chaise longue, sat two china dolls that Dexter had given her in Europe, when they were dating.

Earlier, Anne had scoured through the double-tiered row of dresses, evening gowns, jackets and hundreds of shoes to find some old things so the girls could play dress-up while she got ready for the Cancer Ball. She could hear them giggling as they pored over a pile of clothes and furs, with the shared enthusiasm of two delighted children discovering a pirate's treasure.

"What about jewels, Mommy?"

"Look in the middle drawer, Gracie, under the sweaters," Anne told her, while putting on her mascara at the makeup mirror.

The two hovered over their mother's trinkets like birds, soft whispers passing between them.

Anne paused a second, listening. Usually there was no need for speech; the twins were not dependent on language for communication between themselves, preferring their own special twin-sister telepathy to pass thoughts.

"Here we come, ready or not!" exclaimed Gracie, with a sly sparkle in her eye, as she paraded behind Carrie, back and forth across the room, a long pink train of material following.

"Will you be staying for tea?" inquired Anne of the grand ladies.

"Of course, my dear," replied Carrie, in a very proper British accent.

Anne laughed. Last month Gracie had dominated the drama field, now it was Carrie.

"Anne," Dexter snarled impatiently, appearing in his black-tie finery.

"Daddy, Daddy!" screamed Carrie effusively, kicking off her heels, running toward him.

"Princess," replied her father proudly, scooping her up immediately. He grinned from ear to ear, enjoying the fuss she always made over him.

Dexter had been the one to push Anne into getting pregnant so soon. He'd had an ulterior motive, of course—he wanted to keep her here in Palm Beach to help him socially, instead of gallivanting all over the globe. He had not been prepared for the mental security these two green-eyed, fair-skinned, blond offspring brought to him. Especially Carrie. From the beginning, Carrie just seemed to *like* him. When they took walks together, she would link her little arm around his. When he came home, she'd always be waiting for him, waiting to jump onto his lap and hug him. His heart melted when he looked at Carrie. She, far more than Gracie, eased the residue of that old childhood obsession that still haunted him—that mixture of humiliation and hatred, and the fear of being mistaken for a Jew.

"Daddy will take you to lunch tomorrow, Carrie. Just the two of us," Dexter whispered.

Yes, Carrie was his favorite, *his* child. She was like him. Over the years, she had become something very important to him; he loved her with an intensity he had not dreamed possible. It was an intensity that sometimes frightened him. He had never been as possessive of any lover, not even Anne. He had never felt as attached to another human being, had never felt as passionate toward another person.

"Oh, boy," Carrie gasped, thrilled by the upcoming adventure of eating out all by herself with her daddy.

"Run along, my grand dames. Mommy will be down shortly to tuck you in," said Anne.

"Good night, Daddy," the girls retorted in unison, hugging him before they ran off.

Anne frowned. He favors Carrie so openly, she fretted, looking down at her fifteen-carat matched set of diamond necklace, earrings and bracelet.

"Dexter, please remember how vulnerable twins are to the pangs of enforced separation," began Anne composedly. "Even for an hour. Last week you took only Carrie for a riding lesson. I don't think you understand how deep the effect of that can be."

Dexter's face grew drawn and sharply thin.

"Let them follow their own instincts," she continued. "Leave the way open for them to separate in their own normal, healthy fashion when they're ready."

There was a strained silence as Dexter assumed his most casual posture, strolling around the room, perusing the framed photos on the walls. This sparked his competitive urge.

"Never again tell me how to conduct myself with *my* child," he said acidly.

"That's the point," she said. "Your *children.*"

He walked out of the room as if he had a cape floating behind him in the wind.

"Never," she heard him add, with a gravity that impressed her, in spite of her own misgivings and, yes, she had to admit to herself, fear.

Carrie and Gracie heard their mother's high heels clicking down the hallway tiles. They hid in the closet.

Carrie and Gracie's walls and ceiling were hung with white silk. The rich material was drawn up in the center in canopy fashion. There were two single beds, a dainty dressing table and stool, a desk, an easy chair, a chiffonier—all of white mahogany inlaid with quaint wreaths of mother-of-pearl. Their snowy beds were embroidered in blue forget-me-nots. All brushes, mirrors and combs were of Dresden china, covered with pink roses, and with the monograms CP and GP.

"Boo," the girls shrieked.

"A-ahh," screamed Anne playfully, knowing all their hiding spots. "You scared me to death. Have you brushed your teeth?"

"Not yet," replied Carrie, skipping off.

"We'll do something fun tomorrow, if Carrie goes to lunch, darling," Anne said, pulling up the spread over Gracie. "We'll have a scavenger hunt!"

"I *want* Carrie to go, Mummy. I'll be okay," replied Gracie, wrapping her arms around her mother's swanlike neck and kissing her.

Anne was taken aback by the solidarity and reciprocity between these very young souls.

"Carrie and I have an invisible blue rope, Mummy, that you can't see," Gracie whispered. "We're never separated."

Anne smiled gently upon her daughter. She had read all about the symbolic umbilical, the permanent link between twins that connects them beneath the surface, with a complex strata of shared sympathies, insights and destinies.

"Let's say our prayers," said Anne, turning off the light, knowing she was once again late.

Anne and Dexter stepped out of their Bentley in front of the Royal Poinciana Playhouse, where Broadway's best was brought to the South, into a blaze of lights, clicking cameras and paparazzi. Reporters focused on Anne's tall, slender figure, scribbling notes about her paisley, sequinned Fabrice gown, in silver on royal blue with the V back, which showed off to perfection her full breasts and long legs.

The police kept the fleet of cars from jamming, and there were ropes to keep away the people who weren't invited.

Dexter rubbed his hands complacently. The beautiful people and the chroniclers were all in attendance. He winked at one. Dexter was clever, shrewd and diplomatic, and had secured the favor of a certain portion of the press, for a price. They were always waiting for him.

Dexter watched Anne make her entrance, smiling, exuberant, overflowing with the joy of living. He observed the titled Europeans, the glitterati from the charity ball circuit and the photographers hover around Anne, like bees to honey.

Through the first few years, Dexter had enjoyed living vicariously through Anne. He had seen the world anew with her sense of wonder; it had made the world interesting and exciting again. Before her, he used to see only what his past experiences told him he should see, or what his desires wanted to see. But that shared view was wearing thin now. He knew he couldn't free his mind entirely, like Anne could, of emotions. He couldn't just see for the simple pleasure of seeing. The essence of things was too often hidden from him, except through her eyes, and he was beginning to dislike her for that.

"You look positively dazzling," said a five-foot-two butterball of a man with a clipped British accent, as he thrust his arm through Anne's, leading her toward his table to meet his guests. They all greeted her with eagerness and effusion.

"Let's get together . . . let's go to the avenue . . . let's . . ."

Anne looked back at Dexter with a strange, sad expression, which momentarily marred the gallery of frozen, smiling faces.

Dexter's handsome face was sternly set as he made his way to the bar with his empty glass, shoving it silently toward the bartender to be refilled. The slow fire of an insidious envy began to smolder in his mind.

Anne *had* served her purpose, Dexter reflected, adjusting his bow tie. She was a brilliant hostess, who supervised every minute detail of her perfect dinner parties. She had created an overwhelming feeling of life, color and vitality for his house, always keeping it ablaze with flowers from the gardens and her greenhouse. She *had* helped him socially, but she wasn't supposed to surpass him, goddamn it. Things were getting out of control. She needs some reining in, he mused, his dark eyes glittering like cold steel. She needs to come down a peg or two. Everything comes too easy to her. She mastered it all with effortless amusement. Why did it always seem to fall into place for her—from beginning to end?

In spite of Dexter's arrogance and belief in himself, he was bitter and jealous. He brooded darkly over his glass of wine, as Lester Lanin's Orchestra played.

"Dexter, you look like you could strangle someone," said Patricia Montague, another magisterial dowager one shouldn't tangle with if one wanted to climb to the heights of Palm Beach society. "I just came back from Paul Niehan's Clinic at Vevey, pushkins. Take a rest before those wrinkles turn into permanent roadmaps!"

Dexter's brows contracted a little but he forced a smile as he excused himself and went into the men's room. Who's that bag of bones held together by leather skin to tell me what to do? he asked himself. He wondered why these society sirens, who so eagerly courted his attention over the years, remained so blind and unconscious to the chill of cynicism that lurked beneath his seeming courtesy, the cutting satire that he coupled with apparent compliments—and the intensity of hatred that flamed in his flashing eyes, under the assumed expression of admiring homage.

Dexter washed his hands, every wrinkle jumping out at him from the well-lighted mirrored walls. Shit, he had hated turning forty.

She's so independent and assertive, he thought, handing the attendant a dollar. She had defied him with her untamed will, and gone off to Egypt with the children for a month, to work. Now she's even talking about going behind the lines in Vietnam. Jesus—that could ruin his White House connections. She doesn't come out of the darkroom for hours—ignoring *his* needs. She brings those artist people home, who don't fit in with his friends at all—and then there's the irritatingly condescending Jane. What a pain in the ass!

"Dexter, I need to talk to you," said Harrison Conrad, brusquely. Harrison was the extremely handsome young owner of one of the local restaurants, but he was better known for all the young boys *and* girls who stayed in separate wings at his home. He preferred "little boys"—the girls were for his clients.

"Did you hear Linda Rosenblum is trying to get her son into the children's ballroom dance classes?" he asked incredulously.

"You can count on my support, Harrison," said Dexter, immediately jumping on the issue. "My children attend those sessions." His support would be another piece in the puzzle of the ongoing love-hate relationship he had with Palm Beach. He hated the town for rejecting him years ago, but he loved the town for hating Jews; he could get revenge for his father.

"You know I'll do anything to keep them off this island." His steel orbs fixed on one of the enemy's big noses across the room. "They're insidious, the horrible way they—"

"Pardon me," said Anne. "Malcolm Rosenblum is a friend of Gracie's and Carrie's, a dear friend, and he's at our home frequently." Her bright eyes flashed dangerously toward her husband; indignation flushed her fair cheeks. Dexter knew she was doing all she could to control her temper. "My God, you sound like Nazis! That same old discrimination— I would hate to have seen you two at play during the Holocaust."

"Excuse us," said Dexter, folding his hands with a droll air of penitence, and a mocking glance that seemed to see straight through Anne's clothes and into her mind.

"I'm sure Malcolm is a good little boy," Harrison began, "but that's not the point, Anne." He spoke indifferently, as though he were speaking of the weather. No sympathy was expressed, no pity wasted. His ghastly voice penetrated the very fibers of Anne's consciousness.

She knew that Dexter didn't like Jews. She'd never been able to excuse it, but she always felt it was because he'd isolated himself in high society. She knew if she could only get him to go with her on one of her assignments, maybe even to Israel . . .

"Harrison is right," Dexter said quietly. "Malcolm is not the point. The point is how we are to keep Palm Beach from turning into something . . . something . . ."

"Filthy." Harrison finished the sentence.

"Exactly," Dexter agreed.

"I'm beginning to think," Anne said heatedly, "it may already *be* something filthy."

Conversation stopped all around them as people eavesdropped. Dexter stared at his wife. More than anything he hated public displays. He thought if Anne were to say another word, he might slap her. She met his gaze. Hers was equally hard. But she graciously turned to the frozen crowd around her and said, "Let's take our seats, before we steal the stage from Lester."

Dexter nodded curtly. The expression on his face said that they had not finished their conversation.

When they were seated and the curtain went up, the girl next to her whispered, "Want a Ritalin?" It was Ingrid, a petite five-foot nut-brown-haired girl, who looked so weathered and worn, yet who Anne knew was only twenty-five. "I'm so bored. How do you stand this?" Ingrid added, popping another white pill herself. "The same old ancient people every night—drinks at Taboo, dinner at Nando's, dancing at the Colony. I'll die if I have to have my legs and crotch waxed one more time."

"No, thank you," Anne said to the offer of the pill. But she wondered about Ingrid's question. How *did* she stand it? Perhaps it was because boredom was a condition of brain and body of which she was seldom conscious. She could fantasize; she could go anywhere at any moment.

Dexter turned his head to glance at Anne. He could tell she had drifted away into an absorbed reverie of her own in which he had no part—and which plainly showed how little she cared for anything he or anyone else happened to be saying. His dark eyes shone with a hungry feverishness.

Anne was, in fact, thinking of Dexter, of his cold, sinister beauty— elegant ice. Then she glanced up at the gold and crystal chandeliers, which seemed to dance above her like fireflies whirling in a mist of miasma.

THE PAST

Jane was stark naked except for white cotton gloves, which were creaming her hands in Pond's, while she was being massaged poolside in the open air at her new house.

Her mother did not get on well with Paul, so Jane had purchased a charming and distinguished old island Colonial home, built in 1900, and had completely renovated it. It was a three-story cypress clapboard house with wood wainscoting, shutters and other basic characteristics of the era. It boasted a beautifully matured landscape, with a quiet front garden presided over by a magnificent buttonwood tree, which provided a home to orchids of all colors and species, gardenias and frangipani blossoms. Banks of jasmine and sandalwood flanked the sides of the long brick veranda, which shaded the entrance.

Inside there were soaring ceilings that had moldings which formed circle motifs, yellow pine hardwood floors, masses of antique English country pine furniture, specially designed upholstery fabrics and antique rugs. The latest issue of *Architectural Digest* had applauded Jane's results —"genteel shabbiness."

The furniture was run over by Jane's nine dogs—three Labradors, two golden retrievers, two German shepherds and two dachshunds, as they lounged under the many ceiling fans. The house had no air-conditioning.

Anne sat shielded under a vast cream umbrella, topless, in a madras bikini bottom, watching Carrie and Gracie playing boccie on the side lawn. The sun blazed like a beacon.

"You know, I upholstered my entire bedroom in a floral fabric, covering the doors and the handles," began Jane. "I got up the other morning with a hangover and *I* couldn't even find the bathroom door!" She hesitated. "Earth to Anne, earth to Anne," she said, dismissing the masseuse with a wave of her hand.

Anne had a look Jane had never seen before, a drained passivity as if she did not belong in existence, and could not be reached.

With a feline grace, Anne turned her exquisite head back over her shoulder, toward her friend.

"Dexter's so different lately. He doesn't want me to work or travel anymore," commented Anne soberly.

"It seems to me a tad arrogant for him to expect you, the ambulatory storm, to aspire to conventional life here in Palm Beach, where all you find are self-created prisons for the spirit." Jane took her gloves off and wrapped herself in a large, colorful pareu.

"He's become spectacularly successful," Anne said. "What he does is he ruins his competitors. He indulges in them as an occasional sport, then stages a sudden raid. And destroys them."

Jane poured two cups of Japanese green tea.

"He asked me to lie for him at one of his trials," Anne continued. "I didn't, of course, and he flew into a rage. Why, Jane? Why such ignoble ways, when he doesn't have to?" She looked at Jane, with an eloquent desperate expression.

"My marriage is a sham. A coarse physical interaction and no more. All the finer and deeper emotions which make a holy union of human wedlock are sadly lacking," Anne said gravely. She stirred her tea with a spoon to dissolve the sugar. "The mutual respect, the trusting sympathy, the lovely compatibility of my mind with his . . . They don't exist anymore. Maybe they never did. Why didn't I read him properly? Where was my intuition?" she cried.

"The only gift we're given when we're born is innocence," Jane told her as she watched the girls sneak up on a gray squirrel in one of the banyan trees. "You couldn't have known. There's nothing so deceptive as one's outward appearance. Always pretending to be what we're not. Our physical frames are complete disguises for our actual selves. We're all merely fabrications through which neither friend nor foe can spy." She reached into her straw bag for another pack of cigarettes.

"I don't know . . ." Anne mumbled. "It's almost impossible for me to describe my state of mind. Feverish, irritated . . . fearful," she went on, removing her light-shaded tortoiseshell-framed sunglasses. "My sense of humor is gone. And I feel humiliated. I'm hearing a lot of gossip about nubile parties at Harrison's house. . . ."

"Probably true," Jane told her, putting two gold-tipped crested cigarettes in her mouth, lighting them, and handing one to Anne. "He keeps more drugs in his vaults than money at his bank. How's your sex life?" she inquired, as an afterthought, turning up the Four Tops' "I Can't Help Myself" on the radio, so the children couldn't overhear them.

"All he wants to do lately is pee on my breasts," replied Anne, feeling a flood of weariness, and almost seeing its thickening waves.

"How territorial," Jane said with a raised eyebrow, knowing full well it was Anne's untamed will and spirit that roused in Dexter his love of mastery and his urge to conquer and subdue that which seemed unconquerable. "Be careful, my friend. You could make him afraid he can't break you. You may be in for more than you know . . . *much* more. . . . Why don't you divorce him?" Jane asked as Jugs, one of her black Labs, romped playfully at her feet.

"Here come the reasons now," said Anne, as the twins ran toward them. "I'm afraid of what he'd do."

"What *could* he do? You don't need his money, do you?"

"No. It's not money."

"Would he hurt you, Anne?"

"He might, physically. But that's not what I'm afraid of."

"Then I don't understand," Jane said.

"I'm afraid he would take the children from me. Any way he could."

"But that's crazy," Jane told her. "He wouldn't want—"

Gracie reached them first, interrupting them, jumping on her mother's knee.

"Can we play croquet, Auntie Jane?" Carrie asked airily.

"Your mallets are in the poolhouse, my sweet girls," Jane replied, as they skipped off. "Look at their sandals!"

"I bought them two different colored pairs, one pink and one yellow," began Anne tenderly, "and they simply swapped, so each one had an unmatched pair. Their pediatrician keeps encouraging me to buy them different color and style clothing—but they want to dress *exactly* alike. They're unable to bear a difference of even one button unfastened, and I'm not convinced any of us should force them into it."

"Dexter wouldn't want them, not if you weren't there, Anne. He couldn't," resumed Jane.

"They're beautiful children, aren't they?" Anne asked softly, wistfully.

"They're *very* beautiful children," said Jane, deciding it was time for her friend to try her new mudpack. "It's volcanic. I brought it back from Ischia."

"Dexter's been buying things for only Carrie lately," continued Anne, drying off. "He doesn't seem to care about Gracie's feelings anymore at all." Jane began to scrub her face. "Thank heaven there's no jealousy between them."

"It's because Gracie's too much like you," replied Jane, slapping a thick layer of brown, lightly scented gunk on Anne's face.

"They're *both* like me, in certain areas—not one more than the other," answered Anne, half-smilingly.

"I disagree. Gracie is *much* more like you. Don't smile now till it dries. Did you resolve the problem about the girls being photographed in the charity fashion show?" she added, wiping her hands.

"Dexter's upset I won't allow it."

"He's a stage parent. It's absurd to allow *any* publicity around one's children. What can he be thinking of?" Jane peered at her friend, who didn't look like a woman in torture, but like someone who sees that which makes the torture worth bearing.

"Last one in is a rotten egg!" Jane yelled to the girls, running toward the peacock-blue water and landing on a lime-green frog float.

THE PRESENT

Gracie lay in bed listening to the early-morning birds. She did not feel disposed to sleep any longer; she was burning to write down all she had dreamed while it was still fresh in her mind. Her mother had taught her to keep a journal. She had, originally, restricted it to things that had really happened. But lately, her dreams were as vivid as reality.

Over the past weeks, she had had many more nightmares, and writing seemed to soothe her. Soothed, she could think about other things, happier things. Now, her thoughts went to her sister.

Carrie had come loyally each day to visit, brimming over with all the stories from home. Her sister was the eternal optimist, never acknowledging a problem or a hassle. Always upbeat, always trying to show Gracie the brighter side of life. A half-smile crept onto Gracie's lips, thinking of her sister's attempts to make her laugh. The half-smile turned into a full one as, just then, Carrie came into the room.

"Hi, sis. What are you doing?" She kissed Gracie, as always, directly on the mouth, her lips pursed carefully and daintily.

"I'm recording my dreams," smiled Gracie as she watched a vague expression flit over Carrie's face. It was a look Gracie was very familiar with. Even though Carrie was the most lovable and intelligent creature, she could not often think "beyond"; the mere effort worried and perplexed her.

"How are my little nephews?" Gracie wanted to know, putting her pen and pad down.

"Getting terribly spoiled by Daddy, I'm afraid. I've got to speak to him about it before the boys say something to Michael. He'll be furious!"

"What's he gone and done now?" asked Gracie, shaking her head.

"Yesterday he brought home a new jungle gym, and a trampoline," exclaimed Carrie. "On top of that, he's having a waterslide built. He's just so generous, what can I do with him?"

"Nothing, I suppose. Have you spoken to Michael lately?"

"We talk almost nightly. The boys miss him very much when he's on location. They always do." Gracie sensed a slight tremor of nervousness in Carrie's voice. She watched her sister get up from the bed and walk to the window.

Carrie thought of her thirty-two-room Beverly Hills mansion atop Carolwood Drive. It stood on several acres of impeccably kept grounds. There were sumptuous flowerbeds, flowing lawns, dozens of orange and grapefruit trees, two tennis courts and an Olympic-size pool. Michael was a good husband and father. She had everything. So why was she not happy?

"Is anything wrong, Carrie?" Gracie shifted her position uneasily to her elbows.

Carrie's eyes looked suddenly sad.

"I'm not handling all of it as well as I thought I could," she replied.

"Handling all what?" Gracie inquired.

"The whole *star* thing," muttered Carrie as she turned back toward Gracie.

"I remember you two discussing the movie star thing at length before you were married," commented Gracie gently. "For *hours.*"

"I'm not blaming Michael, Gracie. It's me. He told me how important his work was to him, that I couldn't be jealous of it. He told me how annoying and difficult fans can be on relationships, and how Los Angeles is closed to everything except the entertainment business, et cetera, et cetera, et cetera. I can't say I didn't *know.*"

Carrie began to pace the room, her arms folded.

"I *love* powerful people, Gracie. Their energy and their passion transform me," she continued. "But I'm lost out there. I need some attention, too! I'm so far in the background, no one knows me except as Mrs. Michael Donovan!"

Gracie passed her hand across her forehead. She had spent many a night with Carrie and Michael and remembered that Michael, right at the beginning, had his doubts as to whether anyone who'd never been exposed to show business could suddenly pick up their roots, move to Hollywood and be the spouse of a star. He had been in the business over twenty years and didn't know if it was fair to ask someone into that life. He'd made it clear that if and when he got married, it had to be to the right person and it had to be forever. The right person would ensure that.

"Carrie, you told him you'd do anything for him and your love. You told him you'd put up with all of it. You convinced him," Gracie said softly.

"I was wrong. I . . ." Carrie broke off abruptly with a half-sigh.

Incredulity and surprise showed in Gracie's face. Carrie had often spoken of fights and arguments over the years with Michael, but just the usual marital rifts. She had *never* said she was unhappy. In fact, she couldn't *ever* remember Carrie admitting she was unhappy.

"You'll have to try harder, Carrie. You have a family to think of and protect. Michael loves you and the boys very, very much."

"You're right, I know." Carrie crossed the room and, standing next to the beige easy chair, suddenly recalled being pregnant with the twins. She had been intensely aware of her body then, had felt insecure and sexually awkward. When she had looked at her protruding stomach and breasts, she had been embarrassed. But Michael had loved her pregnant. He had always made her feel good about herself. So what was wrong? A languid feeling of weariness oppressed her, and her limbs ached as if she had walked incessantly for miles. She plopped down into the chair.

"You're right," Carrie repeated. "But I don't think I can explain it. Something's pulling me away from him. I don't know what it is but I can feel it, as if it were a real, physical thing. Does that make *any* sense?"

"I'm trying to understand," Gracie said softly, but she was mystified and puzzled. There was one thing of which she had always felt morally certain—that no truer or more honorable gentleman than Michael ever walked the earth. And under his protection, the loveliest and loneliest woman that ever lived would be perfectly safe. How could Carrie even *think* of breaking her promise to him?

Gracie shivered, and was disinclined to ask any more questions. She sat quietly, lifting her eyes now and then to glance at her sister.

"Do you remember that weekend, Gracie?" Carrie's voice was quiet, even. Gracie practically jumped up to the ceiling.

"You *promised* me you'd never tell," Gracie said.

"And I haven't," Carrie assured her. "It's just . . . well . . . I don't know. I thought it was funny then. Now . . ."

"It was a long time ago," Gracie said. "Now it doesn't matter. Not at all."

"I suppose," Carrie said. "But he's mentioned that weekend lately. And you never really told me what happened."

"Because *nothing* happened," Gracie said. "*Nothing.*"

There was a knock at the door.

"Are you ready for your lunch, Miss Portino?" asked a short Cuban woman.

The two sisters fell silent, both of them remembering when they were young and how *everyone* was an outsider. They still did not relish any intrusions.

"I brought lunch with me, thank you," Carrie replied in a tone of dismissal. "But please leave place settings for two." She turned to Gracie. "Cold pasta primavera from C'est Si Bon," she went on, spreading out French bread and Perrier on the rattan table. "Come on, let's eat. I'm starving."

The two went on easily for an hour now that the subject was changed. They were like young children again, the two of them together against the world.

"Daddy's got all the young girls after him," Carrie said, breaking off another piece of bread. "They call the house all the time and this morning I answered the door and there was this little thing in a skimpy white tank top, no bra and red crotch-hugging shorts. She looked like an over-developed cheerleader!"

Gracie sighed. She knew Carrie thought their father to be highly esteemed and respected, and that these girls were mere golddiggers that went with the territory. However, Gracie knew otherwise.

"Well, anyway, I told her Daddy was busy," Carrie went on, "and then she handed me an envelope for him. You should have seen her fingernails! They were a foot long, and painted down the middle of each red fingernail was a jagged bolt of gold!"

The two laughed. Gracie was an excellent listener. She would give her full attention to everyone, especially Carrie. Even with other people, whether they were witty or dull, intriguing or boring, she loved to listen.

And Carrie loved to talk and make a good story better. She was very theatrical and could lend drama to the most mundane issues.

"You should have seen the way she walked," Carrie went on, getting up from her seat and sashaying across the floor.

Carrie went on and on and they laughed and laughed. As she talked, she reached across and picked at Gracie's plate, a habit that hadn't changed since childhood.

"The house is like a zoo—everybody traipsing through all the time. I'd forgotten what it could be like." Carrie popped Gracie's last piece of pasta into her mouth. Before she was even through chewing, however, there was another intrusion. Dr. Cain stepped into the room without even knocking. He clasped Gracie's hands gently and murmered in her ear. Within moments, Gracie was screaming and crying and kicking, and Carrie had to watch as nurses rushed in to hold, then strap her sister down. She saw them inject something into Gracie's arm. It was like magic. She quieted down immediately, sank into the bed. Her eyes met Carrie's a second before they drifted away into drug-induced sleep. In that second, however, Carrie saw enough sadness to last her a lifetime.

It was three hours before Gracie stirred.

In those hours, Carrie sat in the room, in the dark, and thought of little else beyond Dr. Cain's words: "Gracie, Carolyn is dead."

Carolyn was her sister's best friend in the hospital, a charming and bright girl who, if she remembered correctly, had tried to commit suicide several times before. Gracie always spoke of her incessantly.

"She can't live up to her parents' expectations," she always said. "They want too much of her."

"You can't want too much of a person," Carrie would argue. "Wanting them to be better is for their own good."

"Not always," Gracie would argue back. "Too often it has nothing to do with being *better*. It's usually about being different. Being *safer*."

Safety is not such a bad thing, Carrie used to think.

Gracie's eyes opened, focused. She saw her sister and smiled, then remembered about Carolyn and soon her cheeks were wet with a slow, steady stream of tears.

"She was anorexic," she told Carrie. "She'd been slowly starving her-self to death. It was her way of committing suicide."

"My God," Carrie whispered. She went to her sister, knelt by her bed and hugged her.

"I hope her spirit eventually finds peace," said Gracie tenderly.

Carrie stiffened. "I have very little pity for people who chicken out on life."

"Because it's weak?"

"Because it's *selfish*. Think of all the pain she leaves behind for others to handle."

"It's not for us to judge," Gracie said softly.

Carrie started to speak, then stopped herself. Suicide was a topic the two had never seen eye to eye on.

L̲ong after Carrie was gone, Gracie sat in a loose white dress, with a shawl over her shoulders, in the recess of the window. She gazed out at the brilliant blossoms that nodded their heads at her, like many tiny elves with colored caps on. She prayed that Carrie would keep her promise to Michael, that she'd try to make the marriage work, forgetting about her own ego and insecurities.

She could hear the humming of the bees on the hibiscus, the singing of the birds and voices of people in the garden. They were all united in one continuous murmur that seemed a long way off.

She fidgeted with the gold pen on her lap.

Dear Mother,

Carrie left a little while ago, and I am feeling cut off and alone, as isolated as if I were stranded on an island in the middle of nowhere. There is something going on inside Carrie that is bothering me and I don't know what it is or don't want to face it.

The only time I feel pure comfort these days is when I'm dreaming of you, or when you are with me.

Carrie says you are my good ghost because I told her that I find such comfort in your presence. Sometimes she catches me talking to you out loud. She doesn't understand how close we are.

You would not believe how big Kenny and Keith are getting. She brought them yesterday and they ran into my room and gave me a huge bear hug. It reminded me of your holding me in your arms. Remember? You used to draw me tightly to your breast as if I were the dearest possession in all the world. I hope those little boys get that same feeling of security from my embrace.

They talked incessantly about the great time they were having in their grandfather's home. Kenny told me they were playing in all of Carrie's and my old hiding places and how they ran from room to room playing Captain Power.

My memories of running from room to room in that house leave me with fear and dread. It had such a deserted hollow feeling about it after you left. I would dash about frantically, hoping by some miracle that I would find you hiding. How is it that what brings joy to one, brings sadness to another?

Father is spending all kinds of money and must be trying to buy their love and loyalty, which Carrie doesn't see at all. I know you think I am wrong, but I do not believe him capable of anything good. Father is not made out of the same moral fiber as you, Mother. In fact, sometimes I think he's not even human. I am sorry, Mother, forgive me, but the passing of time has not erased my passions or changed my attitudes. It has only given a new dimension to the circumstances.

The boys have been here in Palm Beach for quite a while now, and miss their father very, very much. When they spoke to me of Michael, their incredibly innocent and youthful look turned to an alarmingly adult look. In their eyes was aged wisdom, as if very old traveled souls had come to rest in these very young bodies. They seem much wiser than Carrie and I at that age.

I was so thrilled to see them. It reminded me of how euphoric Carrie and I would be on your visiting days, waiting for your knock on the front door.

But then there was that ball of ice that used to gather in my stomach when we had to say good-bye.

At least I know they will be coming back soon. Kenny, Keith and I made a pact to pray at the same time each evening so we could think of each other, at the same time, just like you and Carrie and I used to do at eight-thirty every night.

Gracie put her pen down and shivered as if to shake off the cold. A scarcely perceptible wind fluttered in the leaves on the scheffleras against the window. She was reminded of the rising panic that would engulf her when her father used to say her mother would *never* be coming back.

She took a deep breath and continued.

To get back to Carrie, I was overcome today with a feeling of dread that a secret I've kept for a very long time was beginning to unravel.

I've never even shared this secret with you, Mother, for a reason I'm sure you'll understand.

It started way back with all the childish pranks Carrie and I used to play over our identities, when we were growing up. Even Father couldn't tell us apart. You're the only one we could never fool.

Well, as you know, we amused ourselves with this fairly often. When we were fifteen and first started dating, Carrie and I used to fool the young boys, sometimes.

Then we would switch dates and compare them again. There was nothing we didn't share with each other.

Once, when we were seventeen, we liked the same boy, so we shared him completely. He never knew. Both of us were sleeping with him for six months and Carrie and I were perfectly at ease with this. There was no jealousy between us whatsoever.

We graduated that year and moved back to Palm Beach (remember?), where Carrie met Michael. The three of us started going everywhere together happily. We were all very good friends, but this was Carrie's first serious relationship.

I grew very fond of him, too. He was different from Carrie's other boyfriends.

Michael had the smile of a man who was able to see, to know and create the glory of existence. It was a mocking, challenging smile of brilliant intelligence.

Even when he laughed, there was a sense of inner force and vitality that struck me instantly. The flame of a very strong and determined soul burned brightly in him. I can tell you now that from that first day I laid eyes upon him, I felt I knew him.

Father did not like Michael from the very beginning. They were such opposites. Michael didn't use his magnetism to manipulate, as, of course, Father did. It was all so innocent with Michael. He was just delighted with life and his joy rubbed off on everyone around him.

Carrie and Michael began to see each other on a regular basis then, flying here and there to meet each other for a night. Then came that weekend.

Michael and she had planned a romantic rendezvous at the Breakers Hotel. Everything was set, Michael was flying in from Australia. Then, at

106

the last minute, Friday afternoon, just before Michael was to land, Father phoned from his yacht in Cat Cay.

Gracie put her pen down. Yes, she remembered that phone call well.

"I'll get it!" Gracie yelled, dashing to the phone, beating Carrie there by just a fraction of a hair. She grabbed for the receiver, picked it up, smirking at her sister.

"Carrie? Is that you?" Dexter asked.

"It's me, Father. Gracie."

His voice was ice cold, as if he were shocked that she'd even dare pick up the phone. "Put Carrie on," he snapped.

"But . . ."

"Put her on *now.*"

She handed the receiver to Carrie without a word and listened to the excitement in her sister's voice. "What? . . . *What* news? . . . Oh, Daddy, why can't you tell me over the phone? . . . The *Bahamas!*? Of *course* I'll come. I'll go to the Bahamas to hear *anything,*" Carrie squealed.

When she hung up, she couldn't wait to tell Gracie. Daddy had big news for her. What could it be? She was to get on their private plane right away and meet him. Oh, she couldn't wait. But . . .

"Oh no," Carrie said. "I have a date with Michael."

"I'm sure he'll understand," Gracie told her. "I mean, going to the Bahamas . . ."

"He *won't* understand. I've canceled on him a lot lately. And it's almost always because of Daddy."

"Well, you can't do both," Gracie said.

There was a long silence. And then Carrie said, "Oh yes I can."

She begged Gracie to take her place with Michael. Just for the weekend. It would be so simple, so easy.

Gracie didn't want to do it. She wanted to be with Michael, but not as Carrie. She wasn't exactly sure why. Maybe it was just because Carrie seemed so serious about Michael. And he about her. But, of course, Carrie convinced her. Carrie could convince her of *anything.*

Gracie was perspiring now, as she wrote to her mother. She felt dizzy, uncomfortable. But she couldn't stop the flood of memories and she couldn't stop herself from revealing them to Anne.

Carrie was so adamant, Mother, so insistent on keeping both the men in her life happy. I had to help her, she said, so I did.

I walked into the suite at the Breakers that night, and I knew Michael couldn't tell the difference.

He had filled all the room with a wealth of all-white flowers. Their delicious fragrance mingled with the faintly perceptible odor of his after-shave.

We had a wonderful dinner in our room and talked and talked about everything.

We discussed, at length, his latest Oscar nomination for directing his first movie. What I liked was, even though he lost, there were no wailings over disappointed ambitions. Not with Michael. Nor were there regrets over the past, or criticisms or complaints. He had no words against his competitors. Everything and everybody was treated from a lofty standpoint of splendid equality. I listened with deep and almost breathless interest.

I asked him if he wanted me to read him some of his reviews his publicist had given him. "Sure," he said casually, not appearing eager, but I knew he just simply and plainly loved his work.

"I've never seen you this interested in my work before," Michael said to me.

We stayed up till dawn that night, talking, laughing, slow-dancing in our room and walking the beach.

We lay in the sand and watched the lazy progress of the clouds move across the stars.

We listened to the waves, which made a sunburst of sound, as if breaking out of hiding and spreading over us.

In this man's presence, I had the feeling of dreamy satisfaction and a sensation of utter peace.

I remember staring at Michael that night. He was in his full prime of life. His forehead was unfurrowed by care and his face was completely unwrinkled. He gave me a brilliant sense of life I had not known up until that point.

The sun was coming up so we went back to our suite and fell asleep holding each other. It seemed natural not to make love that night. It would somehow have broken the spell that had been woven.

I awoke to the light tap on the door of a bellboy. It was a note from Carrie saying she would be delayed until tomorrow and to please "Continue on. It is of the utmost urgency."

I experienced two confusing emotions, great joy and sheer panic. In the back recesses of my mind, I knew this was not going to end up being a funny prank. There was something much more involved here.

I walked back into the bedroom and Michael flashed his brilliantly gay smile. I felt such serenity of spirit. Even writing about it now fills me with an indescribable longing.

We forgot about food and drink and getting dressed. We stayed in our white terry-cloth robes, sitting on the balcony overlooking the aqua-blue ocean, and talked.

I wanted to know everything about Michael, from the moment he was born. I couldn't get enough. He entered my life that weekend as insistently as a flash of light, illuminating all that had hitherto been dark. With each moment that passed, I knew him better. The flash of his blue eyes; his sudden fleeting smile, which said so little, yet so much; his half-entreating, half-commanding gaze; the turn of his head; and the very gesture of his hand—all of these things were becoming as familiar to me as the reflection of my own face in the mirror.

Michael went in to take a shower and I could hear him singing. Very, very off-key, mind you, but it was such a lovely, rejoicing sound coming from the soul, that I smiled to myself.

The remainder of the day was glorious. Clouds and rain could not have penetrated the radiant atmosphere in which I moved.

Later, we went for another long walk along the beach and watched in silence as the night drew its soft dark curtain around us. The evening was beginning to close on a day of total peace and contentment.

At the end of the path, I involuntarily raised my eyes to his and with one glance, I saw in those deep blue orbs a world of memories. Memories that were tender and wistful. He held my eyes steadfastly and all my inward instincts of my spirit told me that I knew him perfectly. As perfectly as one knows the daisies in the grass will rejoice in the warmth of the sun, and open their golden hearts.

We kissed in mutual desperation and the night air was charged with passion. He set me on fire with his touch and I was completely overwhelmed.

He knew where to touch, and where to touch again; when to kiss; when to push, and when not to push. We moved in total harmony.

Michael was a lover who broke all my bonds. Our lovemaking had the freedom of release and tension of purpose.

When I looked at him, I saw a light of eloquent meaning in the expression of his face. "I'm glad to have met you at last," he said quietly to me. "I've known you in the spirit a long time."

A sense of calm and sweet assurance swept over me and I wanted to be free, to feel all of it, to hold the moment when nothing else was of any concern. My euphoria knocked out the common sense of time. He and I had finally met on a plane of thought where we both had been wandering separately.

He gently pulled my head back by my hair and whispered, "I love you."

I soared to my highest ideal in the blind instinct of a soul seeking its mate.

"I love you too," I whispered for the first time in my life. To confess such happiness was to stand naked. Yet I knew I could let him see it without need of protection.

I will remember that moment forever. It is engraved on my mind.

That night, the moonbeams bathed our naked bodies in a pearly radiance and I watched the light play on the planes of his face.

Perfect happiness is the soul's acceptance of a sense of joy without question, and that is what I felt through my entire being on that never-to-be-forgotten night.

The deep eternal ecstasy can never truly be described or written, but I was the recipient of white light and exquisite felicity. Language fails to describe my feelings for him.

I was so deliciously happy and radiantly innocent, I was incapable of the conception that joy could be wrong. Being with Michael was my secret, mine alone. Immaculately beyond anyone's right of debate or appraisal— even Carrie's.

That night, I slept like a child who is only tired out with pleasure and play.

When I awoke the next morning and looked at Michael, the world seemed all new and brimming with beauty.

At that time, I didn't realize he had already been up a few hours earlier and had met his friend, the manager of Cartier, in the hotel lobby.

Michael sat up on his elbow and a beautiful diamond heart necklace on a silver chain dangled from his hand. "Wear this always with my love," he said, and he clasped it around my neck.

The phone rang that very moment. It was Carrie. Heavy ghosts ran toward me across the Persian carpet of the bedroom.

Suddenly, everything seemed wrong and I didn't know how to make it right. I'll just have to tell her the truth, I thought. I had fallen in love with Michael, there could be no sharing. However, when I walked into the house later that day, Carrie looked as if she had seen the same ghost.

"Daddy's marrying Helena," she screamed. "A wife! This can't be happening to me."

I had nothing to say.

"And I found out Friday just before getting on the plane, Gracie, that I'm pregnant," she wailed.

My heart stopped. Moroseness touched my soul. An icy shiver ran through my veins.

"I can't stay here. I won't," Carrie cried in anguish. "I'm going to marry Michael. It's the only way out."

I remember my hand going to the diamond heart and my chest heaving heavily. Rising panic engulfed me. I stood at bay, my lips quivering and my hands clenched. I couldn't talk. Nothing came to me. Nothing.

"Has he asked you?"

"No," she said. "But he will. I can make him."

I watched the tears slowly fall one by one from Carrie's eyes, and every sob seemed to pierce my heart. Her eyes became darker and deeper with the gravity of each passing moment.

"Help me, Gracie," she pleaded. "I can't make it. I can't handle this. I'm all alone except for you now that Daddy is deserting us."

"Nothing in the world is single," I said to Carrie.

I felt cut in two. I strove to collect my thoughts. I remember clasping my hands and beginning to wonder how and for what I should pray.

"Do you love him?" I asked.

Carrie almost slapped me, Mother. I swear she did. I had never—and have never—seen her eyes flash like that.

"Of course I do!" she said. "I really do! I love him!"

Why couldn't I believe her? I had never in my life disbelieved Carrie. But that night, nothing rang true. I wanted to shake her and say, "No, I love him. He's mine!" But suddenly, I felt myself stepping into a phantasm and I heard this person say, "He must love you, too, Carrie, because he gave you this necklace." Tears of compassion and regret choked my voice. I took the necklace from my neck and fastened it onto her.

"Never tell him it was me this weekend," I said in a low, controlled tone. "This is love and a baby we're talking about. He can never know we intentionally deceived him, no matter how innocent the intention. We must bury this and never bring it up again." The tears stood in my eyes.

111

"I promise," Carrie answered, giving me a hug. We both wore grave and preoccupied expressions as we stood there.

We never spoke of that weekend again, even though Carrie wanted to go through the details. I could never speak of him, even to Carrie.

The next day, a poem by Robert Burns arrived for Carrie from Michael. A month later, they eloped.

All these years, I haven't told this to anyone, but I need to talk to you about this now, Mother. Today Carrie told me she is not happy with Michael. I don't know how to help her, or what to do.

You came to me the other night but you didn't talk. I saw a glimmer of blue, then white, then a rose color. A faint light began to appear for me through the gloom of the night. But then I awoke to find nothing of your character about me, only a shaft of early morning sunshine streaming through the window.

I need you to tell me what to do. Please come again soon.

I love you,
Gracie

Gracie gazed up at the sky, with its gathering clouds, and saw one star. Like a bright consoling eye, it looked at her, glittering cheerfully amid the surrounding darkness. She walked to her box of treasures and put her letter down on the table. She remembered her mother's warm and gentle touch, and also the delicate touch of Michael.

She pulled the poem by Burns out of the box and lay down.

As she read "My Love is Like a Red, Red Rose," little by little, her eyelids closed. The book dropped from her nerveless hand, and in a few moments, Gracie was in a deep and tranquil sleep.

THE PAST

Dexter pulled into the back parking lot of the House of Pancakes on Dixie Highway in West Palm Beach. With a nervous gesture, he lit up another cigarette, cursing Judge Hawthorne's choice of time and place. Dawn was breaking and the restaurant was filling up with truck drivers.

Dexter walked to a rear table where the judge was already wolfing down his breakfast. Poached egg was slivering down the corner of his mouth and he looked like a greedy, malevolent reptile. Dexter controlled his repugnance and shook the judge's hand heartily.

"Good morning, Judge."

"Good morning, Dexter, nice to see you," Hawthorne answered with a southern drawl.

Dexter sat down, the picture of relaxed confidence, and said, "I've been watching you on the eleven o'clock news every night. Your Santiago case has certainly caused a stir these last weeks, but you always did handle the media with a master's hand. Great aplomb, Judge, congratulations." Dexter smiled, knowing just how to flatter this greasy man's ego.

"I'm glad it's about over," the judge remarked. "It went to the jury yesterday." He reached for another waffle.

Dexter plunged in.

"I guess you've heard that Anne has filed for divorce," he said. "It's thrown our plans off a bit. Things will have to be moved up a few months now. I'm meeting with my lawyers this morning to discuss our new timetable."

Judge Hawthorne never looked up, just continued to eat. "Have you had time to establish your 'high moral character'?" he inquired between mouthfuls. "I need lots of witnesses to testify for you, Dexter."

"Don't worry, I've held so many meetings at my house that I can almost recite the Bible from cover to cover! Four hours a week of Scriptures plus a fervent desire to help the poor and needy has got this town convinced of my virtue," Dexter sneered. "Especially the ladies."

"That's excellent," Hawthorne smiled. "You understand how tricky your situation is, don't you? It's highly unusual to award the husband with custody of the children."

Dexter looked straight into the judge's shifty hazel eyes.

"Nobody is going to take my mansion or any of my possessions away from me," he said. "Especially not my beautiful Carrie."

"Well, I think we have good ammunition, thanks to Anne's taking your children off to India when they were so young. How long was Carrie in the hospital in New Delhi?" asked the judge. "Dysentery, wasn't it, then dehydration?"

"Yes," Dexter nodded. "She was in that godforsaken place for nearly a week before Anne finally called me to send my plane."

"And didn't she insist on having a sri, swami, mumbo-jumbo healer come back with them?" Hawthorne asked in amusement.

"Yeah. He sat cross-legged on the floor in the private room at Good Samaritan Hospital for ten days—so we have lots of witnesses. Anne maintains that he saved Carrie's life," Dexter commented sarcastically. "She'll play right into our hands in court," he added confidently.

"As long as you keep watching your p's and q's around town, we may have a pretty solid case," said the judge, wiping his mouth.

Dexter kept a poker face. The judge obviously didn't know yet why Anne had filed so suddenly—she'd walked in on him fucking a minor in their own guest house. Now he was relieved. The last two days he had been worried that Hawthorne might back out of their deal.

Dexter looked straight into the judge's eyes and said smoothly, "I brought you the down payment for that ranch in central Florida we agreed upon." Hawthorne nodded as Dexter stood up and slid his briefcase over to the judge's side of the table.

Hawthorne picked up the breakfast check and handed it to him, saying nothing.

Dexter held his smile and thought to himself, control—only a little longer.

As Dexter drove his beige Rolls-Royce across the Royal Palm Bridge, which adjoined West Palm Beach, the world of the poor and the blacks, to Palm Beach, the world of the rich and the whites, he felt relieved to be back in his realm.

He decided to valet the car at the Everglades Club and walk up Worth Avenue to the oceanfront offices of Goldfarb and Fass. This would give him a minute or two to pick and choose his words carefully. He entered the white stucco building with his usual arrogant bearing that made the receptionist and the other clients in the waiting area notice him immediately. He sat down and spoke to no one.

Samuel Goldfarb came out a few moments later and escorted him silently to a large penthouse suite which had a window view of the public beach on South Ocean Boulevard. Dexter looked down upon all the young, thin girls clad in their skimpy bikinis and wondered how much time Sam spent at the window.

Samuel Goldfarb was one of the most expensive, high-powered attorneys in the United States. His father and partner had founded the Palm Beach firm back in the fifties. When Samuel Goldfarb, Sr., retired several years ago, Sam Jr. had taken over. Now he had thirty-six lawyers working underneath him. Sam loved his work and had not lost a case in ten years.

"Well, Dex, what's the emergency?" Samuel inquired, as his black eyes withdrew suspiciously under his brows.

"The bitch caught me with a young girl," Dexter began. He kept moving, pacing the room, full of a curious energy he didn't seem able to discharge. He hesitated. "A fourteen-year-old."

"Shit, that's why *she* filed yesterday. She's obviously going to use that." Samuel winced, pushing his chair back. He scratched his head and loosened his tie. Goldfarb was furious. How dare this rich asshole jeopardize his case.

"Jesus, Dexter, we told you last year we could hide your other affairs. There were no eyewitnesses, but this . . ." He paused, shook his head, then resumed icily, "*We* were supposed to file, remember? . . ."

"Just handle it, Sam," replied Dexter, angry at being reprimanded. He stared disgustingly at his lawyer and the way his black wavy hair was slicked back in a lounge-lizard style.

"Just handle it," Dexter repeated emphatically between clenched teeth.

The lawyer closed his eyes and sighed. His eyes reopened. "Okay, what's her name and where did you meet her?"

"Her name is Terry something, I met her at Bob Alcori's house. He has three or four young girls living there, like always. You know Bob, one party after another," Dexter said half-smilingly.

"What's his address?" Sam muttered, writing it down on a legal pad.

"Twenty-three Nightingale."

"Did you bring me the other material I asked for, Dex?"

Dexter opened his Gucci attaché case and put a small pile of books on the mahogany desk—Anne's book of the *I Ching*, a book on runes, one about reincarnation and one about the spirituality of the American Indians.

"I also have Carrie's and Gracie's birth charts that Anne had done by an astrologer here in town," replied Dexter.

Samuel just kept tapping his pen on the desk, trying to take in this latest shocking development. A minor, for Christ's sake.

"Don't forget that peyote trip Anne took when she was eighteen. She'll admit she took drugs that year. Anne wouldn't lie. Ever. I could even have some LSD planted on her now, if you want," added Dexter.

"Let's not get carried away, Dex. You told me yourself she's never taken drugs except that one time. We don't even have any witnesses."

"I can *find* a witness, Sam."

Sam Goldfarb stood up and walked to the window, looking down at all the adolescents on their beach blankets.

"Listen to me, Dexter," demanded the lawyer. "We've spent over a year preparing this case. I thought your reputation was all-important to you. You do *not* want to sully your children's names or yours with totally false charges. We'll stay with the religion and what we already have."

"Truth in law, eh?" Dexter smirked.

"No," Goldfarb said, "but we like some small *connection* to the truth. And *I* like to win. So we'll do it my way. I'll be in touch." Dexter turned to leave.

116

"By the way, we drew Judge Hawthorne for the case. He's the one I wanted—extremely conservative," Goldfarb added, trying to lighten up.

Dexter smiled to himself, reaching for the doorknob. "I'll show myself out."

"Just keep away from the fourteen-year-old," Goldfarb warned.

As Dexter walked out into the sunlight and fresh ocean air, he believed himself supreme master of his own life. He knew he was blessed with skills and looks that few had. Things would turn out right for him, they always did. If not, he would simply "buy" them right.

He continued toward Elizabeth Arden's for his ten o'clock facial and manicure.

"Fuck the lawyers," he thought. "They should be called Goldfart and Ass." Stubborn pride settled onto his face. "I'll screw that pretty little pussy whenever I feel like it."

THE PAST

A crowd swarmed around Anne's limousine, their faces pressed against the windows like circusgoers inspecting freaks in a sideshow. The past four weeks of the divorce trial had been a nightmare. Helicopters hovered over her home in Palm Beach, religious fanatics picketed outside and paparazzi on bicycles followed her and the twins on the Lake Trail, making it impossible for her to escape the press's ghoulish scrutiny.

Anne gingerly patted the soft sensitive skin under her heavily made-up eyes, testing for the puffiness that came from several sleepless nights, as she stepped out into the surging mob which blocked her entrance. A phalanx of heavyset bodyguards tried to shield Anne from the crush of microphones, cameras and television lights. A frenzied mob of reporters and photographers jammed the sidewalks.

"Excuse us," said one. "Excuse us!" as a man with a Channel Four newsreel camera stepped directly in Anne's path, and flashbulbs popped in her face.

Dexter leaned against a marble column, his arms crossed. His lawyers had begun gathering affidavits to demonstrate Anne's unfitness well over a year ago. Many detectives and naive new friends had helped him to build up a nearly airtight case.

He had brilliantly kept himself out of the mudslinging. When it came time to pay off witnesses, Dexter was nowhere near the scene. When the press needed to be bought or bribed with special favors, a liaison with only the barest connection to Dexter was found to do the dirty work. He knew that Anne's reputation had to be discredited, without spoiling his own standing in society. He would have to stand aside, lily-white, and feign that his only interest was that "no harm come to my children because of my wife's abnormal religious beliefs and hedonistic, irresponsible life-style."

Dexter and his team of lawyers knew exactly how to manipulate public opinion; the press was trying this case. There had been headlines around the country about her "demonic" and "cultish" acts of worship. The perverse orgies. According to one paper in New York, she had slipped psychedelic drugs to Carrie and Gracie when they were two years old; according to another paper in Florida, she had turned their home into a den of sin filled with instruments used for everything from pornographic films to sexual torture. Sam Goldfarb had built a sympathetic image of his client—the older man used and abused by his young, lustful wife— and would not allow him to testify against Anne. His silence—set against Anne's necessary defensiveness—had Dexter coming off almost saintlike.

Dexter watched Anne walk proudly down the hallway, perfectly groomed in her beige suit. He looked at her as if she were a statue or a matchless picture that *he* had adorned and decked with jewels. Even though she looked unusually pale and tired, and there were dark circles under her eyes, he could have killed her for the mingled loathing and longing which her beauty roused in him. She could still get him hotter faster than anyone else he had ever been with. Over the past months, he had thought about ways to degrade and humiliate her privately, cursing himself for not reading her from the beginning. He had never been able to reach the deep secrets of her soul. He had not given her enough credit for her bloody strength. He had miscalculated.

Anne seated herself at a large rectangular counsel table, directly across from Dexter. Hundreds of spectators and members of the press already packed the courtroom.

The crowd fell silent, then rose as Judge Hawthorne eased himself into a high-backed black leather chair, under a plaque that stated IN GOD WE TRUST. Terror flooded over Anne for an instant; she began to tremble, as she fought to rid her mind of the thick gloom of reality that now threatened to envelop her. She glanced around the room, which was peopled with strangers. All the benches were filled; the overflow crowds were shunted into a fourth-floor courtroom to watch the proceedings on TV monitors.

"Order, order in the courtroom," boomed the ringmaster of the circus, as he pounded his gavel.

Reginald Pearce, Anne's lawyer, sat next to his client. Pearce was an attractive, tall, thin man, with fine, delicate features and iron-gray hair, now wearing a well-tailored, double-breasted, dark-blue pinstripe suit and a somber yellow tie. He was a man of vast legal experience, from an old English law firm in Palm Beach. In the beginning, he had requested the trial be held in closed chambers. His opponent, Sam Goldfarb, had objected—and Goldfarb won. Reginald Pearce's style of operation was light-years removed from Dexter's grandstanding counsel. While Pearce used his polite, elegant manner to soften a witness, many of them broke down in tears under Sam's intimidating assaults. Yet, what worried Pearce much more than style was the power of the tabloids to shape public opinion. Goldfarb had been dispensing bits of information, like jewels, to each paper. It didn't matter that the jewels were paste—the information false. The items ran. And they hurt Anne's case.

Pearce was well aware of the judge's background, too. Hawthorne thought of himself as a good ole Southern boy of simple language and common sense, a man of the people. He was childless and had been married to one rather subservient woman for thirty-five years. She led a cloistered life, sitting at home at night while he went drinking. Anne's successful career and beauty were thorns in the judge's chauvinistic craw. But this custody battle was to be decided solely by his personality and prejudices. He was the one person who would determine Anne's children's future.

Pearce knew he was stuck in a legal maze—every way he turned lately, he found himself blocked. In mounting Anne's case, what militated most strongly against his client were the witnesses who did *not* appear. Everyone from Palm Beach, with the exception of Jane Whitburn, who stood by her, had slipped out of town, feigning to know nothing about the accusations. Her "friends" had put their social standing above any relationship with Anne. Phone calls hadn't been returned, dinner invitations

120

had ceased altogether. They had condemned Anne by their absence and, as a result, his case was weak. Anne had refused to fight back against Dexter's outrageous charges. She would not sully Dexter's name because he was Gracie and Carrie's father. She would also not let the twins testify. She continued to believe that "truth" would win out over expensive lawyers and Dexter's political clout.

"Your Honor, we call Irma Rodriguez," said Goldfarb, who had accompanied Dexter everywhere—fishing in Canada, shooting in Scotland —the past few months.

Irma lumbered up the side steps of the raised platform and plunked herself down in the witness chair. She wore no makeup, and her face looked old and wizened. Around her neck hung a huge gold crucifix. Irma was here for one reason, and one reason only—to prevent this woman from gaining custody of Carrie and Gracie—and she was prepared to say whatever was necessary to accomplish this end for her beloved boss, Mr. Dexter Portino. For twenty-five years she had taken care of Dexter, and for the past five years, she had placated this "other" woman because she wanted to remain close to him. Now her time had come. She placed her liver-spotted hand on the oversized white Bible, and repeated the oath in a high-pitched voice; her Spanish accent spat it out with a strong singsong rhythm.

Sam Goldfarb gave her a reassuring glance and a small smile as she was sworn in. Then in a quiet voice, he began his examination.

"State your name and occupation, please," Goldfarb said.

Irma began her testimony by recounting tales of Anne's "abnormal" life-style. She was encouraged to speak her grievances, so she spent the next three hours decrying that Anne had not even one redeeming trait. One such admission and the twins' custody might go to their mother. It was war.

Anne sat in her seat, tuned out at the moment. Her thoughts were on Carrie and Gracie. Gracie was very high-strung now, crying at the slightest provocation. Her face twitched, and she couldn't speak without stammering. Carrie was not eating well; her ribs were sticking out and she had been having terrible nightmares. Now she was terrified of the dark. Anne had been up very late last night, quieting and comforting the children until their sobs ceased and they fell asleep, curled up like shells.

Inside the courtroom, the questioning continued.

"Do the girls say the Lord's Prayer, Irma?"

"Yes, Your Honor, but *she* never said it with her children. *I* taught them their prayers. I pleaded with her to take them to church," she went on, beginning to cry, all the while fondling her crucifix. "She never takes them to church, *never*, not since their christening."

"Objection, Your Honor. I move to strike that."

"Please, Mrs. Rodriguez, just answer the question," Judge Hawthorne ordered, frowning.

"Did Mrs. Portino have many books around the house?"

"Yes, yes, many," Irma answered, smiling sardonically.

"Did you notice what type of books they were?"

"Yes, yes. They were books about the devil. Yes, the devil." She stumbled in her eagerness to condemn. "She's a bad mother," she continued with absolute moral conviction.

Anne shook her head in negation of the testimony.

"Objection, Your Honor," said Pearce.

"Sustained."

Anne twisted her diamond ring on her wedding finger.

Samuel Goldfarb placed both hands squarely on the thick wooden rail in front of Irma.

"I know this is difficult, Mrs. Rodriguez. I have just a few more questions," he said sympathetically.

"Did you ever find anything unusual in Mrs. Portino's closet?" He was affable now, transforming himself into an angel of innocent vengeance.

"Yes, yes, I did," Irma began, removing a rosary from her purse. Her short fingers began moving rapidly over the beads.

"Will you please tell the court what . . ."

"A voodoo doll with pins sticking out of it." She cut Goldfarb off before he could even finish his question. "With Mr. Portino's hair and fingernails on it! She's trying to kill him!" she screamed.

Anne looked over at Dexter, then at Judge Hawthorne.

"Objection, objection!" screamed Anne's lawyer.

"Sustained," Hawthorne said.

"She's a witch! It's black magic!" Irma's speech was becoming almost incoherent in her urgency to relay this information.

"She's a witch," she repeated dramatically, lifting her gold crucifix and holding it directly in front of her face. Her words hung in the air.

A hum of conversation swept the room, as reporters scribbled furiously on their notepads, and Judge Hawthorne pounded his gavel.

Seated at the long counsel table, Anne's faced turned deathly white with the absurdity of Irma's accusations. Irma could not contain her smile of satisfaction at the reaction her testimony had elicited, and Dexter wore a virtuously injured expression.

"Order, order in the court!" the judge yelled, with lofty severity. Then he declared a recess. Anne followed Pearce, who had stormed into the corridor, trembling with rage.

"Anne, you *must* tell the truth about Dexter and the fourteen-year-old!" he hissed. He was angry, angry at her hesitation and angry at the reality of the legal situation.

"I can't."

"You *must*, Anne."

"No one could believe Irma's testimony. It's absurd."

"They *will* believe it. Just like they believed the psychic who said she made you magic potions. Just like they believed the servant who said he saw you having sex with Dexter's tennis pro. Just like they believed everyone *else* Dexter's had testifying against you. Anne, you're wrong. Did you see the judge's expression? I know this man. Right now, he's got you labeled as dirt. And unless you drag Dexter down into the mud, your case is finished."

"I'm not going to testify against Carrie and Gracie's father. It would be wrong. Integrity is the one and only thing that matters here. When we have that, we have it all. And it will be enough."

"Look—you *have* to allow the children to testify about their religious beliefs and the time you spend with them."

"I will *not* put my children through this! It could destroy them. The judge is *not* going to believe this stupidity."

With that, Anne turned and walked away, her high heels clicking on the terrazzo floor of the corridor. Dexter was at the water fountain. She stood straight and taut, as she always did. Her proud strength was, as always, a challenge to him. The fragility of the need to protect her children, however, was a reminder to him that the strength could be broken. Dexter delicately flicked a piece of lint off his jacket.

At eleven-thirty, Judge Hawthorne called the court to order.

Pearce was unable to shake Irma's testimony concerning Anne, during cross-examination. With a shuffling gait, he moved to the front of the courtroom.

"Do the children love their mother?" he asked.

"The children are not safe with this woman," Irma blurted out. "They're in danger." She spoke rapidly, her words a torrent of venom.

"I'm the one who cares for them," she added, her fat body quivering. "She's teaching them witchcraft."

123

"Please be patient, and just answer the question," Pearce instructed her wearily.

The hours dragged on as the voodoo doll was introduced as Exhibit 42, and the hair and nails positively identified by a lab report as Dexter's. Pearce turned his back on the witness, praying to God Irma's assertions had become such gross exaggerations that no one could believe them.

But he knew everyone would believe Enid Chatsman, the next witness, a heavyset Jewish girl, who sat in the witness chair carefully smoothing her gray skirt under her. She was so discreetly made up, Anne almost didn't recognize her. She only knew her as a woman on the fringe of Palm Beach society, desperate to fit in.

Enid began her testimony by recounting tales of Anne's decadent friends.

"Her companions are people of very questionable life-styles . . . artists, gays, strange religious guys—you know, with the towels on their heads."

"Swamis," Goldfarb prompted.

"I move to strike that out, Your Honor," said Pearce.

"Strike it out," said Hawthorne, sustaining the objection.

Dexter squirmed, thinking of the afternoon he had spent in bed with this pathetic witness. He hoped it would be worth it.

"I walked into Jane Whitburn's studio one day," Enid went on in the dim light, "Anne was there, the two of them staring at a nude man . . . discussing his physical features."

"Jane was doing one of her clay sculptures," whispered Anne to her lawyer, as another wave of sound swept the room.

"We will adjourn until tomorrow at ten A.M.," said Hawthorne, as reporters rushed from the courtroom to their typewriters.

Bailiffs flanked Anne as they pushed out of the courtroom doors through the seething mob of born-again Christians.

One severely pious woman grabbed Anne by the shoulders firmly and screamed in her face, "You are evil—you do not belong to Christ."

Anne looked back at her blankly. Fate—and Dexter—had woven a black, inexorable web from which she felt powerless to escape.

THE PAST

Anne stood in the spacious white marble loggia waiting for Jane. The rising and falling spray from the fountain gave her a chill.

Her thoughts went to the four-story white and beige courthouse on Clematis Street. She was amazed that a building possessed such an aura of power. Human passions lived and died there every day, she thought, and people are permitted to play at being gods. She hoped the verdict would come in soon. The waiting was unbearable.

Dexter had destroyed her in the trial—using everything and anything in his arsenal. Reginald Pearce, her lawyer, was furious with her for refusing to reveal Dexter's affair with the minor. But that was one thing she could never allow to touch Carrie and Gracie. A mother could *never* be responsible for ruining a father in the children's eyes. Not when they were so young and innocent.

For a moment, Anne lost herself in a daydream as she remembered that horrible afternoon. She had returned from a riding lesson earlier than expected. She had walked into the guest house with some roses from her garden to find her husband in bed with fourteen-year-old Terry.

Anne's heart had beat with a suffocating quickness at the sight of Dexter and Terry, the young girl who had baby-sat for the twins several times. The sight threatened to overwhelm her. Anne's mouth fell open, but nothing came out. Some inward restraint gripped her as with iron, and she could feel her spirit beat itself like a caged bird against its prison bars in vain.

Anne ran out of the room, down to the Lake Trail, her eyes blinded by tears. She had been aware of two other transgressions by Dexter during their marriage and had prayed to God to help her look the other way. She believed that holding her family together was more important than what had happened with those two women, but this . . . this was something she could not overlook, or ever forgive.

Anne thought of Carrie and Gracie, tried to imagine them as young teenagers, tried to picture them with a man old enough to be their father. She bent over and started to dry-heave.

She tried to regain herself and stand erect. Too much had happened, too much laid bare. Things were never going to be the same. Everything was all wrong now, and she didn't know how to make any of it right again.

Anne coughed and cleared her throat. She heard Jane's footsteps approaching the fountain.

The two embraced.

"How are the girls?" Jane wanted to know.

"Fine, fine," Anne replied. "I've been able to shield them from most everything. It's going to be harder, though, as they get out of the house."

"Let's go for a walk," Jane said. "This place has ears."

"I've been thinking of calling Dexter," Anne began, as the two strolled through the garden. "If he sees me, I might be able to convince him that what he's doing is wrong. Why won't he let me have joint custody?"

"Because he's a shit, that's why."

"But I loved him, Jane. I truly loved him. I gave up so much for him."

"Unfortunately, that's why they call it *love*, my darling. No one ever said it was logical and certainly no one ever said it was good for us."

"But he loved me, too. I know he did. That's what makes this so difficult. I understand that love fades—but I can't believe it turns into such cruelty."

"Annie," Jane said, taking her friend's hand, "that makes you the last living woman who *doesn't* believe it."

"If he takes my children, Jane, I'm afraid I'd die."

"Your faith has brought you so far," Jane told her. "Let's just hope it brings you a little farther."

"The phone is for you, Mrs. Portino. It's Mr. Pearce," Irma said, as always without any emotion.

"I'll take it in the library, thank you."

Anne kissed the girls and walked to the other room.

"Hello," she said into the phone, her voice quivering.

"I'm sorry, Anne. Dexter won hands down."

Anne listened like a criminal hearing a cruel sentence, her limbs shaking like those of a palsied old man.

". . . Every other weekend . . . Give up custody today before eight P.M. . . . Be out of the marital home within ten days. . . . Leave the religious upbringing to the father. . . . Not allowed to remove the children from the county without the father's consent . . ."

Anne's face was bathed in tears. She put the phone down. Exhaustion and despair subdued her spirit; she was no more than a whimpering child.

She drew herself away from the phone, trembling and sick. All that her consciousness could take in was that she had lost her children.

Anne pressed her hands to her eyes, trying to stop the burning. A sob broke from her lips. The reality of losing Carrie and Gracie overpowered her.

She did not know how she managed to get to the living room. A cold agony gripped her breast when she saw her girls. She kept her eyes fixed on them as if they would vanish if she were to remove them.

Her eyes burned with anguish, but she knew she had to pull herself together for her babies.

She had promised them. Over and over she had promised them: "I'll never leave you. We will always be together."

Slowly, very slowly, words came to Anne like dull throbs of pain beating between her lips.

"I love you," she whispered. "I love you more than life itself."

Then Anne could feel herself being lifted forcibly and rapidly to some terrible limitless space of blackness and nothingness.

THE PAST

The next ten days were a blur to Anne.

She was vaguely aware that Jane had remained at her side through it all, and that Dr. Spivat made daily visits to check on her and dispense pills for her to sleep, but overall, she remembered very little.

Anne's sleep had been so profound and dreamless that she had no idea how long it had lasted, but when she finally awoke, it was with an overpowering sense of the most vivid terror. Every nerve in her body seemed paralyzed. She could not move or cry out. Invisible bonds stronger than iron held her prisoner in her own bed. Then Anne heard Dexter: *You will never see your children again.* Carrie and Gracie cried out to her: *Mommy, Mommy, where are you?* Anne sat straight up, confused, startled. She stretched out her hands instinctively, as a blind man might do.

"I can't get to you, my babies!" she screamed at the top of her lungs. "I can't make it!"

"Anne, Anne, it's all right."

This wasn't Dexter's voice. This was a gentle voice, a soothing voice. "You're having another nightmare," Jane said. "It's all right. I'm here."

Anne's eyes opened, focused on her friend.

"My God, it was so real," she gasped.

"But it's over now."

"Over?!" she cried. "They've taken my children! My children are gone!"

Jane held her friend's hand tightly.

"Justice is an empty word," she said. "It's on the tongues of judges and lawyers, but never in their hearts. *You* know what's right, Annie. Don't let them lead you from your center—not now when you need it the most. You must appeal."

Anne didn't answer. She closed her eyes until she heard Jane leave the room. Then she curled into a fetal position and pulled the comforter over her head.

From the next room, Jane could hear Anne wailing and shouting for Carrie and Gracie. She, too, began to cry. It was all she could manage. There were no words of comfort.

It was only fifteen minutes to six, Friday evening, but Anne could wait no longer. A shiver ran through her limbs as she walked up to the front door. This was her first visitation weekend and she hadn't seen Carrie and Gracie since the decision was announced two weeks earlier. She had called them repeatedly, hundreds of times, she was sure, but Dexter had taken the phone off the hook. The court order prevented her from going to their school. There'd been no way to reach them.

She took a deep breath and rang the doorbell. Dexter opened the door, and the twins instantly pushed past him. The depression that had weighed upon Anne's soul for weeks now vanished completely.

"Mommy, Mommy!" they shrieked with joy, throwing their tiny arms tightly around her neck.

"Have them back by six o'clock sharp Sunday night," Dexter said. A smile of derision parted his lips. There was no contrition for anything that had happened. How could she have loved this man?

She took the girls by their hands and, without a word, led them outside.

Anne did her best to make it a great weekend. They seemed to like her new apartment. They went to the park, the waterslide, shopping for clothes, furniture and toys for their new bedroom. But Sunday night came so quickly, and Anne couldn't believe it was over already. They hadn't really talked about what had happened, what was happening. Anne thought it best that they try to have a *normal* weekend. No stress, no tears, no emotional upheavals.

But the emotion overflowed as the three of them stood hugging each other in Dexter's driveway.

"I don't want you to leave, Mommy. Please, please don't," cried Carrie.

A ball of ice gathered in Anne's stomach.

"Please don't go," Carrie continued. "I want you to live here."

"I know, I know," said Anne, gently holding both girls. She kissed their small faces all over; the taste of their tears stayed in her mouth until she swallowed.

"You *promise* to call us every day?" cried Gracie.

"I promise to *try* every day," Anne said.

"We love you, Mommy, all the way to the moon, the stars and the sun," said Carrie and Gracie in unison.

"And Mommy loves you both more than anything in the whole world." Her voice cracked with a sadness she couldn't hide.

"Carrie, Gracie, *hurry.* Come in the house," Dexter's voice boomed suddenly. He walked toward the twins and pulled them away from Anne's embrace.

The children didn't know what to do as he pushed them into the house, shutting the door between them and their mother. A faint cry escaped from Gracie's lips.

"Dex, you've *got* to let me see them more. You've got to. Please!" Anne cried in despair.

Dexter looked at her with an odd expression. It was not anger or even hatred. It was simply annoyance.

"*You* filed for divorce, Anne. *You* lost. *You* defied me. *You* should have known better."

"Please, please, Dexter. I'll do anything. *Anything.*" Her eyes begged like a tortured animal who desperately seeks mercy at the hand of its destroyer.

"I'll see you in two weeks, Anne," Dexter said, walking toward the door.

"Please! Wait, wait!" Anne burst into uncontrollable grief, her remaining words inarticulate.

The door slammed in her face.

Over the next few months, Anne tried desperately to keep herself busy, but her life, except when she was with her children, was pure hell.

She was unable to work. And, even if, emotionally, she could have, no one in Palm Beach would touch her. She was reviled, she was considered a monster; the sexual innuendos and revelations of devil worship had turned her into a social leper. Worse than a leper, she thought. At least leprosy would evoke sympathy.

Anne wondered many a night, when she lay in the dark, whether she had the strength to go on. She knew she couldn't be there for them when they were sick or hurt. Who was tucking them in at night? Who was singing them to sleep? Why did she lose them? Self-doubt began to plague Anne. But she couldn't leave them completely. She couldn't leave Palm Beach or she'd lose them forever.

Dexter continued to keep the phone off the hook or, if she got through, always insisted the girls were not home, no matter the hour. One night, he even said the girls didn't want to see her anymore. Anne hated having to go two weeks in between visits so she tried going to the Palm Beach Day School. But the teachers and the principal gave her an equally hard time. They insisted she needed Dexter's permission before allowing her on the school grounds.

What was much worse was what was happening to Carrie and Gracie. They were old enough to see what was going on, but they didn't have the skills to deal with it. They were clinging to each other, yet at the same time, they argued more frequently. Dexter was very blatantly favoring Carrie over Gracie and this caused quite a bit of nasty fighting between the girls. Anne even heard them shouting over who was at fault for the divorce. She didn't *want* to imagine all the things their little ears must have heard.

In school, their grades dropped from As to Cs. They were having discipline problems. They defied any authority in school, as well as at home. Both of them were using the name Carrie. Anne urged Dexter to get the children some counseling, but he just scoffed at that idea.

On top of it all, Dexter was fighting the appeal and dragging it out. He found ways to delay each legal step she took. It was taking forever. Because of this, she'd been spending quite a bit of time with Reginald

Pearce. He'd gone from being helpful and empathetic to being cold and supercilious. He blamed her for his defeat. It was as if she had humiliated him in court—as if *he* were the one suffering. He didn't return her phone calls. When he *did* return them, he wanted more money. It was one more web she couldn't get out of—because of the fifty-thousand-dollar retainer she'd already put up. The fifty thousand basically wiped out her bank account—she'd gotten *nothing* from Dexter in the split—so she couldn't start from the beginning with new counsel. Even if she could have afforded it, she didn't have the time to spare.

This morning, Anne stared at the pile of envelopes on her nightstand. She had been receiving a lot of hate mail lately—foul letters claiming she was a sinner.

Anne thought of the people in town and how they were treating her. Some smiled forcibly at her on the street, others feigned a careless indifference. Either way, no one ever signed their names to the letters.

Anne shook her head and threw the unopened mail in the wastebasket. She was, for the first time in her life, doubting everything. And she didn't know what to do about anything. Only silence answered her questions. A silence rendered even more profound by the forebodings of what was still ahead.

THE PRESENT

The morning was fresh and unusually free of humidity. Carrie threw back the lattice and presently the room filled with sweet scents from the garden.

What a glorious day for a party, she mused. Her father was taking her shopping this afternoon and then tonight would be her night. Only hers.

The only gray shadow surrounding the day was that Gracie wouldn't be there.

"Mommy, Mommy," yelled Kenny and Keith, running across the wood floor and sliding on their bottoms, stopping at her feet.

"Good morning, my angels," Carrie said, smiling and taking the two fair-haired boys in her arms. "I love you today."

"We love you, too," they replied in unison.

"They're having a merry-go-round at the church today," Kenny said, his green eyes shining with excitement.

"Yes, Mommy didn't forget." Carrie patted Kenny on the head. "We'll spend the morning together here, the church bazaar doesn't begin until eleven. We'll go there for a few hours, then Mommy's going shopping with Granddaddy. I have to get a few things for the party tonight. Now let's go get some fruit."

The two boys raced downstairs and Carrie followed, watching their long golden locks bounce.

Carrie and Dexter pushed open the door of the St. Laurent boutique to the excessively bright avenue.

"Everything's all set for your party," Dexter said proudly, taking her arm. "My secretary has seen to everything you need. Gigi will be at the house at six o'clock for your manicure, and Dino will do your hair at seven, right after he gives me a trim."

"I can't wait," Carrie replied excitedly.

The two had been in and out of ten stores on Worth Avenue, and Carrie had not been able to find that "just perfect" dress. Most of these shops catered to older people. She wanted something fun, yet dressy, and it was much more difficult to find it here rather than her favorite boutiques on Melrose.

Carrie had always loved getting dressed up, and even when she was little, she had always had a flair for getting into the spirit of things. Gracie had always joked she was the human chameleon, saying, "Stick around and she'll reinvent herself before your very eyes." Gracie, on the other hand, was much more conservative in her dress. She always seemed to know exactly what was right for each occasion, while Carrie usually vacillated between four or five outfits.

Oh, well, if I find nothing, I do have a few to choose from, she thought. She had brought four short, fun cocktail dresses from L.A.—a Patrick Kelly, a Thierry Mugler, a Victor Costa, and a Stephen Yearick.

Dexter smiled lovingly at his daughter. He enjoyed spoiling her; nothing was too good for his Carrie.

That afternoon he had bought everything that she had shown the faintest interest in. New black Maud Frizon shoes, a bustier by Jean-Paul Gaultier, a lime-green Escada jacket. Personally, he thought the color was atrocious—but it didn't matter if it made Carrie happy.

"Where are the boys this afternoon?" Dexter asked as they strolled.

"Tony Robinson's birthday party."

Dexter responded with a look of disdain. "I'm going to give you an 'A' list for them, darling. You've got to watch out who you let them associate with."

"I thought they were friends of yours," she answered. "I remember going to their house with Gracie when we were growing up." Carrie laughed at the memory. "They're the ones who used to have plastic all over the furniture, and sheets, so we couldn't mess anything up."

"He lost all his money a few years ago—or should I say, all his *friends'* money," Dexter snorted. "He persuaded all his friends to invest in a new restaurant here in town that never opened while he lived high on the hog in Lyford Cay with the money that was supposed to be in escrow. I heard he even paid to have his picture in the Shiny Sheet with some of it." Dexter snickered at the mere pathetic thought of that. "Now he's back in Palm Beach talking another big deal. Can you believe it?"

They shopped unsuccessfully for a dress for Carrie until the stores closed at five-thirty. Dexter was clearly more disappointed than she and, as usual, made up for *his* disappointment by buying *her* a present—a magnificent five-carat emerald-cut sapphire necklace with matching diamonds on either side.

"Do you like the necklace?" he asked in the car, as they were driving home.

"Of course," she said. "I love it."

"Because if you don't, I can take it back."

"Daddy, it's *beautiful.*"

"I won't mind. Maybe it was foolish to buy it. You like the one you have on so much."

She hesitated and instinctively touched the diamond heart that hung around her neck, the heart Michael had given her long ago. She had told Michael she'd wear it always when she was away from him.

Her father was looking over at her, waiting with a hurt expression on his face.

Oh, why shouldn't I make him happy? she thought. What difference could it possibly make?

She removed Michael's necklace and put on the sapphire. It sparkled almost as brightly as Dexter's smile.

M illie, Dexter's secretary, was busy seeing to all the last-minute details. She was a very attractive, calm, soft-spoken woman in her early sixties, who had been with Mr. Portino—she would never call him anything but—for twenty-five years.

It was early summer—the "off" season—but Dexter's friends were coming out in full force, flying in from their summer homes across the country.

Eighty-two people out of the one hundred and six invitations Millie had personally mailed had accepted. The crème de la crème of Palm Beach's social register would be out tonight.

Millie, standing tall in her Chanel blue silk suit, inspected the sumptuous food that was being laid out on the white organdy and moiré taffeta–covered buffet tables. She smiled. Everything looked perfect as she strode from room to room. Each of them shimmered with enormous silver and crystal bowls filled with glorious white roses. Voices could be heard in the entrance hall where Carrie and Dexter stood, beneath the vast cut-glass Georgian chandelier, greeting their first guests.

Carrie stayed on her father's elbow in the foyer for the first forty-five minutes, greeting old familiar faces and several new ones. She could hear the party buzz in the living room and watched excitedly as the crowd sipped on their champagne and mingled on one of the many garden terraces.

She already had dozens of compliments and warm kisses from these people she'd known for so many years. This was quite a change from the Hollywood scene, she thought, where nobody *ever* noticed her unless she was on Michael's arm. She liked being the "Princess of Palm Beach" again.

Having stayed at the front door long enough, Dexter took Carrie's hand and they went into the living room.

"That's Morgan Welton. He moved to town after you left and he's really been cultivating his power," Dexter whispered. He took a sip of his Cristal. "Watch him. He used to be incredibly crude, but now he thinks of himself as the sophisticated Englishman. He won't say anything worse than 'bloody.' Morgan is definitely spreading out over America. They call him the octopus—his tentacles are grasping at everything. He's tried everything to get in the Bath and Tennis and now if a board member even mentions his name, that member will be blackballed. I hear he's so obsessed with money that he takes financial reports to bed every night—his idea of foreplay."

"Where I live, they all take *Variety* to bed with them," giggled Carrie. "I'll be right back. I just want to make sure the boys are tucked in."

Dexter looked about the room, as his guests worked at being brilliant. He glanced at old Clifford Borden, already tottering a little but having a waiter refill his bourbon glass. His end of the family had lost almost all their money, yet Clifford was both self-confident and self-assured, wearing what must be his father's old worn-out tuxedo. He jokingly admitted to Dexter earlier that he was selling all the family jewels.

Dexter got a refill and began to work the room, which was abuzz with the music of Peter Duchin.

"Why hello, Dexter," said Marguerite Whitburn, extending her hand and cheek, looking years younger than her seventy birthdays. Her dark brown hair was worn with classic simplicity and her skin had kept a diaphanous quality similar to her daughter Jane's.

"Good evening, Marguerite. I'm so glad you could make it," Dexter said.

Marguerite watched him shape his lips into a smile. Like her daughter, she knew his true feelings were not involved in the smile at all.

"Nothing would have kept me from seeing Carrie," replied Marguerite, withdrawing her hand. "It's a lovely party."

"Thank you." Dexter eyed Marguerite with covert resentment while she stood there in her usual regal and unapproachable manner.

Dexter had never yet been seated in the "right" room for dinner at the Whitburns' mansion. The preferred guests sat in a room full of Van Gogh, Renoir and Manet originals. Mrs. Whitburn, however, always put *him* in the room with the more obscure paintings. They were the only ones in all of the Palm Beach area who still snubbed him.

"I'm so sorry Jane's out of town this weekend," he fawned.

Marguerite didn't answer. Dexter was the father of her daughter's godchildren, so she had always treated him with courtesy, but her behavior toward him was marked by a cold dignity, which, like a barrier of ice, repelled the warmth of his attention.

For once, Dexter was at a loss for small talk. It's probably better for her to say nothing, he thought uneasily. She's too capable of slaying a reputation with a few perfectly enunciated words delivered in her regally high-bred accent.

Mrs. Whitburn excused herself as an array of young girls approached Dexter. He singled out a young wide-eyed blond beauty with a pouty mouth and full, sensitive lips. She confidently held out a cigarette for him to light. For a moment, he didn't recognize her, then realized she was one of his masseuses. He wet his lips with his tongue and decided that tonight she would give him more than a simple massage.

Mrs. Whitburn watched Dexter with disdain. She almost felt sorry for the girl. Almost—but not quite. If she didn't recognize what a phony bastard Dexter Portino really was, she probably deserved whatever was

137

going to happen. The only one who hadn't deserved it was Anne. Anne's blindness had not come from greed, it had come from kindness and a belief in the righteousness of human nature. Anne's error, Marguerite Whitburn reflected, was when she'd decided that Dexter was human.

She felt a gentle tugging on her arm and turned to find a smiling Carrie.

"Aunt Marguerite, I'm so happy to see you," the girl exclaimed as the two embraced. Marguerite had always been one of Carrie's favorite women, filling a sort of grandmother role for her when she was growing up. Her zest and enthusiasm for life had remained undimmed by advancing years.

"Your father has thrown a lovely party for you," Marguerite said. "You must be pleased."

Carrie lifted the new necklace up from her skin. "A present came along with the party," she said.

"Then you must be *very* pleased. It's lovely," Marguerite replied. "And you are looking as beautiful as ever." She held Carrie's hands in hers.

"Absolutely, my dear," interrupted Mrs. Ziphir. "You look stunning tonight." She proceeded to hug Carrie with demonstrative fervor. Mrs. Ziphir who, even at sixty, had a fondness for froth and frills, was in a deep-blue Valentino, tight-hugging on the top with a big pouf at the hips. She gossiped vivaciously with Carrie about the social merits and accomplishments of *all* the people present.

"I ran into Chessie yesterday in Cordially Yours, while she was ordering *the* most divine invitations for her dog's birthday party next week. I wonder if she'll outdo the fabulous soiree Billy Maven gave for his Rolls-Royce at Easter. Everybody is *still* talking about that night."

Marguerite shifted her weight impatiently.

There is no such person as Mrs. Ziphir, she reflected. There is only a shell containing the opinions of her society friends. These people who discuss trivia till discussion is worn thin and the brain is weary are a deadly menace, she concluded.

Myra Wexell was now making her way toward Carrie and Marguerite, looking like a drag queen. They could hear as well as see her. She was waving to everyone and holding her cheek to be kissed, all the while smiling perfectly for the *Women's Wear Daily* photographer. Before the next photo, Myra put her finger into the butter on the buffet table and spread it over her lips.

"Gracie, how *are* you?" Myra asked, her face flushed with drink.

"I'm Carrie," was the soft reply.

Marguerite noticed the dark, sad look cross Carrie's face. But it only lasted a moment, then she quickly smiled again.

"I'm sure *everybody's* been calling you Gracie tonight," Myra said foolishly, glancing at Mrs. Whitburn with apprehension.

Marguerite glared as Myra turned away. "One must make oneself strong enough to be loved or hated in this town," she said to Carrie. "And with that bit of advice, my dear, I shall leave this party to the young and those who want to *be* young. Enjoy yourself."

"Thank you for coming." Carrie kissed the old woman on the cheek, then rushed back in to see where her father was. As she circulated, everyone continued to vie for her attention. Even the reporters were unrelenting—but Carrie was having the time of her life. Dominick Dunne and Helmut Newton were in town doing a piece on Palm Beach and she was a fan of both. She enjoyed chatting with them as she surveyed the dance floor.

She finally spotted her father with a gorgeous blonde. The girl was thin and sinewy and had cascading hair down to her rear; she was gaping at Dexter with open adoration, while he was smiling down at her with a half-seducing, half-taunting smile.

She hesitated, wondering if she should go to him now. A pang of jealousy washed over her. It was *her* party. *Her* night. Why would her father rather be with an intruder than standing with *her*? Why wasn't he proudly escorting her around the room, his hand resting comfortably on her hip, his arm around her waist?

Why wasn't *her* father with *her*?

"It looks like Britty has just played with herself in the bathroom," a tall redhead was whispering behind Carrie. "I bet you she'll race straight to her next victim and stick her finger directly under his nose." Another woman laughed and Carrie turned abruptly, away from her father and the girl and toward the group of gossipers. "Apparently," the woman said, "the aroma of pussy *is* the strongest aphrodisiac in the world."

Carrie choked on her champagne, then listened to yet another woman, Mrs. Pitts, chime in with even more gossip.

"Did you watch the Geraldo about the woman whose ex-husband was still her gynecologist? She went to him after their divorce for a minor operation and instead he sewed her vagina shut!"

For a moment, Carrie forgot all about her father.

"All he wants to do is go down on me," a drop-dead classic beauty from the other side of the group was saying. " 'What happened to *fucking*?' I had to ask him—and he looks at me *puzzled*. 'You know,' I went

139

on, 'when a man gets an erection and puts it in the woman.' I'd like to validate his condom—even *my* condom."

Carrie turned back to her father—enough was enough—but he was gone. The girl was gone, too. Standing in their place was a very attractive man with a comma of black hair hanging over blue-gray eyes. Carrie stared at him, wondering where her father had disappeared to. The man must have misunderstood her stare, for he smiled at her, a roguish grin, and when he smiled, she noticed a tiny white scar on his cheek.

For a moment she held his stare.

"Miss Portino," Irma beckoned from the pantry door. "A fax just came for you over your father's machine."

Carrie looked at the piece of paper. "I'll be arriving in Miami tomorrow on the Concorde. Meet you at our suite at the Breakers. I'm sorry I missed your party. I'm sure you were glorious. I love you. Michael."

"Thank you, Irma," Carrie said. "Please put it in my room."

"Anything wrong, darling?"

Dexter came up behind her, putting his arm around her shoulders.

"No, Daddy. Everything's fine. Michael's arriving tomorrow."

For a moment, Dexter's face froze and suddenly looked tougher, older. *Damn* him, he thought. *Damn him to hell.* Then he smiled, the mask slipped back on. He kissed his daughter on the cheek.

"Some of our guests are leaving. Let's say our good-byes," he said.

The handsome man with the scar approached and Carrie held out her hand in silent farewell. He took it gently and kissed it with graceful courtesy.

The party slowly thinned out. The parking attendants ran a steady stream of Rolls-Royces and Mercedes up to the front door. Carrie sipped champagne and kissed turned cheeks. At last, what seemed like hours later, when almost everyone was gone, Carrie and Dexter finally got to eat a little caviar and salmon themselves.

"So, my darling? Did you enjoy yourself?"

"It was one of the loveliest parties of my life, Daddy," Carrie said. She put her food and drink down and, wrapping both arms around his neck, kissed him.

As her body pressed tightly against her father, Carrie experienced an uncontrollable shiver of physical attraction. It was the same strong desire she used to feel as a growing teenager whenever Dexter held her. Her early sexual fantasies had always included him. She had not had the sensation in a long time, but it had the same effect it always used to; it thrilled her, electrified her—and scared her.

Silence possessed them for a moment. Neither of them cared to move. Then she leaned closer to him.

"I'm very tired," she whispered. "I've got to get up early . . . for Michael."

She let go of him. His hands lingered, not restraining her, just resting on her arm for an extra moment.

"Good night, Daddy," she said. Then Carrie slowly went upstairs to her room.

Dexter felt he was going to explode.

He lurched out the French doors, his fingers balled into a tight fist.

The moon hung over the high walls of his estate. Undefined shadows lurked in the corners and crevices of the twelve-foot-high ficus hedges. He breathed deeply, slowly, and looked at the moon.

"God *damn* him," he said aloud.

Carrie's Paris perfume lingered in the air, on his clothes, in his mind.

THE PRESENT

Michael Donovan sat in the Park limousine. A few last-minute phone calls made sure everything would be perfect. He spoke to the manager at the Breakers, who assured him he had the exact suite he'd requested and yes, it had been filled to the brim with peach roses and yellow orchids. The Taittinger magnum was chilling and the crème brûlée from La Vielle Maison would be delivered exactly at seven-thirty.

Michael put his head back, closed his eyes and pictured Carrie, Kenny and Keith. It had been over a month since he'd seen them and he missed them all. He was immensely pleased to have this one day off from shooting. Flying in from London just for the day seemed the most natural thing in the world. He would have flown in from the moon.

He seldom mustered the courage to visit Palm Beach. It was not his favorite place. The people alternately bored and repelled him. They were snobs, they were racist, they were anti-Semites. They loved *him*, of course, because he was famous. Would they love him as much, he wondered, if they knew his real name was Michael Donawitz? He'd changed his name years ago, on the advice of his agent. It didn't much matter to Michael. He was born a cynic and felt that much of life was a series of cons played out against the years. The best con men sometimes led the best lives. At least he'd felt that way until he met Carrie. He couldn't con Carrie, wouldn't ever want to. Lying to Carrie would be the same as lying to himself—the one thing he'd never do. Michael knew who he was and what he was. That was what counted.

Carrie felt the same way, he was sure. She was a truthful person. There was only one blind spot—her father.

Michael detested Dexter. After all these years, Dexter had still never invited him into his home. He never included Michael in his family celebration at Christmas. Sometimes he didn't even address him. And he still had Carrie under his spell. She thought he was perfect. The only fights they ever had were over Dexter.

God, how he missed his wife. He leaned back, readily yielding to the magic influence of his love for her, experiencing a sudden sense of satisfaction and completeness.

The limo pulled into the palm-tree-lined driveway of the Breakers, the magnificent hotel inspired by the Villa Medici in Florence. Michael picked up the car phone and dialed Carrie's number.

C arrie knocked on the door of Suite 200. She could hear the expectant beating of her heart. She hoped her hangover didn't show on her face.

The door opened and Michael stood there shirtless, barefoot in his jeans, leather belt open, his chin stubbly and his hair wild. He was looking, as always, very untended. That was his greatest charm.

She put her arms around him; he smelled of the cool air of night. They kissed gently and his saliva tasted sweet to Carrie.

"God, I missed you," smiled Carrie, hugging him tightly.

"Me, too," he replied tenderly. "Where are the boys?"

Carrie trembled. "Don't be angry, Michael. By the time I got up, Daddy had flown them to Disney World for the day."

"For Christ's sake," he said. "Didn't they know I was coming?"

"I didn't see them last night, at least not after I got your fax, and . . ."

"But *he* knew, didn't he, Care?"

143

Carrie didn't answer. She looked down at the floor.

"I only have one day," Michael said softly.

"Then let's make the most of it," she said. "Please? I'll go get them first thing in the morning, I swear. And think of what we can do in the meantime, Michael, as long as they're *not* here."

His eyes, deep blue and full of light, studied her face. Carrie felt as though his stare were a searching ray burning into every nook and cranny of her heart and soul. She smiled at him.

"What are you thinking, Michael?"

"Come here," he said.

In the background, a Tracy Chapman tape was playing, and as Michael touched Carrie, she could feel the vibrations of the bass line of the music.

"I've missed you," he told her, breathing in the fragrance of her hair.

The straps of her beige camisole fell from her shoulders as he kissed her neck. His fingers began gently exploring beneath the waistband of her jeans. He held her with his mouth while he moved slowly and expertly to unzip her pants.

Michael could feel her feverish skin and savored the way Carrie began to move, slowly, almost imperceptibly against him.

The lace and satin fell from her breasts and Michael could feel her erect nipples against his bare chest as his tongue filled her mouth.

They kissed in a desperate frenzy.

She watched his every movement as he slowly undressed, feeling as if she might melt from excitement.

Carrie sank down to her knees and began to play with him. Then she took him into her mouth and moved her tongue skillfully.

When he could take no more without coming, Michael grabbed Carrie's shoulders and gently laid her down on her back. She looked at him in the candlelight and began to touch herself. Then she licked her fingers. She put her fingertip in his mouth, watched him lick, nearly devour her, then she reached between her legs again and brought herself to orgasm.

Michael moaned and bent down and buried his head between her legs.

Carrie put her hand softly into his hair and stroked him. Then it came back. The fantasy. *Her father.*

It hadn't happened in over four years. She'd forced herself to stop. But she thought of her father now as Michael's tongue made love to her and she came.

"Make love to me from behind!" Carrie suddenly murmered passionately. "Do it now!"

144

Michael turned her over and pulled her up onto her knees. He put his hands on her hip bones and held them tightly as Carrie began pushing back against him. He caressed her breasts and kissed the back of her neck.

Michael wet his finger and gently inserted it in her. Carrie continued to move back and forth.

He removed his hand and began to enter her very slowly. She'd never let him do this before, not ever, and for a moment she thought she wanted him to stop. Michael sensed this and eased.

But soon Carrie began to open to him and slowly it didn't hurt anymore. She slid back and forth, a totally different pleasure for her.

She began to moan softly. He thrust into her deeply and slowly, riding the slow undulation of her hips. Now, no inch of her body was unexplored to him.

Carrie screamed in pleasure and Michael began to move faster now, finally exploding in ecstasy inside her. Then they collapsed onto the floor, exhausted, drained. After a few minutes, Michael propped himself up on one elbow and grinned.

"So what *other* great ideas have you had while I was gone?" he said.

"Let's Nair our hair off," Carrie said. They'd been lying quietly, listening to music and sipping champagne. Now, she jumped up to go to the bathroom.

Michael laughed out loud.

"Don't be a baby. Come on," she urged, searching in her bag for the Nair.

"I remember the last time we did that," he replied. "It was great until it started growing back in and I thought I was going to scratch my balls off."

Carrie remembered well, too. It had been one of their late nights and the next morning Kenny and Keith had come in while they were in the shower.

"When did you go bald?" Kenny had asked, staring at her completely hairless body, his eyes as big as half-dollars. She and Michael had been in hysterics for days.

"What the hell," Michael said now, handing her his stemmed crystal glass of champagne.

She leaned down to draw the bath and Michael just stared at her. She was tall, big-breasted, narrow-hipped, long-legged, sexy, playful, fresh,

145

yet sophisticated. Carrie was everything a man could want, physically. Yet, he felt something was happening to her. He wasn't exactly sure what it was but *whatever* it was, it had gotten worse since she'd been in Palm Beach. He sensed a certain wildness in her, a craving for risk. He hoped it was a passing fancy, a phase brought on by the boredom of her current surroundings. But he wasn't sure it was just a phase. And it made him nervous.

Michael stood, trying to grin patiently while Carrie spread the white cream over his pubic hair.

"The smell is enough to kill you," he growled.

Carrie pinched him.

"Careful," he replied, sipping his drink. "That's all I've got."

"My turn," Carrie said, handing him the tube. Michael knelt down as she spread her legs for him. He felt an incredible desire for her, but forced himself to rub the ointment carefully over all her hair.

"Ten to fifteen minutes," she said, checking the temperature of the bath.

The two sipped more champagne. He started to tell her about his new film, about the problems they'd been having with the lead actress, who was the director's girlfriend and who didn't exactly speak perfect English —but did apparently give perfect blow jobs to the crew.

"Okay, it's time," she interrupted, taking a wet washcloth and gently wiping the cream off Michael. He immediately got an erection.

Carrie hopped up onto the bathroom sink and spread her knees.

Michael took another wet washcloth and began to smooth off her hair.

When he finished, she leaned back against the mirror and pulled him into her.

As he pounded her against the glass, they both stared at their reflections. They looked perfect together, they fit together.

They they both came simultaneously, their eyes never leaving the mirrors.

"You've been away too long," whispered Carrie.

H̲e was drowsy now. She was asleep, having eaten the last of the crème brûlée and sipped the last of the champagne.

Carrie's blond hair scattered loosely on the white pillows. Her long silky lashes curled softly on her delicately tinted cheeks. Her lips, tenderly red, were slightly parted.

Her robe was open and displayed her round bosom. Michael closed his

146

eyes now. He held his breath just an instant, taken aback by the diamond and sapphire necklace that hung around his wife's neck. He couldn't believe he hadn't noticed it earlier. She'd taken off his diamond heart. Despite her promises. Despite everything.

Her new necklace glittered brilliantly as it rose and sank with her quiet breathing.

It had been a splendid morning for Gracie.

Awaiting her visitors, she slipped on her blue jeans and surveyed herself in the mirror as she pulled her hair into a ponytail, fastening it with a barrette.

Gracie had expected to look haggard and tired after another sleepless night, but her face presented a freshness which astonished her. The heavy marks under her eyes, the lines of pain that had, for weeks, been deepening in her forehead, the plaintive droop of the mouth—all were gone, as if by magic. There was a rose-tinted complexion, a pair of laughing eyes. A happy, mirthful face smiled back at her.

Suddenly, there was a loud ringing in her world of silence. It was so loud, it made her heart skip a beat. Gracie composed herself and picked up the telephone receiver.

"Is Carrie there?" Dexter boomed impatiently on the other end of the line.

"No, Father, not yet. But I expect them any minute."

"I've been trying the hotel for hours. Where could they be?"

"I'm sure I don't know. Maybe they just wanted some time alone with the kids."

Dexter didn't even acknowledge her response. She started to say, "Is there something I can . . ." but she realized, before she'd finished the sentence, that he'd hung up.

Gracie sat down on the bed and laid her head back on the pillow. A sudden coldness in the air made her shiver.

She wished Michael and Carrie were with her. She felt afraid. And it only made things worse that she wasn't sure what it was she was so afraid of.

Michael was in the shower with the twins when he heard the phone ring.

"Soap me, Daddy! Soap *me!*" both boys were screaming, laughing as they all wrestled under the hot water and dripping gobs of shampoo.

Michael strained to hear Carrie's end of the conversation. Her voice was anxiety-ridden. But he couldn't hear what she was saying.

"**D**addy, are you all right?" Carrie said.

Dexter moaned at the other end of the line.

"I was playing tennis," he gasped. "My knee. Hurt it badly. Have to go to the emergency room."

"Is Irma there?"

"She's running errands somewhere."

He sounded in terrible pain.

"Who were you playing with? Jock?"

"He's gone, too. I thought it'd be all right. But it's swelling. I can't walk."

"Daddy," Carrie lowered her voice. "I only have a few hours left with Michael."

There was no answer from Dexter.

"Daddy?"

Again, silence. She could hear him breathing heavily.

"I can't just leave him. Can you call—"

"Never mind," Dexter said tightly. "I'll find somebody else."

Without another word, he severed the connection. Carrie slowly put down the receiver. She cocked her head, listening to her boys cavorting in the bathroom. Then she picked up the phone and, trembling, quickly began to dial.

Dexter folded his arms behind his head on the luxurious brown Chesterfield sofa and eyed the library with a complacent smile. His eyes wandered to the quaintly shaped bookcases overflowing with first editions, then to the wall covered with exotic animal trophies from all over the world.

Anne flashed into his mind. Women are like animals, he thought. Nothing can surpass the thrill of hunting them, capturing them, taming them. *Or killing them.*

He looked out the window at the blossoms that seemed to surge up like the sea to the window's ledge. There was something fantastic in the splendor that surrounded him. He felt as though he were a star in a vast

148

theater where the curtain had just risen on a play. He believed such luxurious living was his privilege; it was the right and custom of men of his stature.

Dexter realized he had to get an ice pack for his knee before Carrie arrived. He stood up slowly and, practicing a limp, edged over to the bar and made himself a drink. A cold, calm smile played on the perfect outline of his mouth. She'll be calling back any moment, he thought, as he settled back in the chair. His whole being plunged into a delicious, throbbing fever of delight to which he could give no name, but which permeated every fiber of his body.

Dexter took another sip of his drink and waited. The phone rang.

Michael stared at her in disbelief.

"Did he break something?" he wanted to know.

"I don't think so," Carrie stammered, "but he wants an X ray to be sure. You can take the boys to see Gracie and I can just meet you there."

"He won't *let* you meet us there. Do you really not see that?"

Carrie looked as if he'd slapped her. "Don't be ridiculous," she said.

"I don't think I am."

"First of all, he doesn't control me. He can't *let* me do anything. Second of all, the man is hurt. He hurt himself. This isn't a game."

"Isn't it?" He spoke softly. Sadly.

"No! It isn't!"

"Care, listen to me," Michael said. "Every time we're together, he tries something like this."

"Like *what*?" She was getting angry.

"Like *this*. An accident. Taking the boys to Disney World. A party! Whatever it takes to keep us apart."

"Michael, this is absurd."

"I don't think so."

"My father loves me!"

"I know he does," Michael said. "I think he loves you too much."

There was a long silence before Carrie said, "I think that's better than you not loving me enough."

"You know that's not true. How can you even think such a thing?"

"I *do* think it," she said, and now her voice was harsh. "My father doesn't leave me for months. My father doesn't spend his time with his millions of adoring fans! My father—"

149

"Your father's not your husband, Carrie. Even if you wish he were, he's not. *I* am."

For a moment he thought she was going to hit him. But the phone rang. After the second ring, she picked up the receiver, listened for a moment, slammed it down.

"The concierge," she told him. "The press found out you're here. They're swarming in the lobby like bees."

"Let's go see Gracie," he implored.

"I have to go to the emergency room," she said. "And that's all there is to it."

The boys came out of the bathroom, dressed and groomed.

"I'll meet you in Gracie's room," she told Michael. "This won't take long at all."

"I'll miss you, Carrie."

"Stop it!" she screamed. The boys' eyes widened and, for a moment, the room was completely silent. "I'll be there," she said to Michael. "I promise I'll be there."

Michael reached over and touched the necklace that lay nestled between her breasts.

"We know how you always keep your promises," he told her.

Michael took Kenny and Keith by the hand and led them outside. The crowd was enormous and, as soon as Michael emerged, cameras started clicking, people started yelling.

"Look over here, Mr. Donovan!"

"Here, Michael, here!"

They passed through the ranks, Michael nodding graciously as he climbed into the limo. When the boys were seated, Michael glanced out the window. His wife was watching them. She didn't wave.

The limo pulled out of the long drive, past the magnificent palms. Carrie's fragrance lingered on his fingertips.

G racie hugged Michael, drawing comfort from his presence.

They were silent, a deeply companionable silence because words were not necessary. Then they both smiled and a curious sensation of pleasure tingled through Michael's frame as he pressed her slender fingers in his own clasp.

"How are you?" he asked tenderly.

"I'm fine," Gracie replied softly.

"Auntie Gracie! Auntie Gracie!" Kenny and Keith squealed as they bounded through the door.

Gracie and the twins hugged each other. Michael enjoyed the pleasure that shone so brightly on Gracie's face.

"Can we play outside, Daddy, please?" begged Keith.

"Let's play football! Please?!" added Kenny.

"Yes, let's all go outside," Gracie said, grabbing a wide-brimmed baseball cap to shelter her from the July sun.

The children ran ahead, playing with their bright-yellow toy football while Michael and Gracie strolled behind. They passed slowly out into the gardens, where rich orange and pink bougainvillea clamored and clustered everywhere. The two walked side by side for some time without speaking, through winding patterns of alternate light and shade from the palm trees. The air about was fragrant and delicate and the two friends relaxed into their own private thoughts.

Finally, Gracie broke the silence.

"Where is she?" she asked softly.

"Your father," Michael replied flatly. That was all he had to say. She nodded.

The boys were tossing the football up ahead of them, scrambling through the grass, lost in the magical world of make-believe.

"Kenny and Keith have been coming regularly to see me," said Gracie, looking on. "They're wonderful children."

"I don't see them enough."

"You make it up to them."

"I mean for me. I *need* them," he said.

They walked a little farther in silence.

"Please don't let my father destroy you," Gracie blurted out suddenly.

"Can he?" he asked.

"The marriage," Gracie said. "That's what he wants to crush."

"It's not his to destroy, Gracie," Michael told her. "Only Carrie and I can do that."

"You don't know Father," she said. "Not really. He can destroy anything."

He stared at her, at the worry in her eyes.

"Throw me the ball, Keith," Michael finally said, running out for a short pass.

A woman in a crisp white uniform came walking across the grounds. It was Mrs. Griffin, their new nanny.

"Mr. Portino has sent me to pick up the children. It's getting to be their bedtime," she said.

"We're waiting for their mother," Michael told her.

"Mr. Portino said she won't be coming," Mrs. Griffin said.

Michael nodded slowly, knowingly. "I'll let you know when they're ready," he told her.

"Mr. Portino said—"

"I'll let you know when they're ready!"

She stopped short at his tone, spun on her heels and retreated.

"I hope you'll come to L.A.," Michael said to Gracie.

"I'll try," she said. "And you remember what I told you."

"I'll try," he said to her.

They hugged one last time.

"Good-bye, Gracie," he said gently.

Gracie watched the three of them walk to their car. They are a beautiful family, she thought. Then she thought of her father. How could anyone want to destroy such beauty?

THE PRESENT

Dexter lay with his eyes closed, next to Zoe, savoring the physical pleasure. A youthful stirring came up from deep inside him.

Zoe had arrived late Friday night from Clifford's, the ultra-exclusive, ultra-expensive etiquette school where Dexter had sent her for six weeks to "improve" herself. She had come back a changed girl, more positive and outgoing. Also, she had lost that last ten pounds. There was no doubt about it—Zoe had bloomed.

Dexter appraised Zoe's naked body through her filmy pink negligee. Her features were soft and round, and her full dark hair tumbled around her face onto the white Pratesi pillowcase. Dexter leaned down close to her neck. He forbade her to wear any perfume because she still gave off the smell of a child's warmth. She had just turned eighteen.

Young girls had always titillated him. Over the years he had attended countless parties where faceless young nubiles had been provided by his

153

friends. To Dexter, the purity of these young girls was the glorious anti-dote to the ugliness of old age.

In his fifty-eight years, Dexter had spent some ugly nights with older women, and they were hard to forget. The ugliness had not come so much from their appearance, but from the sadness and tragedy of their adult lives.

On the other hand, new, young, beautiful flesh was forever being born around him, and his craving for this was almost irresistible. The young ones were untouched by life's hardships. They hadn't been disappointed by love affairs, career blows, children or husbands. They gave off a wild and undeveloped glow. Dexter especially loved awakening in their sweet innocence. They brought strength to his life and satisfied his longing for unfulfilled dreams.

A warm scent came to him again as he lay there. The current of life flowed deeply in Zoe. For Dexter, that meant the recovery of his own youth. She was all future hope and possibility. Zoe offered blind adoration without judgment. She seemed to possess no identity save that which he thrust on her.

Dexter reached under Zoe's nightgown and touched her breast lightly with his finger. Her nipples were small and pink. He felt for her whole breast and held it softly in his hand. Fatherly thoughts came to him and immediately a quiver of something—shame or remorse—changed his expression.

His thoughts went to Anne walking into the bathroom that day, long ago. The anger on her face. The shock . . .

He sighed deeply, not liking the memory. He was beginning to feel like a spider caught entirely in its own weaving.

He walked into the bathroom with his usual catlike tread and surveyed himself in the mirror. His eyes were dark with a brilliant under-reflection of ebony, and his olive-tinted complexion was flushed warmly with the tint of good health. Dexter tossed back his rich black hair which clustered in luxuriant waves.

He turned sideways and scrutinized his naked body, then turned side to front several times, pinching the skin on his hipbones. Something must be done. Teenagers, thirteen, fourteen years old burst into his mind. Snow-white necks, arms and perfect bodies. Dexter felt a surge of loneliness tinged with sorrow for his own youth. Empty longing came over him.

Zoe rolled over, her arm touching Dexter's empty side of the bed. She had only been home for two days and a smile crept over her lips when she heard Dexter in the bathroom.

She and Dexter had been together for almost a year now. They had dated secretly for nine months while Dexter was in the process of divorcing Helena. Once the divorce was final, Zoe had moved into the house.

She loved to bask in the notoriety that came with being Dexter's number-one girlfriend, but more important, she truly loved the man.

Zoe very much enjoyed playing the mistress of the manor, and now, after her new "education," she felt sure she could do it even more convincingly. Before her weeks at Clifford's she had felt like an outsider who had infiltrated the ranks of aristocracy. Now she was closer to being a true Palm Beacher.

With her new confidence, she also felt herself more sexually desirable —no longer just a protégée like the numerous other girls who had preceded her.

Everything seemed to be falling into place for her. Everything was almost perfect—until last night. She had met Carrie for the first time the previous evening and for some reason felt instantly threatened. Competitive—that was what she felt. But competitive with Dex's daughter? It didn't make sense.

Zoe thought how different Carrie was from Gracie, with whom she got on quite well. Gracie was very quiet; she mostly stayed in her own wing of the house, choosing not to socialize much with her or Dexter. On the other hand, all Carrie had talked about when they were together were the social plans her father had organized for her.

Zoe certainly hoped she would be able to be good friends with this daughter, for she knew Carrie was very special to the man she loved.

She looked up as Dexter walked slowly out of the bathroom. Zoe gazed at him, her dusky violet eyes showing open adoration.

"Good morning, Dex," she said, reaching out to him with open arms and feeling *more* than overpowered by the jubilant sense of her extraordinary good fortune.

Suddenly there was a quick knock at the bedroom door.

"Good morning, Daddy," Carrie began, bounding in without hesitation. "I've been waiting for you downstairs for hours." She had two dresses draped over her arm.

"Hello, darling," Dexter replied, giving her a hug and kiss.

"Good morning, Zooooe," said Carrie, the name sliding off her lips with a soft sibilant sound.

155

Zoe grabbed the sheet and pulled it up to her chin, surveying the intruder, astonished at the bold interruption.

"I *desperately* need your opinion, Daddy. Which one of these looks better on me?"

With that, Carrie laid her outfits across the bottom of the bed and, to Zoe's amazement, stepped out of her jeans, then proceeded to lift her oversized aqua sweatshirt up over her head.

She was now standing there completely naked.

Zoe's hands clenched themselves convulsively together and the color drained from her face. For a moment Dexter's eyes skittered between Zoe and his daughter. Then they were magnetically drawn to the grace and marvel of Carrie's unclad loveliness. Her beautiful limbs were rounded and as smooth as pearl. He stared straight and fixedly at his daughter, seeming to note every curve, every gesture of her head and every smile that played on her lips.

Carrie's and Dexter's eyes met. He took one step toward her, then stopped abruptly. He forced his eyes shut. No one could be allowed to see what burned inside him. When his eyes reopened, he fixed them steadfastly on Zoe.

Carrie stepped slowly into one of the black dresses.

Zoe moved her lips in an effort to speak, but no sound came from them.

"What do you think, Daddy?" Carrie flung her hand up with a wild gesture and spun around.

"I like it very much." Dexter spoke slowly. His breath now went in and out of him, slithering like a slow-moving snake.

Carrie now removed the dress and slipped gracefully and slowly into the other. Zoe was sure her eyes were taunting.

"Both are quite lovely," Dexter said. "Certainly on you they are."

Carrie looked at the stranger in her father's bed. She had just learned the night before about Zoe's true role and she didn't like it at all. One more in the long procession of girls who would compete with her for her father's time and attention. To her, Zoe was a vast dark cloud, which had made its way into *her* house.

No one said a word for what seemed an eternity.

"I'll wait for you downstairs, Daddy. I need to talk to you," Carrie said finally, picking up her clothes and walking out as quickly as she had come in.

Zoe sat in bed, motionless, waiting for Dexter to say something about Carrie's behavior. However, he just continued to dress.

156

"I'll be downstairs, sweetheart," was all he said, kissing her on the cheek, and leaving Zoe dumbfounded.

"**I** spoke to Michael last night. He's through with the picture."

"Which means?"

"He wants me home. The boys have to get ready for school."

"My God, it seems as if you just got here," Dexter said with a sad smile. "I was hoping to spend more time with my princess."

Carrie toyed with her dangling earring.

"More important, Gracie needs you. She told me just the other day how much it means to her to have you here. You *can't* leave her yet, she's still not well," he said, patting her on the top of the head. "Think of Gracie. Not of me. Think of your sister."

"I'll think about it," replied Carrie.

"Good," Dexter said. "I'll tell Gracie you're considering it."

He watched Carrie glide out toward the pool, then Dexter went into the library and immediately dialed his secretary.

"I'll need the best tutor in town for Kenny and Keith," he said. "And get me a Palm Beach Day School application.

"I also want videotapes from all the designers' fall collections sent here, so Carrie won't need to attend any showings.

"Arrange physicals for the boys and get me an appointment with Samuel Goldfarb for tomorrow," Dexter said, his thoughts returning to Anne, who had once tried to take his beloved Carrie from him.

"Get me Dr. Cain on the phone—now."

He'd decided that Dr. Cain was the most important element in his campaign to keep Carrie at home, with him. She would stay for Gracie. He knew she would. So it was simple. Gracie would have to remain in the hospital. Indefinitely.

THE PAST

Dexter folded his arms lazily behind his head as he reclined in the gray-and-white-striped chaise longue. Expressionless, he watched Carrie and Gracie taking their scuba-diving lesson in the pool with Joe, their private instructor.

Judge Hawthorne had come through beautifully in the trial, he mused. Everything had gone his way so far. The only snag in his life was Anne's appeal.

A flush of heat moved up Dexter's throat.

Buying a judge had been one thing, but Dexter didn't think that even he could get to all *four* judges who would be sitting on the bench at the Fourth District Court of Appeals.

Hawthorne had told him that he was pretty good friends with the judges at the Appellate Division. Old drinking buddies, he'd said. He also said that, in the state of Florida, only twenty percent of all the final decisions from the lower court were ever overturned. But Dexter liked to have all his bases covered, and this time they weren't. Having always played every competitive game in life as if *his* very life depended on it, he was trying a different angle. He hired a private investigator to see what he could get on Reggie Pearce. The sleazebag detective had come up with nothing so far but a four-year-old DWI.

Dexter relit his cigar and his thoughts drifted back to his wife. For some reason, he couldn't use the word *ex-* when thinking of Anne as his wife.

He had been amazed at her behavior since the trial, her courage and strength. Deep down, he admired these qualities in her very much. Anyone else would have been driven to leave town, he thought.

Dexter had loved Anne as much as he was capable of loving any woman. Unfortunately, she had caught him with Terry that one afternoon. He had been enjoying a purely animalistic act. That's all it was. It was nothing against Anne, it was just his own love of personal indulgence. The truest wisdom is that one must enjoy and satisfy one's own desires and needs. That's the only philosophy to live by. Anne just didn't understand, had never understood. Now she never would.

"Want to go roller-skating this afternoon?" Adrianna asked. She was a tall, buxom redhead, his latest playmate. She was wearing only the bottom of her red string bikini.

"Roller-skating?" Dexter's tone was one of total disgust. He was beginning to feel fatigue in this latest infatuation.

Those pretty human butterflies too often weary the flower whose honey they seek to drain. Where had he read that? The passion of infatuation definitely had a tingling pleasure in it, but it only lasted a short time, it was true. It had touched him that day with Terry and he had yielded to it. Why didn't Anne understand that, if she'd walked in an hour later, it would have been over—forever.

He was very accustomed to following the lead of his own immediate pleasure, with reckless scorn for the consequences. We must all be for ourselves in the long run, he thought. But these brief affairs always came to an end when these little girls felt that their own interests were more important than his, or when they tried to carry it too far—when they thought it was *love.* A scornful smile curved his lips.

Adrianna was reaching that point already.

Anne was the only one who had never wearied him or made a misery of love. She'd probably die for it, too—poor fool. Maybe he should woo her again, he thought. She was so desperate to see the children, she would probably do anything, even drop the appeal. Plus, she was great in bed; no one had ever satisfied him the way she could. Now and then, there was something to be said for intelligence.

Brilliant, he thought. The perfect challenge. I'll get her to move back into the house and drop the legal proceedings. I'll make her fall in love with me again.

The phone was ringing and Gracie heard it. She always did.

"Is it Mommy?" she asked eagerly. Both girls jumped out of the pool and ran to Dexter.

"The wrong number, pumpkins," Dexter replied sweetly, putting the receiver down.

The girls' faces fell. Gracie sighed despondently.

"You know if your mommy *really* loved the three of us, she wouldn't have filed for divorce and left us," Dexter began slowly. "I've told you that before." He paused.

"Maybe we'll get a new mommy," he added as an afterthought.

Carrie's luminous eyes showed complete horror.

"We don't *want* a new mommy," Gracie immediately declared. "We just want *our* mommy!"

Dexter's normally firm nerves quailed. When was this child going to stop whining for her mother? It had been two months now. The week before he was going to take them both to the local fair. But Gracie had been afraid they'd miss Anne's phone call—she'd promised to call at six. Dexter had gotten furious and left Gracie at home. He took Carrie all by herself. They'd had a wonderful day. Carrie never moaned and groaned like this. Gracie was annoying him.

"Run and finish your lesson," Dexter said, waving his hand with a gesture of irritation and impatience. As he thought of Anne now, a shudder of desire quivered through him. It was a desire to own her once again. And it was a desire for revenge at the memory of her filing for divorce.

Anne was confused, preoccupied. Dexter had called earlier that day and invited her over for dinner and to see the girls. She still couldn't believe it.

Dexter led her through the foyer and into the living room.

"I've been considering what you've been saying about it being healthier for the children if they spend a little more time with you," Dexter said, turning and entwining her waist with his arms.

A deep sigh broke from Anne and she put her hands up to her face. A tear slowly dropped through her fingers. Dexter smiled. He knew it was a tear of gratitude.

"Now, go tuck the girls in. They're expecting you," he said, wiping the tear from her cheek with his thumb. "Then we'll have some dinner. I've invited a few people over."

Anne looked at him curiously, with somber, meditative eyes, while she collected herself. She was surprised that others were coming. Yet it made sense. Whatever Dexter's purpose, whether genuine or devious, he was never at his best one-on-one. He thrived in the cover of crowds.

She drew away from his embrace and practically ran to the children's wing. At their bedroom door, however, she stopped dead on her heels.

It seemed to Anne that she stared for several minutes, but it must have only been seconds. Carrie and Gracie were locked like spoons in the fetal position in the same twin bed. Carrie's arms wound around Gracie from behind, and Gracie was sucking on Carrie's thumb. They were gently rocking back and forth, and a slight moan was coming from Gracie.

"My angels," she whispered. She stepped into the room, sat on the edge of the bed and kissed them both.

"Mommy, we've been waiting for you for hours," gasped Carrie. "Climb in."

Anne curled up behind Carrie and put her arm around the two of them.

"Are you and Daddy ever going to be together again?" Gracie asked wistfully. "What would happen to us if he died? Would we be alone?"

"Daddy's not going to die," she said gently, "and you'll *never* be alone. I don't want you worrying about such things."

"Sing us to sleep, Mommy," Carrie said, closing her eyes.

Anne continued to sing the girls lullabies long after they had drifted off, not wanting to leave but finally, she slipped quietly out of the room. Heading toward the dining room, she heard the sound of clinking glasses and boisterous laughter.

Being back in the house felt very peculiar to Anne. It was surreal, unnatural. As if she were an actress in a play, but a play in which she didn't know any of the lines.

Dexter had invited twelve guests to dinner and never had Anne felt more opposed to a group of people, to their thoughts and feelings, than she did that night. She watched them drink, nibble on their food, gossip idly and laugh too loudly. They were bent on enjoying the pleasures offered by the immediate hour, no matter what it took to get that pleasure.

Anne was bored—and she wondered how she'd ever put up with so many similar evenings in the past. Even stranger was Dexter's reaction to the evening. He seemed to be enjoying her discomfort, even enjoying her contempt for his friends. It made no sense to her.

When the evening was over, she attempted to linger. She wanted to find out what Dexter's purpose was for staging such an evening. But he managed to usher her out with the crowd. The perfect gentleman, he kissed her cheek and smiled that smile that had originally made her fall in love with him.

For one brief moment she was tempted to rush back into the house, to say, "Let's start all over, let's forget about the ugly past. Let's return to the safe cocoon of our family!" But she was already being led to her car and she knew that she could never really go back to what once was.

J ane greeted her back at the apartment. She poured herself a brandy as Anne kicked her high heels off at the door and gave her friend every little detail about the evening.

"Very unpredictable. That's the way he likes it," Jane said. "Keep everyone guessing. He thinks that gives him power."

"He invited me back again tomorrow," said Anne, kneading her feet.

"Be careful, Anne. He's up to something." Jane took Anne's foot and massaged it for her.

"But what could it possibly be?" Anne wanted to know.

Unfortunately, Jane didn't have the answer.

O ver the ensuing months, Anne spent more nights at Dexter's than at her apartment. She loved being with Carrie and Gracie again, and the girls were ecstatic to have her back in the house, but Anne had her hands full emotionally.

First of all, the twins had a whole new set of problems as a result of the divorce, and Anne tried desperately to establish some normalcy in their lives. Their behavioral patterns had been altered greatly in the time Dexter had had them alone.

Anne had always insisted they eat properly, make their beds, and keep their bedroom clean. Now, they continually wanted junk food, watched too much TV, didn't do any chores. Anne still pushed Dexter to get the girls some professional help, but he rejected that out of hand. Since he held all the strings, Anne was afraid to push too hard. She was just thankful she had as much time with the girls as he was allowing her.

The emotional trauma of the divorce had also affected how the girls related to other people. They no longer invited friends over, nor did they want to leave the house much. Also, they'd begun retreating into a private language they used only between themselves. They were using it more and more; they didn't do anything without holding secret whispered consultations. Anne did not want to interfere with their special relationship, but Dexter resented it. He was always trying to get in the middle. He felt it was his parental right.

As a consequence, Gracie had become very shy. She wouldn't allow anyone in the room while she was changing or bathing. Carrie, on the other hand, was very open, especially with her father. He spoiled her terribly, buying her far more clothes and toys than he did Gracie, and playing more games with her. Carrie was always the one sitting on his lap, hugging and kissing him, dancing and modeling her new things for him.

Another difficult adjustment for Anne was the fact that her relationship with Dexter was no longer based on love. The pressure of the divorce and the aftermath was an overpowering, corrupting shadow that darkened everything in their lives, and blotted out any romantic feelings she had for him. But they were sleeping together again. Dexter seemed very sexually attracted to her and he wined and dined her with great fervor. She, on the other hand, had become an expert at faking orgasms. If that's what it took in order to be with her children, then so be it, she thought. But it was not easy. At least at first. It got easier. She knew it was wrong, she knew it was not healthy for her, but her children needed her. So when Dexter asked her to move back into the house, she agreed.

When she first moved back in, she accidentally found some nude pictures in his bathroom drawer and a nine-by-fourteen-inch framed gold heart with two benwai balls inside and an inscription, "Thank you for a great time. Love, Denise." She didn't want to know about Denise. She didn't want to know anything having to do with the divorce or the time spent apart afterward. She felt it was all a volcano waiting to erupt and she wasn't anxious for the eruption. For the girls' sake, Anne had decided she could live without a man's love. Carrie and Gracie filled that void for her now.

Christmas came and Dexter went out of his way to please her. He was attentive and caring. He didn't surround them with awful guests—they dined at home as a normal family. On Christmas morning, Anne found a Max Ernst painting under the tree. He was pursuing her on a very grand scale.

It was the new year now and to the outside world, they appeared as one big happy family. No problems. The past had magically been forgotten.

Gracie was helping Clara, the kindly old black cook, make chocolate-cream pie, as Anne came through the door from her yoga class.

"That looks delicious," she said, kissing Gracie's cheek. "I can't wait to try it."

"It's not cooked yet, Mommy," the girl replied, shaking her finger sternly.

"Where's your sister?" Anne wanted to know.

"Upstairs with Daddy. She spilled chocolate *everywhere.*" Gracie's eyes rolled dramatically upward.

Anne went upstairs—feeling quite content and happy, relatively care-free for the first time in a long, long while. She didn't see Carrie or Dexter. Then she heard voices coming from the bathroom. The door was half open. She reached for the door handle but then stopped herself. Her mouth went dry and she stood frozen in the hallway.

"When you grow up, my princess, the boys are going to love touching your body all over," Dexter was saying gently. He and Carrie stood naked in the shower. He shut the water off. "But you must let only very, *very* special people do that—not just anyone."

"Like who?" Carrie asked innocently.

Dexter swallowed and soaped her smooth back. He imagined her as a young woman, with pearly white breasts and light pink nipples. He felt the vitality of her youth coursing through his veins. Anne watched in horror as he got a slight erection.

"Daddy, I'm cold," Carrie said, folding her arms over her chest.

Anne came out of her trance and threw open the door.

"Dexter," she said, startling both of them, "I want to talk to you." Her eyes flashed fire but she tried to keep her voice under control.

"*Now,*" she demanded. She grabbed a bath towel and opened the glass shower door. "Run along and get dressed, Carrie. Mommy will be downstairs in a minute." Images of Dexter and Terry in bed ran through her mind.

Carrie looked back and forth between her parents, not knowing what was wrong but sensing the urgency. She left the room at once.

Dexter shrank back in silence, a black numbness pervaded his body and a maddening anger possessed his brain.

"Enough is enough. I'm going through with the appeal," Anne said, biting off her words. "And *I'm* going to raise Carrie and Gracie."

Rage built in his heart. An all-absorbing feeling of simultaneous love and hate for Anne consumed him. Acting on proud impulse, he raised his head and looked at her boldly. It was a critical scrutiny. A calmly discriminating evaluation of *her,* as if *she* were the one standing there naked instead of him. Anne felt it strongly and it momentarily shocked her. She felt cramped for room. In those seconds, Dexter was able to measure his mental strength against Anne's momentary uncertainty. For the first time ever in their relationship, he was certain of his supremacy. She was afraid and he wasn't.

This awareness filled him with satisfaction. A cold smile crept over his face as he drew in a long breath. No matter what it takes, he thought, this time I will destroy her.

"I'll see you in court, Anne," Dexter said calmly. Then his smile faded, leaving his lips set, stern as the lips on a marble mask.

THE PRESENT

The wind howled furiously outside, flinging gusty dashes of rain against the bedroom window. A glare of lightning blazed and a heavy clap of thunder burst overhead.

Zoe reached for her cigarettes and lit one as she contemplated what she should wear for lunch. The last few weeks had been extremely difficult. Carrie would not give her an *inch* of control over the house or the social schedule, and Zoe could feel herself once again being nipped at the heels by the dogs of doubt. She didn't enjoy having her position as mistress of the house being usurped by Dexter's daughter. But it had definitely been usurped. There was nothing left for her to do. Carrie handled everything, and handled it all so expertly. Zoe had tried to speak to Dexter about it, but he had just stared at her as if she were an idiot.

Zoe looked solemnly out the window, wondering when the hell Carrie was going back to California.

Carrie yawned and opened one eye, too sick and too sore to move, except to reach for the servant's buzzer next to the peach quilted head-board.

After last night's revelry, she felt lucky to be alive. She vaguely remembered joining some friends up at Banana Max in Jupiter for some drinks and dancing. It had been fun. The kind of fun Michael never let her indulge in anymore. She'd smoked some pot, done a little coke—just a little—and remembered flirting with just about everyone. She had laughed a lot, that she was sure of. She wasn't really too sure of anything else—except that her head felt like evil spirits had set up a drilling platform on her temples.

There was a quiet knock at the door.

"Miss Carrie, may I get you something?" Irma asked.

"Maybe you could paint the windows black and replace the shades with sheet metal," Carrie moaned.

"Anything else?" Irma asked, with equanimity; she had seen Carrie with *plenty* of hangovers lately.

"Just black coffee and the paper, thanks."

As Irma closed the door, a flash from last night came back to Carrie. *Oh, my God, Daddy's car!* she thought, a nauseating wave of reality setting in.

She had smashed the Testarossa, of that she was sure. It was on Sloan's Curve while she was racing Kimberly, her old school friend.

It all came back to her now. The front end of her father's favorite car had been totaled. She vaguely recalled the police and her father on the scene after the crash. She'd been too drunk to make any sense.

Carrie tentatively swung her legs onto the floor. Her entire body ached as she gingerly walked to the bathroom.

She examined herself in the mirror, suddenly recalling that Dr. Caupe had come to tend to her in the middle of the night. There were small cuts over her upper lip and left eyebrow, and her chest was sore to the touch. *I must have hit the steering wheel,* she thought. *Daddy must be furious. Michael will be, too, when he calls tonight. Oh God. Maybe it is time for me to go home.* She splashed cold water over her face. *Zoe's driving me crazy, anyway,* she thought. *Her lovesick attitude toward Daddy is nauseating. Christ, she's younger than I am. She's fighting me for his attention, like a wicked stepsister or something. Females come and go. In the end, they all leave, just like Mother. Why can't Daddy see that?* she thought, putting some Visine in her eyes. *Why can't he see that?*

Irma served lunch on the patio. Zoe looked at her salad without dressing and the two thin dry wheat toasts, and sighed, wondering if anything was worth the way Dexter starved her.

Oh well, she rationalized, tonight will be great fun. Dexter had been invited to a private dinner party at La Vieille Maison in Boca Raton for a member of King Juan Carlos's family. She had never met royalty before.

"Where's Mr. Portino, Irma?" she asked, picking at her toast.

"He's in his office with Miss Millie. He said he would join you in fifteen minutes," replied Irma, efficiently as ever.

"Thank you. I'll have a sugarless iced tea while I wait, please."

"Yes, ma'am."

Zoe eyed her luxurious surroundings and felt soothed for a moment, although she was not altogether free from her thoughts on the "Carrie problem."

Zoe rubbed her lean hands together and thought back to the first time she had laid eyes on Dexter. It was a cloudless spring Sunday morning and she and a few of her girlfriends from Florida Atlantic University had heard Prince Charles was playing polo at Wellington that afternoon. Unanimously agreeing they had to get a firsthand look at him, they jumped into Zoe's blue Firebird convertible. Arriving way too early for the three-thirty match, they decided to have a mimosa and observe all the well-dressed BP's as they walked into the grandstand. While they were giggling and gossiping, a jet-black Sikorsky helicopter hovered momentarily, then landed, as everyone hung onto their silk skirts and wide-brimmed hats, waiting for the blades to come to a halt. The sun went behind a cloud and it seemed to Zoe, a sidebeam of radiance shot forth only onto the man stepping down from the helicopter. He was undoubtedly the most attractive creature she had ever seen; Zoe was totally mesmerized by him as he walked to the stands.

Instead of watching Prince Charles play that day, Zoe kept her eyes glued on Dexter sitting in his private box. She didn't know who he was; all she knew was that she had to meet him. After the match, she charmed a young waiter—it was a snap for her—and finagled her way into the private Polo Club. There he was. The rest was easy: a drink together, he asked for her phone number, he called. A few days later she wound up at Clivedon, a lovely palatial estate turned into a hotel in the countryside of

England. Personal maids unpacked their clothes, liveried footmen carried to them heavy silver trays laden with tea and scones. They stayed in the Lady Astor Suite overlooking the Thames and never left the room for five straight days. Their dinner was served every night by white-gloved waiters. Meals were all that interrupted their sexual acrobatics—she had *never* been made love to the way Dexter did it. Gentle and rough, passionate yet clinical and perfect. He had thrilled her by grabbing her hair, firmly holding her down, pulling her head back and fucking her long and hard, over and over again. For weeks afterward, all she had to do to get instantly wet was snake her own fingers around the back of her head and yank her own hair.

"Your iced tea, ma'am," Irma interrupted.

"Yes, thank you," Zoe stammered, blinking back to the present.

She instinctively put her hand on the back of her neck and twisted several strands of hair. She waited for the pleasurable feeling to come— but it never did. With dismay, Zoe realized she was dry as could be.

"M̲illie, get Bob Hutch on the phone at the Palm Beach Police Station," Dexter growled, tapping his pen impatiently on the desk.

"Palm Beach Motors will deliver Carrie's new Lamborghini by six P.M., in time for your cocktail party, Mr. Portino," Millie responded. Then she dialed the number. "Red convertible, beige leather interior with red piping. Everything is just as you wanted," she continued, putting her hand over the mouthpiece. "Chief Hutch, please."

Dexter hesitated until Millie closed the door behind her.

"Hello, Bob. How are you?"

"Fine, Dex. And you?"

"I appreciate your boys bringing Carrie home. Especially since they didn't file a report."

"How is she?" inquired the police chief.

"Fine, fine." Dexter's pencil was still tapping wildly. "But the reason I'm calling, Bob, is that I want you to know I've decided to donate a new ambulance to the town. I'm having my secretary handle all the paperwork this afternoon."

"That's very generous of you. Thank you." Bob Hutch grinned at the other end of the line, pleased with the result of his discretion.

"Well, it's the least I can do," Dexter said. "If I can be of any more help, let me know. And I'll be looking forward to the Policemen's Charity Ball this year. Don't forget me."

"Don't worry, I won't." Bob chuckled to himself. "Have a nice day, Dexter."

Dexter stood up and buzzed Millie.

"Have two dozen white roses delivered to Carrie with a note: 'Hope you're feeling better. I'm glad you're all right. I love you,' etc. I'll have her come in to see you when she gets up, to give you our social schedule for the next few weeks."

"Fine," Millie said, jotting notes to herself.

"Call Martha's and have Lynn pick out a new wardrobe that will be appropriate for Zoe—size eight—and have it delivered this afternoon while she's out." He hesitated. "Better have some flowers delivered to her, too." Satisfied, he walked out of the office.

Dexter's fingers ran over the wide white elastic surgical belt around his waist as he stepped into the front-hall bathroom. He lifted up his fuchsia polo shirt and ripped the Velcro belt open, allowing himself a much needed deep breath as he inspected his most recent operation. His friend, Dr. Peter Sommers, had performed a two-hour liposuction surgery in his Miami Beach office two days earlier. Dexter looked at the small Band-Aid which covered the quarter-inch incision on each hip-bone. Then, looking at himself in the mirror, he nodded with self-satisfaction; his love handles were almost completely gone. No one will ever know, as long as I stay out of a bathing suit for a while, he thought. No one except Zoe. He cursed Peter under his breath as he sealed the uncomfortably tight girdle that he'd been told to wear at *all* times for the next four weeks.

"Fuck, even in the shower!" Dexter muttered, sliding the glass door open to the patio.

Zoe was sitting cross-legged at the white wrought-iron glass-top table. She was wearing a black scoop-neck leotard with her tights rolled up to the knee.

God, he liked her firm body. And so easily pleased, he thought to himself. He enjoyed being her mentor; it gave him control. Dexter knew Zoe would *never* tell anyone about his plastic surgeries. She wouldn't dare. A smile of complacent vanity flickered across his face.

"Sweetheart," said Dexter, kissing her lightly on the mouth.

Zoe gazed at him in mute admiration, forgetting her own problems for the moment in the subtle, strange and absorbing spell cast upon her by Dexter's irresistible influence.

"I missed you this morning," she replied excitedly.

"Steak tartare and salad," he said, looking down at the plate that Irma had just set up for him. "Great. I'm starving."

"Me too," Zoe said softly, staring longingly at Dexter's food. Then she brightened.

"I can't wait to meet the princess tonight," she said, smiling enthusiastically.

Dexter stiffened, sat up straight in his chair and reached for her hand.

"Is something wrong?" she asked. "Aren't we going?"

"I thought I told you that the invitation was only for two."

She didn't understand. "Of course you did. So?"

"So Carrie is an old friend of the king's family." He tried to say it tenderly but he could hear the indifference in his voice. And he could certainly see the tears that were starting to roll down Zoe's cheeks.

He put a deliberate look of babylike petulance on his face; he knew she normally melted at that look. The thought of her tied up to his four-poster bed flashed through his mind.

"*I'm* your girlfriend," she murmured, a quiver in her voice. "Not Carrie."

"Talking about me?"

Carrie suddenly appeared out of nowhere, wearing her tight stone-washed jeans, a white off-the-shoulder Fiorucci T-shirt and sneakers.

"Is this a bad time?" she implored sweetly, pulling out the chair on her father's left.

"Not at all," Dexter said. He smiled at her—and Zoe wondered if he would ever smile at *her* that way.

"I've been going over the brochure for the Golden Door," Carrie said to her father. "I'm going to book us for the five-mile mountain walk."

"The Golden Door?" Zoe asked.

"Yes," Carrie said. "Didn't you tell her, Daddy?"

Dexter shook his head. It was a moment before he was able to turn and look at Zoe.

"I thought I would take Carrie to the spa," he said slowly. "Before she went back to California."

"When are you going?" Zoe asked.

"Next week," Dexter told her.

"It's Couples Week," Carrie said brightly.

Zoe stood up abruptly, knocking her chair over backward.

"Excuse me," she said, controlling herself the best she could.

She almost made it all the way to the house without bursting into tears.

"What was *that* all about?" Carrie asked, but Dexter said nothing. He stared after Zoe. Carrie saw him put his hand on the edge of the table, ready to push himself up. He was going to go after the slut.

"Michael called this morning," she said suddenly.

Dexter eased himself back into his chair.

"What did he want?"

"Me," she said. "He wants me home now."

"I thought we'd been through all this. With Gracie still—"

"I know. I know we have. But *he* hasn't. When I told him I might stay here till Christmas, I thought he was going to have a heart attack."

Dexter didn't respond.

"Daddy?" she said, after a few moments of silence.

"I have a present for you," he said, finally.

"*Another* present? You shouldn't. Michael doesn't give me a lot of presents. He says I'm already too spoiled."

"Go look in the driveway," he told her.

Carrie, excited, dashed away. She was back in a flash, squealing with joy.

"Oh my God!" she screeched. "A Lamborghini! I should smash up your car *every* day!"

"Let's not get carried away," he smiled.

"Daddy, I love you. I thought you'd be furious. Instead . . . I *love* you."

She sat in his lap, her legs dangling over his thighs, her arms around his neck. She nuzzled his neck, kissing him softly.

"I love you, too," Dexter breathed. "More than anything in the world."

The silence was unsettling to both of them. Their faces were only inches apart, their eyes wide open, each staring at the other.

Z oe stared out at them through the living room windows. She watched as Carrie spotted her. Zoe flinched but Carrie just smiled, triumphantly. Never taking her eyes off Zoe, she leaned forward, just a slight tilt of her head, closer to her father. Zoe watched her kiss him. It started slowly, then Carrie, still smiling, still staring in at her rival, threw her arms around her father. Her mouth opened. She pushed harder. . . .

Zoe turned away. She thought she was going to be sick. She felt as if these two people were driving a stake through her heart.

Her mom had always had a bad feeling about Dexter. "The most powerful events in our lives are not always the *best* events," she said. "But they *are* often the quickest—they come, our lives are changed, *then* they go."

172

Dexter had certainly changed Zoe's life. Was he leaving now? There were hot tears in her throat, and the air, all at once, grew suffocating and sulphurous.

Zoe, as if in a daze, went upstairs. Restlessly, she wandered through the master suite, gazing at Dexter's belongings with sorrowfully wondering eyes.

I'll write him a letter and leave it under his pillow, she thought, sitting down at his Louis XIV desk. Zoe opened the top drawer and took out a Cartier pen. Setting aside Dexter's silver-gray linen stationery, she searched further for a sheet of plain paper. She wanted something that *didn't* have his name on it. In the bottom left-hand drawer there were some photographs lying facedown. She automatically began flipping through them. Many were of Carrie and Gracie as toddlers and young girls, others of Dexter and a beautiful woman she had never seen. Zoe smiled sadly. Dexter still looked exactly the same, she marveled.

Putting the pictures back in their place, Zoe noticed some yellowed newspaper clippings sticking out from underneath a strongbox. Unfolding them carefully, the first headline leapt off the page: PALM BEACH TWINS KIDNAPPED. Another read: SCANDALOUS SOCIALITE GOES TO JAIL.

Zoe's mouth dropped open.

"What are you doing?" Dexter said coldly, a dangerous flash of steel in his eyes.

Zoe's whole body convulsed. "Jesus! You scared me," she gasped.

His gaze was deep and intense. Zoe could feel the tension coiling up.

"I . . . I was just looking for some paper," she stammered, "and I saw these headlines. I'm sorry. I was just curious as to what they were."

"Restrain your curiosity from now on," Dexter replied, with a blazing glare. "These are of no importance to you." He lifted the newspapers from her hand.

Zoe dared say nothing.

"I know you're upset," he said. "But you have no reason to be."

"No," she agreed, shivering. "Of course not."

"We'll do something together tomorrow. Just the two of us. Won't that be nice?"

"Yes," she nodded. "Very nice."

She wasn't exactly sure why, but Zoe had never been this afraid in her whole life.

He smiled at her and reached over to her. His hand went to the back of her head and he slowly twisted her hair between his fingers. She felt her head being pulled back, the hair stretching, tight and taut.

With his other hand, Dexter unbuckled his belt. His pants dropped to the floor. He ran a finger down her neck, to her breasts. *Oh, my God,* she thought . . . I want him. I want him *now.* I have to have him!

He pushed her onto the floor. He got on top of her. She started to say something, anything, but couldn't because he was inside her now, deep, deep inside her, and she forgot about everything except her desire to please him.

He came, then she came.

Without another word, Dexter pulled on his clothes and left the room. Zoe lay panting on the floor.

Jail? she thought. *Kidnapping? What the hell kind of family had she walked into?*

THE PRESENT

"I'm sorry I'm late again, sis. Really I am." Carrie's unbound blond hair streamed over her shoulders in loose, glossy waves.

"Don't be silly," responded Gracie tenderly. But she was upset. She'd sensed a change in Carrie over the last month. There was a certain irresponsibility. She seemed a bit fuzzy. Even dissipated.

"I've decided to stay until Christmas," Carrie said suddenly. When Gracie didn't respond, Carrie said, "Aren't you glad?"

An expression of fear swept over Gracie's face.

"What about Michael?" she asked.

"Daddy thinks *you* need me more than he does. I'm sure he knows best."

Need, Gracie thought. *Father's ultimate seducer.* She gazed at her sister with sorrowful eyes.

"What about *your* family?" Gracie asked gravely.

Carrie didn't seem to know how to respond. Lately, Gracie realized, Carrie never knew what to say about her own children or husband.

"I've been *impossible* with Zoe lately," she said to Gracie, resting her forehead against the cool glass of the window, and looking down at the lawn below.

Gracie said nothing. She was used to her father's conversational shifts, he was a pro at it. But Carrie usually didn't do this with her.

"I don't even know the girl, but I haven't given her a chance at all."

A smile of compassion parted Gracie's beautiful lips. "She's innocent enough. Just a young girl completely devoted to and in love with Father."

"I know, I know," Carrie replied wearily. Her face welled up with anxiety and distress. "Gracie, what's wrong with me?" she asked.

"What do you *think* is wrong with you?"

Carrie didn't answer.

"You have to realize," Gracie said softly, "that no one can ever take away Father's love for you. It's total and absolute. And unconditional. There's no need for this jealousy."

Carrie turned her back to the window to shut out the bright sunshine. Still, she said nothing.

"Please promise me you'll talk to Michael in person before you make any decisions," Gracie said. "Please?"

"I promise," Carrie replied, picking up her bag. "Now close your eyes, I brought you a surprise." Her pearly teeth gleamed with a mischievous smile, and Carrie then proudly displayed a huge black vibrator, topped with a red bow, in the center of the coffee table. She surrounded it with an amazing assortment of attachments.

"Okay, open," she ordered.

Gracie gaped wide-eyed and fell backward onto her pillow, overcome with laughter.

"I thought you must be needing something by now," howled Carrie uncontrollably. "Maybe *I* should get one too!"

It seemed as if they'd never stop laughing. This was the way they used to laugh as little children, Carrie thought. Gracie was thinking the same thing. *And maybe this is the way we'll laugh for the rest of our lives.*

"What's the emergency *now*?" Dr. Cain sighed, as Dexter strode through the door.

"It's good to see you, Rob," Dexter said, as he sat down, leisurely crossing his right leg over the left.

Cain's gray brows drew together in a slight frown.

"I trust everything's going well with the hospital," Dexter began. "Of course, under the direction of such a fine and respected physician as yourself, it would have to." He smiled mockingly.

Cain knew it was no use trying to stem the flow of Dexter's bullshit. He watched him take a peach from the fruit bowl on the table.

"I like the balance sheets I saw last month."

Dexter began to peel the peach slowly with a deft movement of his fruit knife. It made Cain think of some sentient thing being flayed alive.

"I want you to keep Gracie here until further notice," Dexter ordered calmly.

An ashy paleness spread over Dr. Cain's face. What the hell was he doing in this complex web of human destinies?

"I told you last week, Dexter, that Gracie's about ready to go home. You know she almost *chooses* when she's sick and when she's well."

A little river of peach juice glistened as it dripped from Dexter's mouth onto his hand.

"Dexter, I beg you, let me get her a doctor she can fully trust *or* let her go home."

"Until further notice," Dexter said, "she stays." He put his knife down and ate the last of the peach.

Totally dumbstruck for a moment by Dexter's cruelty, Cain composed himself.

"Then let *me* help her. Tell me why Gracie feels guilty about her mother."

"How much money do you think you'll need to keep operating this year?" was Dexter's response, a remote smile creeping over his face.

Rob Cain refused to look up.

"*Why* won't you let me help her?" he asked.

"You didn't answer *my* question," Dexter said. "How much?"

"You already know the answer," Cain mumbled.

"That's right. I do. The answer is: a lot. And that's why you'll keep my daughter here until further notice. Is that clear?"

Dr. Cain didn't answer. He nodded, ever so slightly, then turned his back on Dexter.

"I'll get back to you," Dexter said and closed the door behind him.

"Selfish son of a bitch!" Cain bellowed, slamming his fist on the desk.

177

THE PRESENT

Carrie unfastened the seat belt on her father's sleek black Gulfstream III. The interior of the jet was all done in beige leather and soft brown polished woods. It boasted two bathrooms, a bedroom, a galley for preparing gourmet meals, a large living area and two flight attendants. Adjusting her white silk blouse and ivory pleated trousers, Carrie gazed solemnly out the window. At her insistence over the phone yesterday, Michael had agreed to meet her in New York for an early lunch. However, he told her he had to be on the one-thirty Concorde back to London. He had no choice, he said. As if a star of his magnitude couldn't *make* other choices, couldn't make people do what *he* wanted. Why couldn't Michael be more like her father—he wasn't dependent on other people. He made his *own* rules.

Why had she promised Gracie she'd speak to Michael in person? What was she going to tell him? She'd already promised her father to stay until

Christmas, and he'd gotten so upset with her last night when she told him about this New York trip. Daddy was kind enough to let me use his plane though, she said to herself. Would Michael be so kind as to let me stay in Palm Beach?

Carrie glanced at the pile of international newspapers on the table in front of her.

What had gone wrong in her marriage? Had she married too young? For the wrong reasons? And why was she drinking and smoking pot so much lately? It was all a numbing and coping thing. Would these feelings pass?

Carrie recalled what Dr. Cain used to tell her when she and Gracie went for joint therapy. He used to talk a lot about the pain of a divorce and how it could linger in children's lives for years, causing confusion and heartaches well into adulthood. The ruined marriage of her parents certainly was the single most important cause of enduring pain and agony in Gracie's life. The trauma had always haunted her sister. The doctor once told Gracie she was struggling to escape a lingering shadow that darkened her own search for love. Am I doing that too? Carrie thought. She was used to forcing all doubts and questions out of her consciousness, but Dr. Cain had said she shouldn't repress them, she should let out all the memories and fears. Could she ever? She seemed bound, as if by chains, by her memories.

Carrie took out her handkerchief and blew her nose. She was tired and thought she was coming down with something. Standing up, her posture was careless and uneasy; she put her hand on the roof of the plane to steady herself.

"Please allow me," said the young steward, pouring a mimosa into a cut-crystal glass with the initials D.P. emblazoned on it.

"Why, Michael, how lovely to see you again."

The speaker was a tiny woman in a black Azzedine Alaïa dress, which curved around her body like a second skin; her brown hair was pulled back into a French braid.

"It's been . . . what? . . . since the beach at Cannes? Two years ago?" she added demurely, just loud enough for everyone to hear, as if it were their little secret.

"At least that," he said. He hadn't a clue who this woman was.

"I've just bought this *gorgeous* chalet in St. Moritz," she added, leaning over to kiss him on both cheeks. "Come anytime!"

179

Michael ran his fingers through his hair impatiently, a habit he'd developed in childhood whenever he was uneasy. He was anxious to see Carrie; she'd be a particularly nice change from the obsequious people who flocked to his Hollywood fame.

"More coffee, please," said Michael to the flight attendant. He thought of Carrie's voice in the middle of the night. She had spoken in disconnected sentences about the urgency to talk with him in person, immediately, assuring him at the same time the children were well and happy. As the stewardess gawked at him, she overfilled his cup.

"Thank you, ma'am," he said, not realizing he was smiling that automatic smile that made millions of women weak in the knees.

"I'm *so* sorry, Mr. Donovan," she gushed like a high schooler.

He didn't even notice the spilled coffee. A deep sense of dread hung like a cloud over his mind. Michael caught himself dimly speculating as to what lay behind the cloud, and his forehead beaded with sweat.

Picking up his movie script, he forced himself, by degrees, with each line of dialogue, into comparative calmness.

Carrie tapped her French-manicured fingernails on the table at Le Cirque, having decided to lunch in public rather than in the suite she'd reserved at the Mayfair. What she was asking for would seem less monumental this way, she thought, taking a sip of her second Bloody Mary. She felt confident—at least confident in her beauty and her position in society as Dexter Portino's daughter.

Michael walked across the crowded room, meeting Carrie's nervous look with a sad, questioning one of his own. He folded his arms around her, kissing her passionately, not caring to move, even as the maitre d' held his chair.

"God, I've missed you," he whispered. "And the boys? They're fine?" He finally took his seat, nodding at the maitre d'.

"They're wonderful. I told you that last night," Carrie replied. It was good to see him. She was surprised how good. She loved his hair slicked back in a ponytail. "They look so much like you now," she said. "Both boys."

"May I get you something from the bar, Mr. Donovan?" a waiter asked.

"A Perrier, thank you," he replied.

"And another Bloody Mary," Carrie said, winking at the young waiter.

"Are you sure?" Michael asked.

"I've only had two," she said, with a wave of the hand and an enigmatic smile. "Who's counting, anyway?"

Michael took a deep breath.

"Well, what's so urgent?" he asked. He ran his hand through his hair again.

A silence followed, a long and weighted one. Michael looked steadfastly at Carrie, biting his lip. He knew what was coming but it was still a shock to hear it.

"I want to stay in Palm Beach until December," Carrie said. She looked away from the intensity of his eyes.

"We settled this a month ago," he told her as calmly as he could manage. "You promised to have the boys home in time for school."

"Well, I've changed my mind. I want to stay."

Carrie's words burnt into his brain like fire.

"You can't!" he told her with a force that surprised him. He caught her arm in a resolute grip, carried away by a passion that seemed almost outside his own identity. "You *can't*," he added adamantly, lowering his voice as a girl approached their table.

"May I please have your autograph?" the slightly overweight teenager gurgled.

With a violent effort, Carrie wrenched her arm from his clasp and sat straight in her chair. Her eyes flashed a warning to him.

"Carrie," Michael said slowly as the maitre d' ushered the young lady back to her table, "the boys need to be in their own school and their own home. I'll be finished with this picture in a few weeks. Then, we can—"

"Would you care to order?" asked the waiter, putting Carrie's drink down.

"No, thank you," she said impatiently. When Michael shook his head, the waiter scurried away.

"You're doing that Paramount picture after this one. I'll be by myself again."

"Then we'll figure out a way for you to come with me."

"Daddy feels Gracie needs me more than you do right now."

"Your father doesn't always know what's best for you, goddamnit!" The harshness in his tone elevated the tension between them. "When I spoke to Gracie on the phone, she told me she was coming home soon. Maybe this week." His voice softened when he discussed Gracie. "What does she have to say about all this?"

"You know her. She'd never ask me to stay," Carrie told him. "And she's not coming home soon. She can't. They're keeping her there."

"Maybe your father has a selfish stake in all this," he said.

Carrie's eyes blazed fire.

"You don't know what you're talking about!" She seethed with pent-up anxiety and anger. "Just because you've never liked my daddy—"

"You're right, I've never liked him. But at least I can see him for what he is. And he's hurting you. He's not good for you. Look at yourself. Are you happy? Do you feel good about yourself?"

She didn't answer.

"Would you like to know what he is?" Michael continued. "He's a selfish, egotistical son of a bitch who doesn't give a shit *what* happens to you or Gracie as long as he gets his way."

"*Stop it!*" she screamed.

The entire restaurant froze; all heads turned. Carrie pushed herself up from the table and ran toward the ladies' room. Michael ran after her, grabbed her before she could disappear.

"We'll get through this, Care," he said gently, taking her cheeks in his hands and wiping her tears with his thumbs. "I swear to God we will. So let's try. Okay?"

She hesitated.

"Please?"

She took a step toward him, relenting. His fine blue eyes lit up with relief. Then he stopped dead in his tracks. Dexter Portino stepped through the entrance.

Dexter stood with the natural autocratic bearing that made everyone pay attention to him. A man on whose every lineament was expressed a profound belief only in himself, and an equally profound scorn for the opinions of anyone who might ever possibly presume to disagree with him.

Dexter smiled condescendingly and saluted Michael's stare with a gravely pompous air.

"I didn't know your father was in New York," exclaimed Michael incredulously. His temple began to throb.

"I . . . I didn't either," Carrie said with a frozen smile. "Michael, I swear . . ."

"Aren't you glad to see me?" Dexter asked his daughter.

"Of . . . of course. I'm delighted." The smile on her face now seemed genuine.

Shit, Michael thought. *I had her. I had her back and I just lost her.*

182

"You know I completely forgot that tomorrow was the last day of the Degas exhibition at MoMA," Dexter said.

"What an amazing coincidence, then, that we should all run into each other here," Michael said facetiously.

"It certainly is," Dexter agreed with a solemn shake of his head. "The Lord works in mysterious ways."

"Well, we can go back home together," Carrie said, trying to steady her gaze.

"Yes, I had to charter a plane this morning." He pinched Carrie's cheek, his voice softening. "I'm meeting my accountant for lunch, sweetheart, then I'm going back to the apartment at the Carlyle. Then perhaps we'll go to Bulgari and get Gracie a little something to cheer her up."

"Yes, of course," Carrie concurred immediately.

"I hope you children have worked out your problems," Dexter said to Michael.

"We're still working on it." Michael met Dexter's arrogant gaze.

"Would you like to be my guests for lunch?"

"Of course," Carrie started to say, but Michael cut her off with a "No, thank you. We've still got some things to discuss in private."

He immediately led Carrie back to their table, leaving Dexter to be seated by the maitre d'.

"Well, do you think you could have been any ruder?" she snapped as soon as she sat down.

"For Christ's sake, Carrie—don't you see what he's doing?"

"I see that he's looking out for his daughter. For *both* daughters."

"He's trying to destroy our marriage!"

"Our marriage is *already* destroyed!"

There was a painful silence. Michael felt helpless, stunned. He had no idea how they had reached this terrible place in their relationship. This wasn't the woman he'd fallen in love with. This wasn't the woman he'd sent off to Palm Beach just a couple of months ago. This couldn't be the mother of his beloved children. This wasn't Carrie.

"I'm staying with Daddy until Christmas," she said quietly.

Michael slammed his fist down on the table. Carrie's drink toppled off, spilling all over the floor.

"You're staying with Daddy! You're going to Couples Week with Daddy! You're wearing Daddy's jewelry! Are you fucking Daddy, too?!"

Carrie stood up, wild-eyed.

"Shut your filthy mouth," she said. "How dare you? How *dare* you!"

"Sit down, Carrie," he said. "Sit down, please."

"Daddy's jewelry?" she said. "You want to know why I'm wearing Daddy's jewelry?" She fingered the necklace that had replaced Michael's. "Because he gave it to *me*," she hissed. "Not Gracie. To *me*."

"What's that supposed to mean?"

"Whatever you think it means!"

"Goddamnit, Carrie!" He stood up now, too, yelling. He grabbed her arm and yanked her closer to him. "What the hell are you talking about?"

She screamed at him now, a wild woman.

The people at the surrounding tables were staring.

"You never gave me your precious heart. It was Gracie you were with at the Breakers! Don't talk to me about fucking! You don't even know that you fucked my sister!"

He let go of her arm, stunned into a catatonic silence. Carrie sneered at him, a terrible triumphant sneer, then spun on her heel and walked out of the dining room. Michael was only vaguely aware that Dexter was right behind her, his arm on her elbow, guiding her.

He slumped down into his chair. He sat frozen. He could hear the regular beating of his heart and the blood rushing through his body, but no other sound was audible. Michael weakly signaled the waiter for the check. He felt sick, dead inside.

How many times had they exchanged places? Why hadn't Gracie ever told him? Was it because Carrie had been pregnant? She must have put Carrie before herself. Is that why the magic of that weekend had truly never been recaptured again?

Michael stared vaguely at the floor as he put his platinum card back in his wallet. Rising, his legs felt like rubber under him as he stumbled out of the restaurant.

Michael scarcely noticed the crowd of people outside. Recognizing him, they waved their hands, elbowed each other, shouted words of greeting. Oh, how he wanted desperately to walk a while, to think things out before heading to the airport. But it was impossible. His fans enclosed him like a thick wall on all sides.

Michael forced his way into his limo, haunted by Carrie's words. As the car pulled away from the curb, all he could think about was that he had married the wrong twin.

Dexter lay in bed, preening. The last few days he had made sure Michael's calls had not reached Carrie and that she was kept too busy to even think about him.

He stretched out languidly, anticipating his masseuse's arrival. Then he looked over at Zoe lying next to him, wondering if he would be able to balance the two women in his house. He hoped he could have it all and keep them both. Why not? Yet, if he had to sacrifice Zoe for Carrie, would he? Yes, of course he would.

Zoe yawned and extended herself luxuriously. Lately, she had been remote and distant—in competition with Carrie. That excited him, though. He liked it.

Zoe ran her hands the length of her smooth body; she looked very beautiful to him, her dark tousled hair shining with chestnut highlights. She was vitality and innocence personified, and right now he needed both. He needed her.

"Olga's here," he whispered.

Dexter put his hand under her chin, lifting her face to his, and kissed her tenderly. Feeling the warmth of her skin, he pressed the servant's buzzer under the mattress.

For some time, he and Zoe had had their own little ritual. Almost daily, Olga, the Swedish masseuse with the flared cheekbones, wide-apart hazel eyes and magic fingers, would massage Zoe with scented oils and creams, rubbing and lubricating every part of her body—preparing her for Dexter. Watching this sensual rubdown never failed to excite Dexter, never failed to make him hard. Sometimes Olga would stay and watch them make love. That excited him, too. He liked to finish coming, then roll over and see Olga's eyes glistening, her nipples taut under her shirt.

Zoe lay facedown now on the white padding of the portable table; Dexter watched Olga run her fingers deliberately along the small of Zoe's back, letting her hand linger on the perfectly rounded cheeks of her bottom. Zoe flowed with the rhythm, in perfect harmony with the expert hands that knew her body so well. The hands pushed her pelvis into the table and stroked lightly up and down the cleavage of her buttocks, spreading the warm lotion. Zoe felt a hot, moist excitement between her legs; Olga slowly pulled them apart, letting one hand slide all the way up to Zoe's pubic hair. She moved her fingers in small circular motions, deliberately, sensually.

Dexter swelled as he gazed at Zoe, glistening under the cream. He had to possess her now. Olga took Dexter in her warm soft hands, greasing

him, just before he climbed onto Zoe. From behind, he thrust into her
. . . then again . . . and again . . . and again . . .

A Japanese gardener, working in the flowerbeds, glanced up curiously, bowing to Zoe, before returning to his labor of love. As she walked up the terra-cotta steps, she looked at her reflection in the glass sliding doors. Alone again. Dexter had taken Carrie to yet another cocktail party.

Everything had changed since Carrie had come to live with them—especially Dexter. Zoe thought back to that morning and a faint tremor shook her. She was used to Olga now, after a year; in the beginning, she had thought it strange to have a woman play with her like that, but Dexter had eventually taught her to think of it as erotic. However, after Olga left in the mornings, Dexter wanted and demanded more. She wondered if it had to do with the fact that he couldn't get as hard anymore. Today, he had commanded her to dress up in a schoolgirl's uniform and parade for him, slowly and tauntingly, then strip, as if she were an exhibitionist, flamboyantly trying to turn her teacher on. When she was completely naked, he spanked her, rather firmly, then forced her into oral sex. She was willing to put up with this—in truth, it excited her—as long as she had Dexter to herself. Their sex games were her security blanket; they kept Dexter right where she knew she had to have him. But she didn't have him anymore. She knew that. Carrie had him.

Jealousy crept anew up Zoe's spine, along with a tinge of revulsion, as she tapped her cigarette against a silver case. She thought of her girlfriends, and envied their carefree lives. She was fed up with going to the opera, art galleries and museums. She hated her French and Italian lessons, and having to learn how to greet royalty—just in case she ever met any. Which, with Carrie in town, she never would. Why had she even bothered to learn how to give a dinner party? Carrie was having all the fun! She, on the other hand, was up to her miserable neck in thin glossy women who lived on lettuce, champagne, drugs and vicious gossip.

Zoe angrily tossed back her long brown hair, longing desperately to chat with someone—anyone—about movies, boyfriends or makeup. The doorbell rang.

It rang again and again. Realizing no one was going to answer it, Zoe ground out her cigarette with an annoyed gesture. Opening the door, a sensation of complete awe stole over her. There in the flesh stood the best-looking creature she had ever laid eyes on.

186

"I'm Michael Donovan," he said grimly. "I'd like to see Carrie, please." He looked even more handsome to Zoe in person than on the screen.

"I know who you are," Zoe began, a delicate flush rippling up her skin. "Uh, she's gone out with, uh . . . her father," she stammered. "But, please come in. They should be home soon."

Michael ran his hand apprehensively through his tousled blond hair. "Are Kenny and Keith here?"

She shook her head. "They're spending the night at a friend's. Jane Whitburn's."

Zoe watched him eagerly. His blue work shirt was opened two buttons, leaving the hair on his chest exposed.

"Please come in," she repeated.

Without a word, he followed Zoe to the terrace, past a beautiful place setting for one, strewn with pungent gardenias. On the table were pink shrimp, lobster, freshly poached salmon and an iced soufflé on a silver tray.

"Dexter makes sure I'm taken care of," was her comment. "Especially when I'm alone," she added with a slight touch of sadness.

Michael looked solemnly at the girl. She was so young and fragile, like a butterfly freshly emerged from its cocoon. Then he gazed at the magnificent panorama before him. It was a fairyland. Everywhere were colorful pots of geraniums, hibiscus and bougainvillea. The wide expanse seemed to meld magnificently into the moonlight over the water. Yet, Dexter Portino lived here. Dexter created a morass of evil and mischief around himself, for which others were always having to pay the price. That did not belong with beauty.

"Would you like a drink?" asked Zoe.

He shook his head. He didn't want anything to interfere with his mission. He would wait, sober and determined.

He didn't have long to wait. Carrie's boisterous laughter soon broke the silence in the living room.

She and Dexter appeared, arms linked in the open terrace doorway.

"Michael! What are you doing here?" gasped Carrie, astounded. Her eyes were a little glazed, her attire disheveled.

Dexter stared insolently at the unwelcome visitor; a burning hate gleamed in his eyes. Michael met the stare, eyes locked with Dexter's.

"I've come for the twins," Michael said. "The film in London's finished and I've canceled the next one. I'm going to take them home, get them in school—get them back to a normal life."

"That's impossible," Carrie said. "You can't!"

"Can't I?" Michael smiled, though it was a smile without much humor. "Why don't you ask *Daddy*? I'm sure he won't mind if I take the children. Then he'll be able to have you all to himself."

"As usual," Dexter said through clenched teeth, "you're talking nonsense. Keith and Kenny can stay here as long as they want. They can stay as long as their mother stays," he said pointedly.

"I won't let my children live in this house. They're coming with me. And I think you should come with them. We've got a lot to talk about and I want you to come home, Care."

"I can't. And I won't let them go," Carrie said. "They're mine!"

"I'm not taking them away from *you*," Michael said. He turned to stare at Dexter. "I'm taking them away from *him*."

"No!" Carrie said. "No, no, no—"

"Let them go!" Zoe screamed suddenly. The room went instantly silent.

Almost sobbing, Zoe went on, staring at Dexter. "They don't belong here. Let them *all* go. You don't need them. *I'll* stay with you. Don't you see what's—"

Carrie took three quick steps across the room and slapped Zoe across the face. Zoe staggered back, frightened and hurt.

Instinctively, Michael grabbed for Carrie's arm before she could strike the poor girl again, but before he could reach her, Dexter seemed to leap across the room and punched Michael brutally in the face.

Michael fell to his knees and Dexter kicked him, aiming for the neck but missing and catching him full in the chest. Michael gasped in pain but managed to grab Dexter's foot. He twisted it, bringing Dexter to the ground in a heap.

Chest heaving, gasping for breath, Dexter was scratching and biting and kicking, but Michael had recovered somewhat. He threw a jab at Dexter's chin, knocking the older man's head straight back. Bellowing in rage, Michael grabbed Dexter's throat, held it, squeezed as hard as he could. Dexter's face reddened and his eyes bulged. Michael tightened his grip.

"Let go of him!" Carrie howled. She jumped on Michael's back, frantically pulling on his forearms.

But Michael didn't let go. He squeezed even tighter. Dexter's body started to go slack. Michael raised one arm, ready to smash a fist into Dexter's face—but suddenly he let go.

Dexter crumpled to the ground, gasping for air. He looked suddenly twenty years older and pathetically weak.

Michael ran his hand through his hair, rubbed some of the blood off his own face with his finger.

"You'll never get my children!" Carrie screamed at him, cradling her father's head in her lap. "You will never get me *or* my children!"

"I don't *want* you," he said to her. Then, as if to make himself believe it, he said it once more, very softly, "I don't want *you.*"

Michael Donovan surveyed the wreckage of the room—the shattered furniture and the broken lives—then walked out the front door, hoping he'd never have to return.

THE PRESENT

Zoe awoke after a restless night. Tendrils of hair stuck to her cheeks —tears of fear and bewilderment had flowed until the early morning hours. Dexter had never come to bed. Reaching for his pillow, she prayed it had all been a terrible nightmare.

Dexter knew it was no nightmare. He was already springing into action. There was a lot of work to do.

Carrie had slept in his arms last night. His eyes never closed. He just stroked her hair and whispered to her and stared at her all through the night.

By 6:00 A.M. he'd swum thirty-five laps in the pool and taken a cold shower. Carrie was still asleep. Dexter suspected she'd sleep most of the day.

He pressed his intercom buzzer and told Millie to come in and bring her pad.

"Get Sam Goldfarb on the phone as soon as possible," he said. "Notify all the servants that Michael Donovan is forbidden to set foot on my property. If he attempts to, they're to call the police immediately." He enunciated his words deliberately, in a dictatorial manner. "None of his phone calls are to be accepted, either."

"Even to his children?" Millie asked timidly.

"*No* phone calls are to be accepted—*especially* to his children."

"Yes, sir," she said.

"Also, start the process to have Carrie's name changed back to her maiden name. Make sure it's changed on all her credit cards, driver's license, whatever." He lit up a Montecruz, hesitating.

"Anything else?" Millie inquired.

"Yes. Have Irma pack up all of Zoe's personal things. If she's already started packing, have Irma check through her suitcases for any of *my* possessions." He spoke coldly now, calmly, thinking of Zoe only as an encumbrance. "That will be all for now," he added, putting his feet up on his desk. In just a few seconds, Millie buzzed him to say that Sam Goldfarb was on the phone.

"Sam, how the hell are you?"

"Worried, now that you're acting so friendly."

Dexter laughed heartily.

"I've got another divorce for you to handle—my daughter Carrie's. I'll need a detective to check up on all of her husband's activities. I want a restraining order put out on him. He was violent, and I think Carrie and the kids are in danger. And I want the case heard in Florida, not California. I'm going to show that son of a bitch who's boss."

"In the investigation—what is it you want me to find this time?" Goldfarb asked.

When Dexter told him, even Sam Goldfarb had to shake his head. The look on his face was a mixture of awe, shock and self-revulsion.

Gracie turned when she felt his presence. Without seeing him, she knew he was there.

Once she saw him, she knew what had happened.

"It was you," Michael said. His cheeks looked sunken; his eyes were weary.

Gracie nodded. "Do you hate me?" she asked. "I think I could bear almost anything except your hating me."

"You were the one I fell in love with," Michael said. "How could I possibly hate you now?"

Gracie stood there white as marble, her breath coming between her lips in quick, frightened gasps. She unbraided her hair, avoiding his eyes. Finally, breathing deeply, she controlled her emotions and forced herself to speak calmly, though her voice shook.

"I'm sorry I lied to you, Michael. But Carrie was pregnant. Well, I . . . I thought it was the best decision for everyone." She began to cry, and pressed both hands firmly against her bosom.

Michael gently took her hands away from their folded position and held them in his own.

"I loved you so much," he said.

"I loved you, too," she replied. Her angelic smile brightened gloriously around her lips.

"Oh, Gracie."

He gently cupped her face and she trembled at his caress.

"As I told you then—you're my other soul," she whispered gently.

"Then you had no right tampering with everyone's fate," Michael replied, turning away.

There was a sense that things were closing around them like a wall. She felt as if her love were suffocating her.

"You're right," said Gracie. "You're so right. And I'm so sorry."

"Come here," he implored sweetly, and Gracie took a step closer to him. She moved with the soft tread of a forest animal; her head tilted upward on her splendid shoulders.

"We'll help each other," she told him. "We'll help each other through this."

"It's too late for that," he said. "We're going to have to do much, much more for each other."

Drawing her to him, he kissed her, a long, wonderful, passionate kiss. For the first time in years, Gracie felt truly alive.

Dexter had never heard of Joey's Public Health Club in Lantana. He drove impatiently, nervously tapping the wheel for miles before spotting it.

He didn't want his nerves to show, so he did some deep-breathing exercises before he entered the dilapidated stucco building posing as a gym. Offhandedly, he asked for Frank Guido, the private detective he'd used on and off for twenty years now. A pale-faced, wiry young boy directed him to a back room where Guido was stretched out naked on a massage table. In one hand he held a lit cigar; in the other, a glass of gin. A dog-racing form rested on his ample stomach.

Frank Guido was a short, greasy man about sixty years old; his face was deeply lined. He didn't move as he assessed Dexter Portino from across the room. Guido was used to seeking out the flaws in a man's character, and Dexter had plenty of flaws. Must be anxious, he thought. This guy always did want everything done *yesterday.*

The radio blared rock 'n' roll; the masseur was busy talking with his bookie on the phone.

"Do you mind leaving us alone?" Dexter asked the masseur, who looked to get Guido's okay before leaving. When he was gone, Dexter closed the door and handed the detective a plain white envelope. It was thick with cash. "Like I told you on the phone," Dexter began, lowering his voice, "I need a beautiful woman who's lived in Paris the past few years—and who'll testify that she was Michael Donovan's mistress. I also want a few other bimbo types on the side."

"And you want them right away, I imagine."

"Tomorrow. Today, if possible."

"Well, Mr. Portino, those other dalliances just might cost a little more of your hard-earned money." Frank sipped his drink. "And I'll have to postpone my present job for a while. I was makin' pretty good dough on that assignment."

Dexter folded his arms over his chest. He was used to this.

"And I'll have to hire an interpreter over there," Frank continued.

"I'll get you some more money, you lying son of a bitch. But I also want you to leak a tidbit or two to a columnist at one of the rags."

The wiry man from the front room wheeled in an oxygen tank and began hooking up a clear plastic tube to Frank's nostrils. Dexter looked at Guido to see if the detective needed any more information. He shook his head—all was understood.

"I'll be in touch," Dexter said brusquely.

Walking out the door, he thought of the repulsive little bloodsucker he'd just hired. "Scum," he thought.

At Dexter's next stop, he was escorted immediately to the open doorway of Samuel Goldfarb's office by a flirtatious adolescent secretary. Her face was by no means beautiful, but watching her curvaceous body wiggling in a short tobacco leather skirt and cream jacket, Dexter found her almost irresistible.

Papers and books were neatly piled on Goldfarb's desk and floor, and Sam had a frown on his face, as though the very act of writing was too slow for the speed of his thought. Dexter, of course, had no compunction about interrupting him.

"Did you get my . . . ?" Dexter let his words trail off.

"Tip?" Goldfarb finished the sentence for him. "Yes. It was most generous."

"Well, you've done a lot of work for me over the years. I believe in taking care of my friends."

"Is that what we are, Dexter?"

Dexter looked at the little Jewish lawyer and tried his best to disguise his contempt. "Aren't we, Sam?"

"Maybe," the lawyer said. "But this is certainly my last job. I'm using your 'tip' and I'm retiring to Hawaii."

"That's your prerogative," Dexter told him. "Just make sure this last job gets done—and done well."

"It's already in motion." The lawyer handed over a sealed manila envelope. "Are you sure you want Carrie to go for full custody?"

"I told you—they're in physical danger from their father."

"That's going to be hard to prove. Especially with someone of Michael's stature. It's not as if you're taking on . . ." Goldfarb clamped his mouth shut. He wished he could bite off his tongue.

Dexter twisted his neck slowly; he glared at the lawyer, a penetrating, terrifying glare. "It's not as if I'm taking on *whom*?" he asked.

"Anne," Goldfarb said. "I'm sorry. I was going to say, 'It's not as if you're taking on Anne.' "

Dexter, perhaps for the first time in his life, was afraid. He didn't understand it—it was an emotion so totally foreign to him, at first he didn't even recognize it.

Ridiculous, he thought. *What do I have to be afraid of?*

Losing? Losing what? Carrie? Kenny and Keith? Yes. They were his, his possessions. They were like his Jasper Johnses or his yacht. He *owned* them. He would never relinquish what was rightfully his. But *were* they his? Were they?

And then he thought of Capri.

God, he hadn't thought of that night in years. Hadn't *let* himself think of it.

194

It was five and a half years ago now. He had rented a villa on the small island off the Italian coast and had taken Carrie. They spent a lot of time partying, visiting friends; they were like a deliriously happy couple. He'd loved escorting her, leading her around on his arm, picking out clothes for her to wear, watching her sunbathe topless on the beach, rubbing suntan lotion on her back, on her neck, down the back of her tanned legs . . .

"Are you all right, Dexter?"

It was the Jew. What the hell did he mean? Of course I'm all right!

But his thoughts wouldn't leave the villa or the island.

One night he'd gone out late, looking for a drink and some easy companionship. He wound up in this local café, Florian's, and he'd picked up a little raven-haired beauty, seventeen years old. God, she was luscious. She also introduced him to a wonderful pill, Ecstasy, which affected him like no other drug he'd ever taken. They went to the beach where he was overcome with desire. He remembered making love to her in the sand, rolling into the waves. . . .

That was all he remembered about that night. But he remembered the morning.

He woke up in Carrie's bed. He didn't know how he'd gotten back to the villa or how he'd ended up in her room. Or what had happened between them. But they were both naked.

He lay frozen when he realized where he was. Carrie was asleep, unmoving. He stared at her. God, she was beautiful. He reached his hand forward to touch her, then drew it away in horror. Dexter lifted the covers off, stepped silently out of bed. Carrie never stirred.

They had *never* discussed that night. Never. Yet, six weeks later, Carrie's doctor told him she was pregnant, and he had immediately married Helena.

"Dexter?"

Dexter felt the sweat streaming down his forehead and his neck. What the hell was he doing? What was he afraid of? He was Dexter Portino and he had done nothing wrong! There *was* no right and wrong for the likes of the Portino family.

"I want those boys with me and Carrie," he said. "That's all there is to it!"

Dexter walked past the luscious young thing in the reception area.

"Here's my card," he said, and handed it to her without even slowing down. "Call me sometime," he added, with his most charming grin.

"I just might do that," she replied excitedly. Then she licked the flap of an envelope with a small pointed pink tongue. She could not have been more thrilled. Dexter Portino! He was a legend. He was so handsome. He had *all* that money!

THE PRESENT

"**I** have to go home," Gracie said. "Carrie needs me."

Dr. Cain took a long time before answering.

"You know it's not as easy as all that," he said.

"Yes, I do. I know my father's ordered you to keep me here."

"Gracie, now, now, now . . . let's not be ridiculous. I'm here to help you get better. No one gives me orders on how to care for you."

"Dr. Cain, I'm not an idiot. I hear things and I see things. When Michael Donovan's lawyers hear the same things . . ."

She didn't finish the sentence. She didn't have to. She could see the doctor crumple in front of her. She felt pity for this big man with the unhappy eyes. She wondered if he had told so many lies about Dexter over the years that he'd be unable to understand the truth. But she decided to give it a try anyway.

"I think you're a good doctor. Despite it all, you've helped me. I'm struggling with a lot of thoughts inside my head and on my conscience. I think I'm ready to talk about all of them. And if I do, I think it might help *both* of us."

"Yes," Dr. Cain said. He wanted to take her slender hand and lift it to his lips. "I think it might."

"Carrie is first."

"I'm ready to listen," he said.

She started slowly. To begin with, she loved her twin. More than anything or anyone. They were almost one person. But lately, Carrie was . . . different. She'd stopped coming to the hospital. When she *did* come, she wouldn't talk. Nothing had ever stopped them from talking to each other. And without that communication, Gracie was feeling less than whole. She needed Carrie. And Carrie needed her. Carrie needed many things.

Gracie told Dr. Cain about Michael. About their past and about their present. She loved Michael, she said. But now it was all right, because Carrie no longer loved him.

"Why not?" Cain wanted to know. What had changed?

Gracie told him about her father. About his relationship with Carrie. His feelings for Carrie, his possessiveness toward her boys. She told him everything. She told him what she never told anyone. She told him of her greatest fear. Could her father and Carrie ever have been together?

"Gracie," Dr. Cain said, "how can you possibly? . . ."

"Mother warned me about father," she said.

There was a long silence.

"That's impossible," Cain breathed. And yet, somehow, against all his logic, he believed her. It *was* impossible. But this girl had some magic about her, a serene strength that defied logic and all that was merely possible.

"Mother talks to me all the time, Dr. Cain. There. I've told you. Does that make me crazy?"

"I don't know," he said. "I don't know what's crazy anymore. I just know that you don't deserve what we've all done to you."

"Yes, I do," Gracie said calmly.

"Don't be silly. Don't do that to yourself."

"I'm not doing anything. Except trying to tell you the truth."

"This has to do with your mother, doesn't it?"

"Yes."

Cain took a deep breath and stood up.

"You could *not* have saved your mother," he said. "You were only seven years old. It was her choice. Free will is the divine condition attached to life. Each person determines his own fate." Cain watched her eyes well up with tears.

"Your mother *chose* to do what she did. Why should you feel any guilt over that?"

"Because *I* asked her to kidnap us," Gracie said quietly. She had turned pale. "It was *my* idea, not hers."

Dr. Cain looked puzzled, almost disbelieving.

"I begged her," Gracie added. "I thought I had the perfect solution. I thought I could make us be happy again." She began wiping her tears on her sleeve. "I remember it all so clearly. I remember Mommy . . ."

THE PAST

The offices of Reginald Pearce were as luxurious as Dexter had expected—soft carpets, good paintings, the unmistakable air of opulence that goes along with great success. Dexter was sure that Pearce had already composed an acceptance speech in anticipation of his judgeship. Surely that was this man's lifelong goal. Had to be, from looking at things he'd surrounded himself with.

"What brings you here, Dexter?" Pearce asked. His accent was refined; his bearing was that of a gentleman. However, he did not offer his hand, nor did he leave the seat behind his antique tulipwood desk.

"Well, Reg," began Dexter. His features were hard enough to have been carved out of wood. "I need you to do a little favor for me." Dexter, without having asked, took a chair with his usual soldierly dignity. "Then, if you're lucky, *I* might do one for you in return."

"Get to the point." Pearce began tapping his string-bean fingers. "Or show yourself to the door—the same way you showed yourself in." He had nothing but contempt for Dexter Portino. The man was despicable. What he'd done to Anne and his children proved he had absolutely no feelings for other human beings. He had nearly tricked her into dropping her appeal. Dexter had few if any of the nobler emotions and ambitions which put man above the evil of his companion—the beast.

Dexter, expressionless, threw a large white envelope at the lawyer. He was looking forward to seeing Pearce's contemptuous smirk wiped off his lips.

As Pearce pulled the pictures out, he stopped breathing for a moment. His heart began pounding so violently, he wondered if he would ever breathe again.

The office was tense and still until Dexter spoke. He spoke graciously —because he knew his enemy had been crushed.

"It looks to me," he said, "as if you're having an awfully good time with that young boy." Then Dexter laughed as clear and cold as a sleigh bell on a frosty night.

"Your present duty, my friend, is to listen, not to speak," Dexter continued with a satisfied smile. "So listen discerningly, pick up your pen and take notes." There was a gleam of triumph in his eyes. "This is what you're going to do for me."

At Petite Marmite on Worth Avenue, Anne picked at her tortellini filled with mousse of chicken.

"The appellate process is *so slow*," Anne began dispiritedly. "The more I'm away from the girls, the less they seem like mine. It's been over a year. What is taking them so long?!"

Jane played with the five strands of pearls hanging around her neck. She understood her friend's disappointment at yet another motion by Dexter to delay. But she wasn't able to offer her the slightest consolation.

"Just remember, honey," she said. "They're not judging *you*. They're judging your reputation now."

"Gracie told me they both slept in the same bed with Dexter and his new girlfriend the other night." Anne shook her head worriedly, moving a piece of green pasta round and round her plate. "I only see them four days a month. How can I help them like that?"

"They know you love them," Jane said, grasping her best friend's hand. "That's all you can do."

"How could I have loved the wrong man and loved him so much?"

Unfortunately, neither of them had an answer for that question. While they pondered, the maitre d' came up to Anne and told her she had a phone call. Everyone in the restaurant turned to watch the most-talked-about woman in Palm Beach walk to the phone.

"Anne, it's Reginald Pearce," her lawyer began. "I'm sorry to interrupt your lunch, but your housekeeper told me where you were."

"What's so important?" she asked, turning toward the wall for privacy.

"I have a plan, Anne," he said, hating himself more with every word. "I want you to come to my office first thing tomorrow so we can discuss it."

A ray of hope began to relieve the cold weight in her heart. "I'll be there first thing," she said.

"Happy birthday to you both," their grandmother smiled. The love in her eyes clearly shone through her creamy, yet slightly careworn face. Alice Graham, Anne's mother, was Carrie and Gracie's only living grandparent. She was a very elegant-looking woman, with her gray hair sleekly pulled back into a black bow that wrapped around the nape of her neck. She wore ruby and diamond drop earrings and today was dressed in a Karl Lagerfeld red suit.

"Grandma!" Carrie and Gracie cried, their bright faces lit with pleasure. "You came!"

"It was really three days ago," Carrie grinned. "Our birthday is February twelfth."

"Well, then, you're very lucky. You get *two* birthdays," replied Grandma Alice. She ran a comforting hand over Carrie's blond hair.

Since the divorce, Dexter had not permitted Anne's mother to visit his house, nor did he allow Anne to leave Palm Beach County with the children, so, since her heart attack, Alice made as many trips to Florida as her health would permit.

"Is there anything I can help you with, Anne?" Alice asked, watching her daughter carefully place seven candles into the vanilla and chocolate ice-cream cake. Their relationship had always been strained, yet Alice had never really understood why. She felt that Anne had somehow wanted more than she, Alice, had ever been able to give. Perhaps that was Anne's problem—she always expected too much. She wondered if that had been passed on to the twins.

"Thanks, Mom, but everything's taken care of." Anne wished the two of them weren't alone in the kitchen. She still needed to think. Reggie Pearce's plan had thrown her for a loop. It was so bold. So final. It excited her—but it scared her to death.

"Anne," her mother said, watching her closely, "you can't possibly be considering what you told me earlier."

"I am," Anne said.

"But it's crazy!"

"It's *all* so crazy! Reggie thinks I won't win my appeal. *That's* crazy. I was married to the most diabolical man who ever lived. *That's* crazy. Lies become truths and love becomes hate! What could be crazier than that?"

"If you go through with this, Dexter will hunt you down wherever you are. You know he will."

"So what's my choice? To let him have Carrie and Gracie?!" Anne was angry now. "To let him *destroy* them? Because he *will*, Mother. He will destroy them. He's destroying them now."

Alice had never seen this kind of passion in her daughter. Not in all their years together—not in their arguments, not in Anne's schoolwork, not in her photography, not in her marriage. Alice wondered if it always took tragedy to evoke the kind of love and passion she was seeing Anne exude.

"What do you want me to do, my darling?" Anne's mother asked her.

"I need you to release the cash in my trust fund," Anne told her. "I need you to help me kidnap my children."

That evening, Gracie, clad only in a white silk nightgown, was sitting on the edge of her bed. Her small, rosy toes peeked out beneath the frilly hem. Carrie was in the bathroom, brushing her teeth.

"It was a wonderful party, Mommy," Gracie said eagerly. "I loved it." She swung her legs back and forth nervously.

"What is it, my Gracie?" Anne asked.

"I want to live with you." Gracie began to cry. "And I heard what you said to Grandma. I want you to kidnap us. Please do it." She stretched out her arms, clinging to her mother's neck.

Anne's eyes went wide.

"Please, Mommy, I beg you," Gracie cried. "I'm scared of Daddy."

"We'll see, Gracie. We'll have to see." Anne kissed her daughter. The taste of Gracie's tears stayed in her mouth until she swallowed.

"Please, Mommy?"

Carrie came running and jumped into bed with her sister. Anne bent over, pulled the covers up and pressed her warm fingers on each child's brow. Softly, she rose and stood erect, staring at her twin daughters.

"Good night, my angels," she whispered. "I love you."

"We love you too," was the bright reply.

Only minutes later, Anne sank, exhausted, into a huge, luxurious marble bathtub filled with hot water and perfumed oils.

My God, she thought. *What am I about to do?*

It was Mother's Day, one of the five days during the year she was allowed to take the girls to dinner. Anne stood waiting at the front entrance, fidgeting with a wisp of her hair.

Did Dexter suspect anything? Could she really get away with this? Christ, it seemed so crazy all of a sudden! How did she ever wind up in this position? For a moment, Anne was caught up in a memory of her past life—a successful photographer, traveling around the world, free and easy. How had she reached this point? She was lonely, she'd been celibate for over a year and, let's face it—she looked like shit. How had it all happened?

Carrie and Gracie came running out the door and into her arms. Oh, how she loved them. They belonged to her and she belonged to them.

There was no going back now. She must help her children escape the dreadful man who was their father. She was in the right. It was no longer an alternative—it was a mission.

She had decided not to tell the children of the plan until they were safely on the plane and in the air. Reaching the airport, stalling, Anne drove around the circle at Butler Aviation twice, while the girls chatted merrily. When they realized where they were, they bombarded her with questions.

"I thought we'd go for a little plane ride tonight and eat our dinner up there," Anne told them, a bit nervously. "It'll be fun," she added half-heartedly.

Gracie knew immediately her mother was going to answer her prayers and her heart pounded excitedly. Carrie knew something was up; she didn't know what, but she was nervous. She wondered if she should call her father. Gracie, who always knew what she was thinking, shook her head. This wasn't for Daddy. Carrie nodded back—she trusted Gracie with her life.

Anne finally parked the car in the last lot at the end of the private airport, where the blue Citation jet was waiting. The children said nothing. Moving stealthily, holding Carrie's and Gracie's hands, she led the way.

The door of the plane was open, the stairs were lowered. The three of them made their way across the tarmac. It was going to work! She was going to get them away from Dexter, somewhere he'd never find them.

Anne first saw the figure out of the corner of her eye. She stopped. There was no sound, only the unchanging shining of a few cold, quiet stars. She grasped Gracie and Carrie tightly, pushing them forward. She started to run—when floodlights came on, blinding her from every direction.

"You're under arrest, Mrs. Portino," a police officer boomed.

Anne squinted, shielded her eyes with her arms as people ran toward them. There was mass confusion! She felt someone grabbing the girls, pulling them away from her.

"Mommy! Mommy!" The girls made a violent effort to reach her.

Then she saw him standing in the cold shadows. Her trance was broken. She was no longer speechless. Never had she hated anyone so much. Never had she had such fear.

"Dexter!" A shriek, half fierce, half despairing, broke from her quivering lips, piercing the suffocating air. Suddenly, Anne was dizzy, as if she was gazing down from some lofty mountain peak and could see nothing below but white, deceptive blankness.

"Mommy!" Gracie cried at the top of her lungs. It was an agonized scream and it made Anne cover her ears in horror.

She fell to her knees and began to sob.

THE PRESENT

Carrie was hung over again.

Her bloodshot eyes were half open and that was as open as she could get them. Her mouth felt as if she'd just eaten a plate of cotton—and then washed it down with a gallon of vinegar.

Good God, what had she taken last night?

With a grimace, Carrie realized a better question would probably be what *hadn't* she taken.

It had started innocently enough. She'd gone with some girlfriends to Ciao, a great little Italian restaurant in West Palm. Daddy had begged off, said he wasn't feeling well, but insisted she go have fun without him. She felt a little guilty, but she went. Earlier in the day, she had signed the papers filing for full custody of the twins. She didn't feel right about that —but Daddy had shown her the detective's report. Michael had had a mistress when he'd made that film in Paris. *Several* mistresses. One of them even had a baby. Maybe it was Michael's!! Miserable, she'd signed the papers. She would have signed anything at that point. So she needed to get out of the house last night. It felt good to go out by herself. It made her feel mischievous and reckless. She had forced herself not to think of Michael.

She remembered commenting on Christina's skin. "It looks fabulous," she said. "It's flawless. What's your secret?"

"Baden-Baden," Christina told her. "Mummy was there last week for her annual physical. She had a lovely suite at Brennor's Park Hotel, so I joined her."

The four of them—Carrie, Christina, Nikki and Alicia—had known each other since Palm Beach Day School. They loved catching up on all the town gossip whenever possible.

"Did you know Ned Blumfield was found dead in his sauna this morning?" Nikki asked. She was tall and amber-haired and quite beautiful in a haughty, well-bred and understated way.

"I can top that," Alicia giggled. "Garrison Kingston has a penis implant."

The girls howled at that one.

"It's true," Alicia went on. "A permanent erection now—and he must be over sixty."

"I don't care if it's King Kong's penis," Christina said, "I can't *imagine* going out with a man that age."

Carrie flushed. Her father was almost sixty. That wasn't so old. He was attractive still. In fact, he was *very* attractive.

"I *can* imagine going out with Michael," Christina went on. "Come on, Carrie, tell us what he's like in bed."

Michael, Carrie thought.

She hadn't talked to him in almost two weeks. And then he'd lied. He told her he'd been trying to call, several times a day, but that Irma always told him she or the boys were out. Irma denied it, of course, and Daddy said Irma would never lie.

No, Michael was the liar. With his mistresses. He'd made a mockery of their marriage, of her.

She couldn't trust him. She couldn't trust any man—except her father. She knew he'd always be there for her. She knew he loved her.

"Come *on,* Carrie. Give. What's he like?"

She didn't want to talk about Michael. It made her too sad. So she just smiled knowingly, as if he were too sexy to even discuss. The girls sighed happily—it was even better than they'd hoped.

After Ciao, they went to The Speakeasy for a drink. Alicia decided she had to have a dinner party and invite Garrison Kingston. "We'll arrange to spill something on his lap and when he stands up, maybe we can see the implant."

While they were all laughing, a man came up to Carrie and asked her to dance. He looked vaguely familiar. The girls all egged her on, so she agreed to dance with him. Why not? He was astonishingly good-looking. Dark, piercing black eyes, slender, with broad shoulders, a mysterious scar on his right cheek. It was the scar that gave it away. Daddy's party, the one he'd thrown for her. That's where she'd seen him. The scar did more than remind her—it also gave him a sex appeal that was downright combustible.

A fast song came on. As always, Carrie abandoned herself to the music. Her lips parted, her hair flew in all directions. She didn't just move, she slithered, she stalked. She danced as if dancing was her greatest sensual pleasure.

Her partner matched her, step for step and sensual look for sensual look. When the song ended, his fine-boned Italian face glistened with sweat. He licked his lips.

"Paolo," he said, introducing himself. His smile was dazzling.

Carrie told him her name, but he clearly knew it already.

"We are going to make love, you know," he told her, almost matter-of-factly.

"You think so, do you?" she asked.

"Oh, yes. I *know* so. Shall it be tonight?"

"It was nice to meet you, Paolo. But I think one dance was quite enough for tonight."

He smiled and she turned to walk back to her table.

"You will find," Paolo said, stopping her, "that there is no such thing as enough, Miss Portino. When you realize that, I hope you will give me a call."

He smiled, an infuriatingly superior smile, and handed her his card.

I'll have to tell Daddy about this one, she thought.

Then she realized it was late, she should go see how Daddy was feeling.

When she got back to the table, the girls were beside themselves.

"That's the man who bought the Gubel estate," Alicia squealed. "No one knows anything about him except he's richer than Trump."

"Well, I found him quite rude," Carrie said.

"*This* should make up for the rudeness," Christina noted.

They all looked up to see a waiter carrying over four bottles of Cristal champagne—one for each of them. Courtesy of Paolo.

"You can't leave now, Carrie," Nikki pleaded. "*That* would be rude."

So she'd stayed. After finishing off the Cristal, they drank Armagnac. And did some Quaaludes that Nikki happened to find in her purse. Then smoked some incredibly good pot in the ladies' room.

She'd danced with Paolo again. And again. At some point in the evening he kissed her. One gentle, lingering kiss. Her nipples had instantly gotten rock-hard. Then he'd stepped back, kissed her hand and disappeared into the crowd.

C arrie's hangover was her worst ever. She struggled to stand up, groaning. The room was spinning, but she made it to the bathroom and the shower, then to her dressing room, where she put on her favorite silk robe. Her nipples still tingled from the night before.

Carrie decided to see how her father was feeling. Surely he'd be awake by now.

But no. There was no sign of him. She made her way toward his bedroom. The door was closed. Still asleep?

She decided she'd wake him up. They were going to spend the day together, just the two of them. They'd planned it for days. Maybe they'd have breakfast in bed. Then a workout in the gym. Then they'd go shopping. Perhaps she'd buy *him* a present for a change.

Carrie opened the door to Dexter's room. He was still in bed. He was naked, mounted on top of Steffi, one of his secretaries. Steffi couldn't have been more than eighteen years old. There was an older woman in bed with them. She was Steffi's mother.

Dexter turned toward the door. His penis was swollen, erect. His mouth opened, but no words came out.

Carrie wouldn't have heard him anyway. She was too busy screaming. Louder and louder and louder still . . .

THE PRESENT

Dexter leaned back in the green leather chair in the library, his hands clasped lightly in front of him. It was four o'clock in the morning. In another few hours, she'll have been gone twenty-four hours, he thought. Where could she be?

Dexter rattled the ice in his glass, marshaling his thoughts. After Anne left, he'd worked long and hard to prepare Carrie to become his female companion. He'd turned to her for emotional support and, in return, had given her everything she ever wanted or needed. He'd treated her as if she were his wife. He almost smiled at his next thought: He'd treated her far *better* than any of his wives.

He was, by nature, a man who craved female support and who feared its abrupt removal. He knew that. It was why he had to seduce almost every woman he met. He remembered when he had been sent away at a young age to school in England, removed from the arms of his adoring mother. He had to face alone all the horrors of British boarding school. Dexter recalled vividly his one homosexual affair. It had been brief, but very real. With a boy named Dominick. Dexter wondered if he'd been in love with Dominick. He couldn't remember.

He stood straight up, the muscles of his throat pulled taut. He forced his thoughts back to his mother. He'd felt the pain of separation acutely. Before going to bed at night, he'd habitually prayed to God to have her come and retrieve him. He had craved the warmth of her affection.

Dexter's fingers lay still on his glass. He had no intention of being deprived of such affection again. He *must* get Carrie back. She was the emotional anchor of his home. Kicking a footstool angrily out of the way, he walked toward the bar, poured himself another drink and stood admiring his possessions. He did love them—all of them. The Chinese vases from the Third Dynasty, the Fabergé eggs, the Caffieri clock, the rare books that lined the wall. He smiled, thinking of his priceless collection of erotica hidden behind a fake wall in his dressing room. His smile faded just as quickly as it had come. Where *was* his Carrie?!

The sun was coming up. Dexter felt completely exhausted and drained. Back in his chair, he lowered his head onto his chest. He'd always been so precise and sure of himself without emotion getting in the way of his actions. He loved Carrie. He loved her as he'd loved no other woman. He had to have her back. At any cost.

Dexter heard something—a footstep?—as his eyes were about to close and sleep was about to come. His head jerked up and he peered into the shadows of the hallway. Could it be? Yes! She was back!

Dexter leapt up, took one step toward his daughter, then froze. Carrie had never looked at him that way. Carrie *would* never look at him that way. No matter *what* had happened.

"Hello, Father," Gracie said. "Where's Carrie?"

Dexter was speechless, bewildered. His eyes instinctively went to the telephone.

"Yes, it's all right to call Dr. Cain," she said. "In fact, he'd like to speak with you."

"He let you out?" Dexter asked hoarsely.

Gracie didn't answer.

"Where are Kenny and Keith?" she demanded.

"Asleep. Why do you want to know?"

"I've come for them. I've come to take them away from here."

She expected an explosion. But there was nothing, no response at all. Dexter simply closed his eyes.

"Where's Carrie?" Gracie now asked.

Dexter's eyes opened. She saw how bloodshot they were, how old he looked deep down inside them.

"She's gone," he told her.

Then her father did something that Gracie had never seen.

He began to cry.

Carrie awoke, disoriented, frightened, a blinking pain flashing across her brow. Where was she?

She glanced around the room, which was filled with white lilacs and hundreds of candles in crystal holders.

Carrie lifted herself groggily onto her elbow. She noticed a pink silk robe spread neatly across the foot of her brass bed. Slipping her robe on, she sauntered through the twelve-foot-high, stained-glass French doors, pushing them wide open to the outside second-story porch decorated all in white wicker.

It all came back to her a split second before she heard the voice. She smiled now, remembering the look on his face when she'd appeared.

"Good afternoon," Paolo said from below. He lay beside the pool, his body stretched into a straight line on a chaise longue, arms folded behind his head, dark glasses on. The deep tan of his skin implied months of days spent in that position.

"Take a shower. You'll find clean clothes in the closet," Paolo told her, and stood up. "I'll join you when you're finished."

Carrie took a hot bath. Usually the steam felt so cleansing, but even scrubbing her skin till it almost bled didn't make her feel clean.

What the hell was she doing here with this man? What had she done?

When the last of the water ran out of the tub, she got dressed—he had an entire closetful of beautiful women's clothing. When she stepped out of the bathroom and into the bedroom, he was waiting for her.

"I think I'd better leave," she said.

He smiled at her and didn't move. There was something vaguely threatening about the smile, although when she headed for the door he still didn't move a muscle.

It was only when she went to open the door that she realized why he could stand still. She was locked in.

"The door seems to be stuck," she said nervously.

His silence was beginning to scare her.

"Please say something," she told him. "If this is a game, I'm not enjoying it."

Her eyes widened as he pulled a silk scarf from one of the bedposts.

"I don't play games, Carrie," Paolo said. "I told you that last night."

"Could you please let me out of the room?"

"I'm afraid not."

"What are you doing?"

"I'm going to fuck you."

"It seems to me we already did that."

"No. Yesterday we made love," he told her. "Now we're going to fuck."

"Open the door," Carrie demanded.

He smiled. Still smiling, he hit her, just once, but that was all it took. She went down hard on the floor and felt her eye start to swell immediately.

Paolo pulled her by the hair over to the bed, effortlessly tossing her onto it. When she made a move to struggle, he hit her again, a short hard jab to her jaw. Carrie fainted.

When she woke up, she was naked. She was also tied, spread-eagle, to the four posts of the bed. Paolo was pacing before her. He, too, was naked.

He saw her eyes open as he walked over to her. She feigned unconsciousness, but he knew she was awake. He slapped her, once gently, once so hard she felt her jaw rattle. Carrie groaned with pain.

"I'm going to tell you what I'm going to do, Carrie," he began. And, for the first time, she began to panic. The terror of her situation struck her deeply, like one of Paolo's punches. She was helpless. She was a prisoner.

"I'm going to fuck you, of course," he said, quite softly. "I may do it several times." She could see he was getting hard. "I'm going to hurt you first. I'm going to get great pleasure out of inflicting pain in this particular case. Do you know why?" She shook her head.

"Because of your father. Fifteen years ago, he stole my father's company. *Stole* it. With his lawyers and his brokers and his Palm Beach bullshit. You don't know what suffering is, not yet anyway, but my father suffered. He was broke, humiliated. He was ruined. And do you know what? I don't even think Dexter Portino knew my father's name! He just needed another possession. Well now, I'm going to take one of *his* possessions. I'm going to take it but then I'm going to return it to him. So he can see how it feels to have something you own broken. Finished."

213

Paolo went to a drawer and pulled out a small whip. Carrie's eyes widened as he cracked it across the room.

"I think we are ready to begin," he said.

When she heard the word *begin*, Carrie fainted again.

"**D**addy?" The voice was raspy, almost a stranger's voice.

"Carrie! Where are you?!"

She could barely hold on to the phone. Her legs were like rubber and her back throbbed. Paolo stood over her.

"Are you still there, Carrie?!"

Daddy sounds worried, she thought. *Worrrieeeddd . . . How nice. He loves me. He looovvvveeessssss meeeeeee . . .*

"Carrie! Where *are* you?!"

She gave him the address Paolo told her to give. Her voice sounded broken, so harsh. She began to cry again, deep, wrenching sobs.

"Carrie, *please* talk to me!"

She could not talk for long. She was in too much pain. She had no idea how long it had been since Paolo had first tied her up. She didn't care. She just wanted to sit, to lie down, to sleep.

Gracie came with him. She insisted and he didn't really resist. He didn't have the strength to resist. Dexter could focus on one thing only: Someone had hurt his Carrie. Someone had raped her and nearly killed her.

Dexter knew one other thing: He would destroy whoever had done it.

Dexter drove grimly, his hands wrapped tightly around the steering wheel. They reached the house in fifteen minutes.

He pulled the car to a stop in the driveway. Without a word, Dexter went up to the front door. Gracie stood behind him.

Somehow, he knew the door would be open. He turned the knob and stepped inside.

There was a man standing in the entryway. He wore a white terry-cloth robe with nothing on underneath. There was also something on the floor. It was a person, lying there. Helpless. Not moving. It was a woman.

Her face was swollen, one eye was shut completely. She showed no recognition when her father and her sister approached her.

Dexter turned away. He couldn't look at her.

He'd been expecting to find Carrie. But this wasn't his daughter. This wasn't Carrie Portino! Carrie was beautiful, regal, a magnificent creature. This person was . . . ugly. Hideous. No, this was not Carrie. This was a stranger.

Gracie ran to her sister, crying, and cradled her. She tried to get through to her father, but he was in some never-never land.

"Father! Call a doctor!"

Dexter didn't even look at her.

"Father!"

No response.

A tear rolled out of the stranger's eye and down her cheek.

Paolo arrogantly turned his back and now, without a care in the world, walked away from Dexter. He actually heard the two shots—they sounded like explosions—before he felt the searing pain in his back, then in his chest.

He was never even able to turn back toward the door. He simply fell to his knees, balanced there for just a moment, and then pitched forward onto his face.

THE PAST

Dexter had not visited Anne the entire time she'd been in prison. She'd served one year of her ten-year sentence—no parole allowed—and she now sat directly across from him, behind a sheet of glass, staring into her palms. It was Mother's Day.

Anne was ageless. She never seemed to grow any older, he reflected, only more beautiful. She did have some fine wrinkles at the corners of her eyes, though, like paper that had been crumpled, then smoothed out. Marks of past joys and sorrows, he thought. It gave her astonishing character.

There was silence.

Dexter rubbed the back of his neck. It was her mouth that had changed the most, he mused. Her lips were drawn downward.

The silence continued.

Dexter tapped his fingers on the shelf before him. He thought she owed

216

him all the anger she could command. But there was none. She showed him no strain as a result of this meeting.

When he lifted his eyes to hers, he realized there was no caution necessary. She would have no reaction to his scrutiny. Her expression would remain the same.

"Where are the children?" Anne asked. There was no emotion in her voice.

It was the question he had been waiting for.

Dexter pulled a letter out of his jacket pocket. He'd drafted it over a month ago and had been painstakingly working on his daughter ever since.

"You must do this for me," he'd said to Carrie. "If you love me."

"I *do* love you, Daddy! I *do* love you."

"Then if you want *my* love, forever and ever, you'll sign this."

"Gracie will *never* sign it. Never," Carrie stammered nervously.

Dexter caressed her hair, his hand resting lovingly around her neck.

"You can sign it for her," he said softly. "No one will ever know."

"I can't," she said and started to cry.

"You must," he'd told her. "If you love me."

Now he handed the letter to Anne. It would destroy her once and for all.

She unfolded the piece of paper and read the words:

Dear Mommy,

Daddy told us we could visit you on Mother's Day. He even showed us the letter from the judge. But we don't want to. We spend our Sundays with Daddy and we like it that way now. You left us so how can we love you?

Carrie and Gracie

He marveled at her self-control. She wouldn't break, not in front of him.

"What do you think of me, Anne?" he finally asked her. He said it so quietly, he wasn't sure she'd heard him. Her only response was that she unfolded her hands.

"I said . . ." he began again, but she cut him off with her eyes. Those eyes told him she'd heard.

"I *don't* think of you," she replied simply.

217

Something cold and shadowy seemed to possess the room. Dexter felt momentarily deprived of strength, of motion. She smiled gently, softly, an almost imperceptible movement of her lips.

Suddenly Dexter stood up, knocking his chair over backward. His breath was heaving, labored. He slammed his fist down on the ledge in front of him. He watched her face for a reaction. There was none.

Running outside, running away from her, he made it to the cement curb and sat down. He didn't move for quite a while, then realized it was getting dark. Dexter shuddered, then stood and walked toward his car. He never looked back at the prison that held his ex-wife.

Alone, back in her bare, all-white room, with the very dimmest light, Anne thought of the inside of an egg.

The calm sadness of her eyes changed to a look of longing, compassion and tenderness as she gazed at the photograph of Carrie and Gracie next to her bed. Her eyes moved slowly from face to face. She ached. It had been over a year since she had seen them. Jane visited faithfully each week with information, letters and drawings, but it wasn't the same.

What had gone wrong with her life? Dexter? No, that wasn't it. He was a tool, perhaps a lightning rod, but she couldn't blame him for her choices or her life. One only became a failure, she knew, when one pointed the finger at someone else.

Anne poured herself a glass of water. She moved restlessly about her cell, her limbs trembling slightly. The fear was back, the same fear that had crept insidiously through her veins like a shuddering cold. It had been getting worse over the past months. It was a terror which she could give no name.

Anne sat, her hair tied into a single ropy braid in back. She opened the locket around her neck; it contained another picture of the twins. Tears ran slowly down her cheeks. Oh, how she worried for them. Would the children of such a pain-filled union be heirs to that pain? Would Carrie and Gracie be able to survive the treachery? Could children grow up to love when they had been exposed to such hate?

What was the answer? What was the lesson to be learned here? Perhaps there was none. Perhaps *that* was the terror.

Or perhaps the answer was to try to *eliminate* their ties to their past.

Anne did not want to go on without her children. Lately, she would wake up each and every morning and wish she were dead—wish that her eyes wouldn't open. Oh, how she loved them. But it would be better for them if she were gone. As long as she was alive, Dexter would never let them have any peace. That letter told her more than its printed words. And she was so tired, anyway. Too tired.

There were dull, unceasing throbs in her head now. Then, suddenly, at the very height of pain, as despair threatened to overwhelm her, Anne felt a strange and comforting calm. She walked to her tiny closet, retrieved a handful of the precious Nembutals Jane had been sneaking to her slowly over the past few months. Her dearest friend. How could she ever thank her? Their deep respect for each other forged such trust between them that Jane had never asked her not to do what she was about to do, but Jane *knew* she could no longer live without her children.

Anne put the glass to her lips and sipped from it. She washed the pills down with a series of controlled gulps.

Picking up a pen and paper, she sat at the small table. The stillness deepened, pulling at Anne. What could she say to her beloved children? Could she say she was not going to measure up to life's expectations? Would they understand? Would they judge her harshly? Was she failing them after all?

Her heart thumped hammer strokes of fear. Her eyes were growing heavy.

Her forehead fell to the table. She was staring into a moving glow, where Carrie and Gracie were running and playing. A cry rose involuntarily to her lips. *My babies . . . my babies.*

The sharply defined edges of consciousness began to wear smooth. Darkness clung and closed about her. Its advancing weight rolled over her like a huge waveless ocean. Totally absorbed in it, she was drawn down toward some hidden, all-supreme agony. Cramped for room, she struggled for existence, for motion and breath. Then she plunged coldly into a depth of inextricable blackness.

Time was ending. . . .

Alone, all alone, Anne confronted death.

THE PRESENT

Gracie sat huddled next to Michael outside Carrie's room at Dr. Cain's hospital. The twins, Kenny and Keith, were inside the room, saying good-bye to their mother.

Carrie had lost a lot of weight over the past few weeks. She'd had a concussion and several broken ribs. Her lower back was badly bruised. Dr. Cain had assured them that plastic surgery would heal the facial scars. But the mental scars . . .

She had taken on a haunted, sallow look. And what was worse, since the news of the shooting, she hadn't spoken a word. She'd said nothing when Michael flew in from L.A. to be with her, not a word when the boys came to visit and hug her.

"You could come with us," Michael said to Gracie. "You *should* come with us."

Gracie shook her head.

"I love you," Michael told her. "I've loved you for years."

"I have to be with Carrie now," she said softly. "She needs me."

"*I* need you," he said.

Gracie took his hand. "One day, maybe I'll come," she told him. "I'll come and the boys will be wrestling on the carpet and you'll be learning the lines of a new script . . . and I'll just walk in unannounced and surprise you."

"Will we be together again?" Michael asked.

"I love you," Gracie said. "But Carrie's my twin."

Dexter followed his young escort, as a man would walking in his sleep—uncertainly, with unseeing eyes. His heart was beating loudly, and he felt a sick sense of suffocation in his throat.

He walked behind the guard in absolute silence. He did not ask for warmth or pity—he asked nothing.

Taking a key from his belt, the guard watched Dexter closely. There was something in the stooped grandeur of the old man's bearing that touched him with a sense of compassion. He unlocked the door, threw it open and signaled for Dexter to step in. He did, and found himself in a green plastered room. Obscene graffiti covered the walls. There was one small bed, a table, a chair and a cupboard for clothes. There was no mirror. A bathroom adjoined the cell.

Dexter ran to the door, pulled at it angrily. The guard had gone—he was a prisoner. He stood, breathless and amazed, as a wave of terror swept over him. Drawing back from the door, he paced around the room.

He had finally reached Sam Goldfarb in Hawaii. When he told the lawyer he was in jail, Sam had said only, "I can't help you." Zoe had refused to take his calls.

Dexter sat down on the bed and tried to calm himself. Everything had suddenly been wiped out. He was left with nothing. Even his desire was gone. He had no appetite, no lust left in him.

There were furrows on his face. His brow bore lines and wrinkles of pain and anxiety. They were the soul's marks of a devious and tragic life.

He lay his head back on the pillow and felt a coldness in the air. He listened, hardly drawing a breath—there was not a sound. He seemed to be in a place apart, where no human, no human touch, could reach him, and he felt as he had never felt before in all his life—that he was indeed utterly alone.

He thought of Anne. Lately, he often tried to conjure her face in his mind. He was having trouble seeing her, though. Even she had abandoned him. He remembered their last conversation together.

"What do you think of me?" he had asked that last day.

"I *don't* think of you," she had replied so easily.

The guard stood at the end of the hallway, lighting his cigarette. From behind Dexter's door came a sobbing sound. It was the sound of a wounded animal—or a spirit damned.

THE PRESENT

Gracie walked quietly along the sun-dappled path under the trees. There was the smell of fresh-cut grass, and she enjoyed having the sunlight playing on her skin, and the soft breeze blowing on her face and hair, which flowed loosely over her shoulders.

The last two months had flown by swiftly—so much responsibility had come her way since she had returned home. A rich color flushed her cheeks as she thought of the past, and how she had survived it.

She had lost her fire at times, but she had regained it. Somehow she had always known that the fire was not to be betrayed.

As she walked on, she reached for her mother's locket, which hung on her breast. She felt the love that had emanated from Anne and felt, too, her gentle presence.

Gracie knew it was time for her to evolve and move onto another stage of learning, of accepting and of life.

Back in her bedroom, Gracie sat at her desk, jasmine placed in a silver bowl next to her elbow. She looked into her mother's box of treasures and smiled. Her hand was unhurried as she reached for a pen.

Dear Mother,

I have been so busy since I arrived home. I have so much to tell you, I don't know where to begin.

Over the past months my fears have subsided, except at times when I think of Kenny and Keith, and recognize patterns repeating themselves. They rock each other to sleep every night, as Gracie and I did. They truly are the innocent victims. What did they do to deserve this? Do children come into our lives to fulfill their own destinies or their parents' destinies? Do they come to teach us? Or are we totally responsible for the children we have created? Isn't it amazing how all of our paths are so interwoven?

Michael has put his career on hold these past months to be with the boys, to help with his children. I'm not surprised at his selflessness. He is everything I knew he would be when I first met him. However, of what we shared together nothing more can be said. It must remain in the past. At least for now.

Carrie, my beloved twin, is still in the hospital. I visit her daily, but her progress is so very slow. I have known since we were young that Carrie could never accept your leaving. But I cannot live for her the hard road she has chosen for herself in passing judgment on you—she must follow her own path.

I have at last forgiven myself for the useless guilt that I carried for so many years. I thought that I had been responsible for your death. I know now you chose your own destiny and that I took on a karma that wasn't mine.

At the moment, I think I have a fair understanding of where I stand spiritually. And thanks to you, I have grasped one of my harder lessons: Forgive yourself. That's what you always told me, that's what I've finally done.

My world is no longer shadowed with hatred. Not even for Father. I have not yet forgiven him for what he was with you—or me, or Carrie—but perhaps one day.

As always, it is hard to say good-bye, but I do so with all my love. Forever.

Your Gracie

Gracie put down her pen. The stillness was suddenly made fragrant by the scent of her mother's tea-rose perfume.

Gracie folded her last letter to her mother and slipped it back into its final resting place—near her heart.

ABOUT THE AUTHOR

*R*OXANNE PULITZER is the
author of the best-seller
The Prize Pulitzer.
She currently lives in
West Palm Beach, Florida.